River's Call

Other books by Melody Carlson

Limelight (Multnomah)
The Four Lindas Series (Cook)
Christmas at Harrington's (Baker)
Love Finds You in Martha's Vineyard (Summerside)

RIVER'S CALL

The Inn at Shining Waters Series

Melody Carlson

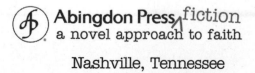

Abingdon Press fiction
a novel approach to faith

Nashville, Tennessee

River's Call

ISBN 978-1-4267-1267-8

Published by Abingdon Press, P.O. Box 801, Nashville, TN 37202

www.abingdonpress.com

Cover design by Anderson Design Group, Nashville, TN

Library of Congress Cataloging-in-Publication Data

Carlson, Melody.
  River's call / Melody Carlson.
     pages cm. — (The Inn at Shining Waters series)
  ISBN 978-1-4267-1267-8 (trade pbk.)
  1.   Teenage girls—Fiction. 2.   Mothers and daughters—Fiction. 3.   Grandmothers—
Fiction. 4.   Siuslaw Indians—Fiction. I. Title.
  PS3553.A73257R57 2012
  813'.54—dc23

                                                                           2011045026

Printed in the United States of America

1 2 3 4 5 6 7 8 9 10 / 17 16 15 14 13 12

1

October 1959

Anna's dugout canoe sliced a quiet path through the glasslike surface of the river. Today the Siuslaw was the color of topaz, with reflections of trees along its edges. Interspersed between spruce and firs, maple trees shone in shades of gold and rust and red. Anna turned the canoe around, paddling back to the inn where she would start breakfast, when the silvery form of a good-sized fish shot out of the water. Soaring nearly a foot into the morning air, it arched then gracefully came down with a quiet splash. The third one she'd seen this morning.

Spawning season. The salmon were beginning their annual migration upriver, and in a day or two, the whole river would be hopping with them, with fishermen not far behind. Grandma Pearl used to say that the salmon were practicing their jumping skills, getting strong enough to make it up mountain streams and small waterfalls in order to lay their eggs in the same spots their ancestors had been procreating their young for hundreds of years.

October was Anna's favorite month on the river. With mild weather, good fishing, harvest moons, and gorgeous sunsets, who could complain? And this year—her first October back on the Siuslaw in twenty years—she was sharing this special month with Clark! Only two weeks since returning from their honeymoon, Anna and Clark had already fallen into a comfortable pattern. It was amazing how compatible they were. Both enjoyed the quietness of the morning, a good cup of coffee, and the great outdoors.

Clark was nearly finished with the first cabin, with a good start on the next one. Meanwhile Anna enjoyed puttering around, putting up produce from her garden, catching up with neighbors, making plans for the inn, and being a wife again. She was just entering the house when she heard the phone ringing. Surprised that anyone would call this early in the morning, she hurried to answer it. Perhaps it was a guest wanting to book a room. So far the reservations had been few, but both she and Clark agreed that was a blessing in disguise since it allowed them more time to enjoy being newlyweds.

"*Mom?*" It was Lauren, and she sounded upset.

"Yes, dear, it's me. How are you?"

"Not good, Mom. Not good at all."

"Oh, dear, are you sick?" Anna had heard there was a bad strain of influenza going around in the cities. Lauren had been on campus less than a month. Surely she wasn't sick.

"I don't know . . . maybe."

A wave of worry washed over Anna. She remembered the time when Lauren had been seriously ill with scarlet fever as a young child. "Tell me what's wrong, Lauren. What are your symptoms?"

"I've been throwing up and I just feel awful."

"Oh, dear, that sounds like influenza. Do other students have it too?"

"I don't know."

"Maybe you should go to the doctor."

"I don't know who to go to here."

"What about your sorority mother? Can she help you?"

"Mrs. Ellis is just horrible, Mom. She's a real witch. Everyone hates her."

Anna controlled herself from correcting her daughter's judgment. "Well, is there a clinic on campus you can go to?"

"I don't know, Mom." Now Lauren was starting to cry.

"I'll talk to Clark," Anna said quickly. "Maybe he can bring me up there and we'll figure out what's going on with you."

"Okay . . . ." Lauren's voice sounded weak now.

"You'll be all right until I get there, won't you?"

"Yeah, I'm going back to bed."

"Good. Stay warm. And I'll call your sorority and leave a message about when we'll arrive." As soon as she hung up, Anna ran outside to where Clark was just coming up the stairs to the house.

"Hello, darling—" He stopped, studying her closely. "What's wrong?"

She quickly explained and Clark, without questioning her, said he'd be ready to go as soon as they had a quick breakfast. Anna hurried to cook eggs and toast, explaining to Clark about the time Lauren had been sick with scarlet fever. "She was so little and so ill." Anna set his plate in front of him. "Her fever was so high, I really thought we were going to lose her." She sighed as she went for her own plate. "Even after she recovered there was some concern about heart problems. Although she's been fairly healthy since then. Until now that is."

"Don't worry, honey." He patted her hand. "We'll be there by afternoon and we'll stay as long as you like."

"Or maybe we can bring her home with us."

"Sure. If you think she'll be comfortable in the pickup." He frowned. "Times like this make me wish I had a car instead."

Now Anna thought hard. "I wonder if Dorothy might be able to help. She lives near the college. If she could bring Lauren here in her car . . ." Already Anna was heading for the phone.

"If Dorothy can bring her, Lauren could be here by this afternoon," Clark pointed out. "Then you could nurse her back to health."

"Yes," Anna said eagerly. She was already dialing the operator. Before long, Dorothy was on the other end and Anna quickly explained the dilemma. "I hate to bother you, but—"

"It's no bother," Dorothy assured her.

"But I hadn't considered—what if Lauren has something contagious?"

Dorothy laughed. "Don't you worry. I'm strong as a horse. My girls come home sick with some new illness every year and I never seem to catch a thing."

"Okay . . . if you're positive."

"You just give me the details of where Lauren is and I'll head over there straight away. I'll pack blankets and pillows and maybe a thermos of tea. And my girls are in school. Even if they get home before I do, they're capable of being by themselves for a few hours. Ralph gets home by six. Really, I'd enjoy the drive, Anna. Don't give it another thought. I might even stay into the weekend, if you have the room."

"Of course we have room. And you know you're always welcome here." Anna told her Lauren's address and they estimated the time she'd arrive in town. "I'll take the boat and meet you at the grocery store," Anna promised. "I need to get some things anyway."

Next Anna called Lauren's sorority and explained to Mrs. Ellis that Lauren was ill and that her friend Dorothy would arrive there soon to pick her up.

"She's sick?" Mrs. Ellis sounded surprised, and a bit grumpy.

"Yes. I think it may be influenza. She's been vomiting."

"This is the first I've heard of it."

"Yes, well, it may have just come on this morning. She can stay with us through the weekend and we'll see how it goes. Perhaps she'll be well enough to return to classes next week. But if she's contagious, it might be best if she's not there."

"Yes, that sounds wise. I'll let Lauren know your friend is coming."

Anna hung up the phone and returned to the table where Clark was filling her coffee cup. "Sounds like you've got it all worked out."

"Yes." She sighed and sat down. "Thank goodness for Dorothy."

"I wouldn't mind driving up there, but for Lauren's sake, I'm glad Dorothy can transport her." He patted Anna's hand. "Now, try not to worry."

"Yes . . . you're right. Worrying doesn't help anything."

"But this does make me wonder if I should consider getting us a car."

"The road is so terrible, Clark."

He nodded. "We could keep the car parked in town. That way, if there was an emergency, we'd zip down in the boat and have a car to use."

"Oh, I don't think we really need a car."

"But what about when you have guests at the inn? Perhaps you'll want a car if you need to pick them up or take them somewhere, Anna. You never know."

Anna was embarrassed now. "I don't even know how to drive, Clark."

He chuckled. "Well, I've seen you handle a boat. I'm sure you'd be just fine behind the wheel of a car too."

She smiled. "It might be nice to know how to drive."

"Then we will see that you do."

"I just hope I don't put you through too much stress. I remember how Eunice complained when Lauren was learning to drive."

Now he told her about teaching Marshall to drive a couple of years ago. "And that boy had a lead foot and an attitude to go with it. So I'm sure teaching you will be a piece of cake."

After the breakfast things were cleaned up, Anna went to work getting a room ready for Lauren. Although the weather had been temperate, she decided to put a heating pad in the bed, as well as an extra quilt. She also put a water pitcher and glass on the bedside table, along with a small vase of garden flowers. Then she made a grocery list and called in her order, saying she would pick it up around two.

To keep herself from worrying about Lauren, she decided to make some of Lauren's favorite childhood foods, including baked custard and snickerdoodle cookies. Staying busy was good medicine for her. Instead of fretting, she began to look forward to this unexpected visit. Focusing more on the time they'd get to spend together, she put her worries about Lauren's illness behind her. It was wonderful that Lauren had called her—and not her paternal grandmother, Eunice. That alone gave Anna great hope that her relationship with Lauren was already much improved. What Anna's former-mother-in-law would have to say when she found out (and, knowing Eunice, she *would* find out) was beyond Anna's control.

As Anna removed the last batch of cookies from the oven, she mentally compared her new mother-in-law—Clark's mother, Hazel—to Eunice. Could two women be more different? Anna never met Adam's mother until *after* they had married—against his mother's will. But she had met Hazel even before meeting Clark. Perhaps that was a better way to plan a successful marriage—meet the mother-in-law first.

"Hello, darling!" Clark came up from behind her, slipping his arms around her waist and hugging her. "Something smells good in here."

"I'm keeping myself distracted by cooking." She turned around, kissed him, then handed him a warm cookie.

"Am I a lucky man or am I a lucky man?" He grinned and took a bite. "Yummy."

"They're Lauren's favorites. I hope she'll feel up to having one."

"Poor girl. I just hope their trip is going smoothly."

"I hope Dorothy thought to bring a bucket." Anna made a face. "In case Lauren gets sick, you know."

He made a face. "Oh, I didn't even think of that. Anyway, if you like, I can pick up the ladies in town. I put the full cover on the boat so it'll be warmer for the patient."

"I planned to go myself," Anna told him. "I've got groceries to pick up."

"You want a hand?"

She smiled. "I'd love it."

"We could put a cot in the boat if you think Lauren will need to lie down."

Anna nodded. "That's a good idea. And I'll get some blankets and things. And I already called Dr. Robertson. I explained that I wasn't sure what was wrong and he actually offered to come out here and look at her."

"A doctor who still makes house calls?"

She smiled. "He said he saw the article in the newspaper about our wedding. And he was so impressed with what he read about the inn that he's been wanting to come out and see it anyway."

"Ah, so an inn comes in handy for lots of things."

Anna felt worried again. "I just hope she's okay, Clark."

He hugged her again. "Even if she's really sick, she will have to get well quickly with you caring for her, Anna. Like Mom says, you have a gift when it comes to healing."

Anna wasn't too sure, but she didn't want to argue. She hoped Hazel and Clark were right. After returning to the old ways, Anna's grandmother had been a gifted healer. Anna remembered several times when traditional medicine had failed her family or their friends on the river. Without fanfare, Anna's grandmother would step forward, often when Anna's mother wasn't looking, and she would quietly recommend herbs and poultices and other treatments, and before long, the ailing person would recover. Anna wished she knew more about those ancient remedies, but mostly she was thankful for the quiet healing elements of the peaceful river itself. That alone had brought health and wholeness to her life. Maybe it would work its magic on Lauren as well.

2

Anna was pleasantly surprised when she stepped out of the grocery store and spotted her daughter. Lauren looked perfectly fine as she waved from Dorothy's car. Dorothy beeped the horn then pulled the Buick into the small side lot that river families leased for their parking convenience. Anna hurried over to the car, opened the door, and soon had her daughter in her arms. After a long reassuring hug, she looked into Lauren's eyes. "How are you doing?"

"I still feel kind of weak and tired, but at least I haven't been throwing up."

Dorothy got out of the car. "That was a relief," she admitted. "I can remember when Jill got carsick on our way to Yosemite a couple years ago. The car stank for weeks."

"Well, let's get you onto the boat. Clark just took a box of groceries down ahead of us, but we're ready to go." Anna put an arm around Lauren's shoulders. "We fixed it up like a floating ambulance."

"And I'll get our bags," Dorothy said.

"I'll send Clark back to help."

"Meet you at the dock."

"Thanks." Anna smiled gratefully at her old friend. Dorothy had grown up on the river too. She knew her way around as well as Anna. If only she lived here full-time.

Before long they were back at the inn where Anna thanked Dorothy again, telling her to make herself at home, or to use the boat to go and visit her parents if she liked. "I'll get this girl into bed."

"I'm not that tired," Lauren protested.

"I don't care," Anna said with authority as she led Lauren to the room she'd prepared. "I'm in charge here and I think you should just rest."

"Okay." Lauren gave in easily and Anna noticed her usually vivacious daughter did look a little pale and weary as she peeled off a soft pink cardigan.

"Do you feel like eating a little something?" Anna set one of Lauren's bags on the bench at the foot of the bed.

"I guess I could try. I didn't feel much like it on the trip here." Lauren kicked off her shoes and sat down on the chair by the window, sighing as if bone-weary.

"You get yourself into bed, sweetheart, and I'll bring you something."

Lauren made a weak smile. "Thanks, Mom. You know, there's no one like you when it comes to taking care of me when I'm sick. Grandmother was always hopeless at it. Remember?"

Anna chuckled. "Your grandmother never could stand the sight of a sickroom or even something as innocent as a thermometer—and if there's a bedpan anywhere near the poor woman, she might actually faint."

Lauren made a face. "Well, at least I don't need a bedpan, Mom."

"Thank goodness for that." As Anna went to prepare Lauren a tray, she remembered the long, hard years she'd spent caring for Lauren's father when Lauren was a girl. Adam had returned from the war minus an arm and a piece of his soul. Anna had cared for him for about ten years before he'd finally taken his own life. As far as Anna knew, Lauren was unaware of this sad fact. For years Anna had assumed she was the only one with those suspicions. However, she'd been blindsided when Eunice brought up the subject of Adam's death last summer. It was possible Eunice might've informed Lauren about her father by now, but Anna did not intend to bring the subject up herself. Some things were better left unsaid.

Anna carried a tray with tea, custard, and a couple of cookies into Lauren's room. "See if there's anything here that can tempt your appetite," she told her as she set it on Lauren's lap. "And I'm making chicken soup for dinner."

Lauren smiled. "Looks good, Mom. Thanks."

Anna sat down, making small talk as Lauren picked at the food. She told her a little bit about their honeymoon trip up the Oregon Coast. "We stayed at different beachside hotels all along the highway, clear up to Astoria."

"That sounds fun." Lauren took a sip of tea. "But I plan to go somewhere more exotic my honeymoon. I think maybe Honolulu or Jamaica."

Anna chuckled. "Already planning your honeymoon?"

"Doesn't hurt to think ahead."

"How are your classes going, honey? Do you like school?"

Lauren shrugged. "You know me, Mom. I've never been the scholarly type. But I like the girls in my sorority. And it's fun seeing Donald on campus."

"Are you feeling a little better now?" Anna got up now, placing her hand on Lauren's forehead, like she used to do when Lauren was a child. To her relief, it felt normal.

"I guess so. But I'm surprised because I really felt sick this morning. I barely made it to the bathroom on time. And I couldn't eat a thing for breakfast."

"Maybe you just need some rest." Anna picked up the empty tray. "A weekend on the river will put the roses back in your cheeks. Now just close your eyes and relax, honey. Enjoy this leisurely rest." She quietly left the room, closing the door.

By dinnertime Lauren said she felt like getting up, and Anna didn't discourage her. The four of them enjoyed dinner together and even played cards until ten. Feeling as if Lauren was making a swift recovery, Anna went to bed feeling happy. But at five in the morning, she heard groans coming from the bathroom and hurried out in time to see Lauren hunched over the toilet.·

Anna stayed with her, comforting her until she stopped retching. Then after giving her some water and washing Lauren's pasty forehead with a cool washcloth, she walked her daughter back to her bed and tucked her in as if she were a small child. "I'll put the wastebasket right here," she told her, "in case you feel ill again."

"Thanks," Lauren muttered with closed eyes.

Later that morning, Anna went to check on Lauren again. She seemed to be sleeping comfortably, but Anna checked her forehead, which felt normal. And Lauren's cheeks weren't flushed or splotchy or spotty. Mostly she just looked very pretty, sleeping sweetly in her lacy pink nightgown. Fair-haired and blue-eyed, Lauren didn't have any traces of the Native American blood she carried. Lauren resembled her father's side of the family.

Anna remembered how relieved Eunice had been at this. Prior to Lauren's birth, Eunice had fretted vocally, although not when Adam was around, over the possibility that her first grandchild would come out looking like, "heaven forbid, a real Indian." As if Eunice expected the baby would spring forth wearing a headdress and holding a tomahawk the way they were so often portrayed in motion pictures.

As Anna sat down in the chair in Lauren's room, she wondered how much Eunice's relationship with Lauren would've been altered if Lauren had looked more like her mother's side of the family. Of course, Anna knew that would've changed everything. Eunice never would've pampered and spoiled an "Indian squaw" granddaughter. Even so, Anna still questioned whether Lauren's fair looks had been a blessing or something else.

"Mom?" Lauren sat up in bed, rubbing her eyes. "What are you doing in here?"

Anna smiled. "Just thinking, sweetheart."

"Oh." Lauren yawned, stretching lazily.

"How are you feeling now?"

She shrugged. "Okay, I guess."

"You look perfectly fine," Anna told her. "You don't seem to have a fever or anything to suggest a serious illness."

Lauren nodded. "I know. It's weird. The illness just comes and goes. I get so sick in the mornings that I wish I were dead. Then I throw up and feel okay for the rest of the day."

Suddenly something hit Anna—something that had happened to her when she was about Lauren's age. She recalled it as vividly as if it were last week. Anna remembered how she'd felt when she'd first been pregnant with Lauren. She let out a little gasp and closed her eyes.

"What is it?" Lauren asked with concern. "You look like you just saw a ghost, Mom. What's wrong with you?"

Anna opened her eyes, pressing her lips together, and tried to appear normal. Surely she was wrong about this. Of course she was wrong.

"What is it?" Lauren demanded. "Why are you so upset?"

"Oh, I know it's perfectly ridiculous." She tried to hide her nervousness, but went ahead and explained how there was a time when she got sick in the morning too. "Then I'd feel perfectly fine throughout day."

"Really?"

"Yes, and it went away after about a month or two."

"That long?" Lauren frowned. "What caused it?"

"You did, Lauren."

"Huh?" She looked truly oblivious.

"I was pregnant. With you."

Now Lauren's eyes got big and her lower lip quivered.

"Oh, Lauren," Anna said quickly. "You don't mean . . . you and Donald . . . well, you don't think . . . is that a *real* possibility?"

With both hands over her mouth and tears filling her eyes, Lauren slowly moved her head up and down in a frightened nod. Now Anna felt sick—truly sick. But instead of saying all the things that were rushing through her mind, Anna gathered her daughter into her arms and together they cried.

"It will be all right," Anna said as she stroked Lauren's hair. "It will be all right."

3

Lauren stayed in her room for the rest of the day. Crying off and on, refusing to speak to anyone, and barely touching the trays Anna brought in for her, Lauren seemed inconsolable. By that evening, Anna wasn't sure what to do. But she felt certain she must be handling this all wrong. Still, what was a mother supposed to do in situations like this? Who could she ask for advice? Dorothy would probably be shocked to hear the truth of Lauren's "illness." After all, Dorothy's daughters were too young to get into this kind of trouble. Consequently, Anna was too embarrassed to mention it.

It wasn't until Dorothy had gone to bed that Anna explained to Clark what was actually wrong with her daughter. "I don't know why I feel so humiliated by this," she finally confessed as she wiped tears. "It makes no sense, but I feel as if I've made a mistake. I feel ashamed."

Clark took her into his arms. "It's because you're her mother, Anna. You are linked to Lauren by invisible ties. I'm sure it's perfectly natural that you take her problems onto yourself. That's what parents do. Remember how concerned I felt when Marshall started acting like James Dean? How worried I was that I'd done something wrong?"

"I know . . . but it's more than just teen rebellion now. Oh, I feel so many emotions I can't even sort them out," she continued. "I'm angry at Lauren for getting herself into this place. At the same time, I blame myself. What if I'd never left her behind this past summer? Maybe I could've prevented this."

He made a half-smile. "These things happen, Anna. Usually there's nothing a parent can do to stop it. Kids will be kids."

"But I saw signs that she was running around too much. Eunice just let Lauren do as she pleased. She never even asked where Lauren was going, or with whom, or when she was coming home. But I can't blame Eunice for this. Lauren is my daughter. I should've been there for her."

"I don't mean to minimize this, Anna, but I honestly think there's nothing you could've done. This thing happens in all kinds of families—no matter how vigilant the parents think they are."

"Remember when we were there last summer? I should've said something right then. I knew that Donald was a womanizer."

"A womanizer?" Clark frowned. "That seems a strong accusation for the young man."

"I know. It does sound harsh." She sighed. "But it was an impression I'd had even before he and Lauren began dating. Donald was always going with a new girl, breaking hearts left and right, and leaving them strewn along—" Her hand flew to her mouth.

"What is it?"

"What if Donald refuses to do the right thing?"

"The right thing?"

"You know, to marry Lauren."

Clark's brow creased. "What if marrying her is the wrong thing?"

Anna felt confused. "I suppose I don't even know what the right thing is anymore. Really, how am I supposed to have all these answers?"

"Right now, it's out of your hands, darling. The best thing you can do is just exactly what you've been doing."

She looked into Clark's eyes, feeling herself being pulled in as he rubbed her shoulders. "And what's that?"

"Keep loving her, Anna. Keep being her mother. Give her time . . . it'll work out." He ran his hand over her long hair, kissing her on top of her head.

Anna gave in now, relaxing into his arms. As much as she wanted to resist and continue blaming herself, she knew Clark was right. Being anxious and upset was not going to make anything better. It would not change a single thing. "You're right," she conceded. "But I will take her for an appointment with Dr. Robertson tomorrow. He made time in his schedule to see her in the afternoon."

"What, no house calls now?" he teased.

Anna glumly shook her head. "Under the circumstances, I think not."

———

The doctor's appointment seemed to confirm what Anna already knew. However, the doctor offered to send a specimen out for a test—just to be sure. "Thank you," Anna told him as Lauren was getting dressed. "And I'm sure you will respect Lauren's privacy regarding, uh, this," she added a bit anxiously.

"Of course." He chuckled. "In a couple of months, Lauren will have to figure out other ways to keep folks from guessing her secret."

Anna sadly shook her head.

"I figure she's about three months along, Anna. If Lauren's young man is in a marrying frame of mind, I wouldn't waste any time with it."

"Yes, we'll discuss it." Anna waited as he wrote something down. Then Lauren came into his office and the doctor began to tell her some things.

"It's time to take it easy, young lady," he said in an almost fatherly way. "No strenuous exercise, no heavy lifting, and get plenty of rest." He lit a cigarette and let out a long puff. "And you need to eat sensibly. Not too much, mind you. We don't want you getting fat. But, remember, you are eating for your baby too."

Lauren looked on the verge of tears again. "So, it's really true? I really am pregnant?"

He flicked ashes into the large glass tray and nodded. "Yes, I'm 90 percent sure. But I'll send out for a test just to be 100 percent positive."

Now Lauren burst into full-blown tears.

"I can prescribe a sedative," he offered. "It will do the baby no good to have hysterics." Already he was writing something down.

"I think we'll be all right," Anna said nervously. She put an arm around Lauren's shaking shoulders. "Just give her a moment."

"Then if you'll excuse me, I have other patients."

Anna nodded, thanking him again. She handed Lauren her handkerchief and waited for the tears to subside. Finally Lauren set up straight, looking at Anna with a blotchy face and puffy eyes. "What am I going to do?"

Anna forced a smile. "For starters, you're going to do what the doctor said. You'll take it easy, eat sensibly, get plenty of rest and—"

"No, Mom. I mean *what about my life?* What am I going to do about this?"

She pointed to her abdomen. "I don't want to have a baby!"

"Well, darling, it's a little late to be—"

"But I've heard stories of other girls, Mom, ones who are like me. They get rid of it."

Anna stared at her daughter. "You mean an abortion?"

"I guess that's what it's called." Lauren's eyes were desperate. "Can I do that? Does this doctor do that?"

"Lauren, that's illegal. Of course, Dr. Robertson doesn't do that. And why would you want to—"

"Because I'm young, Mom. I don't want to be stuck with a kid. I want to have fun and be with my friends."

Anna reached for her handbag. "Maybe we can discuss this further at home, Lauren."

"You're sure Dr. Robertson won't help me get rid of it?" Lauren stood and glanced around his office. "He seems like a nice old guy. Wouldn't he know how it's done?"

"Hush, Lauren. We don't want anyone to hear you talking like that." Anna felt angry now. How could her daughter be like this—so callous and unfeeling? "Come on, let's get home. I need to start dinner soon."

They were barely in the boat when Lauren began pestering Anna again, begging her to find a way to "get rid of the baby." Finally Anna could take no more. She turned off the boat engine and, allowing the boat to float with the incoming tide, slowly going up the river, she told Lauren that was enough. "I don't want to hear another word from you about getting an illegal procedure like that," she firmly said. "Not only is it illegal, but I'm sure it's very dangerous. I will not allow you to take that kind of risk."

"But I don't want a baby!" Lauren howled so loudly that Anna looked over to the riverbanks to see if anyone was around to hear.

"Then you can let a family adopt it, Lauren. That happens all the time. There are couples who can't have children who'd be happy to have—"

"You don't understand, Mom."

"What?" Anna stared at her. "What do I not understand?"

"That I do not want to be pregnant. It will ruin my life."

Anna felt desperate now. "What about Donald? This is his child too. Do you think he has a right to an opinion?"

Lauren's chin quivered. "He warned me, Mom."

"Warned you?"

"To not get pregnant?"

Anna sat up straight and shook her head. "If Donald didn't want you to get pregnant, you never should've—"

"I don't want to hear that, Mom." Lauren pointed at the water outside of the boat. "If you keep talking like that I will jump into the river and drown myself."

"You know how to swim." Anna kept her voice calm, but the idea of Lauren floundering around in that cold water was unnerving. She wouldn't even put it past her high-strung daughter to do something that foolish. "Lauren," she said gently. "We don't have to figure everything out right now. Let's just go home and talk about this rationally. I'm sure we can come up with some answers."

Now Lauren went to the back of the boat, sat down, and folding her arms tightly across her chest, turned her back to her mother. Anna turned the engine back on and nervously continued up the river. The clouds had rolled in and it felt like rain was in the air. The river and sky were drab and heavy looking, shades of gray blurring together. She revved up the engine, picking up some speed so that they could get home without getting wet. She glanced back a couple of times, just to be sure that Lauren was still on board. But she was there, hunched over, her arms wrapped around herself, looking small and helpless and confused.

Anna prayed silently as she guided the boat upriver. Begging God to come up with some good solution, she prayed for Lauren's state of mind and her heart as well as her body. She even prayed for Lauren's unborn baby. When Lauren had started to speak of getting "rid" of it, something inside of Anna had reacted almost violently. Whether it was Anna's own maternal instincts or simply a longing for a grandchild, Anna knew that, without a doubt, she would fight for the life of this vulnerable baby. If necessary, she would offer to raise the child herself. Surely Clark would understand. He would have to!

4

To Anna's relief, Dorothy went back home to her family the next morning. Anna knew that Dorothy suspected something more serious was wrong with Lauren, something beyond influenza. Perhaps she'd even guessed what it was by now. But until Lauren's moodiness stabilized a bit, Anna decided it was best not to discuss her daughter's "delicate" condition with anyone. She even avoided the subject with Clark, and he seemed to appreciate this. She hoped that in time, Lauren would realize that this wasn't something she could run away from . . . or sleep away. In time, Lauren would have to face up to the consequences of her choices.

"Do women in, uh, Lauren's condition, do they usually sleep all the time?" Clark asked uneasily as he and Anna sat outside enjoying the river. Today it sparkled like diamonds and the moist air had a musky, almost spicy, aroma reminiscent of autumns past. Anna had made a pitcher of iced tea and they were soaking in some of the afternoon sun. Unfortunately Lauren had no interest in fresh air and sunshine. She'd spent most of the day in bed.

"I don't think so," Anna admitted.

"Do you think it's healthy?"

She shrugged. "Probably not. Although the doctor did tell her to take it easy."

"Oh. . . ." Clark sighed.

"I wanted to give her time to settle into it," Anna told him. "Sort of adjust to what's going on with her . . . maybe even consider the fact that she's got a living human being inside of her." What Anna didn't say—what she couldn't bring herself to say—was she hoped that Lauren's maternal instincts would kick in and she would decide that she loved and wanted her child.

Clark nodded. "That sounds like a wise plan."

"And she's obviously not going back to school now. Not this semester anyway."

He cleared his throat. "Have you informed Eunice yet?"

Anna pressed her lips together.

"I know it will be hard to do, but it might be best just to get it over with, Anna."

"I asked Lauren to call her."

"And . . . ?"

"She pulled the covers over her head and started crying again."

"Poor Lauren."

Anna appreciated his compassion toward her daughter, especially since her own sympathies were waning just now. She wondered if Clark would be as kindhearted if he knew how badly Lauren wanted to be "rid" of her unborn child. However, this was a topic she wasn't ready to discuss—not with anyone.

Anna heard the chortling sound of a boat engine coming down the river. "That sounds like Babette." She stood and peered across the glistening water to see a motorboat in the distance.

"Are you going to tell her about Lauren?"

Anna considered this. Babette was like family. She'd been around as long as Anna could remember. She was one of Anna's best friends. Surely she should tell her . . . but how? "I don't know. Of course, I'll tell her . . . eventually. But I'm not sure when."

Clark's brow creased slightly as he set his glass back on the tray. "I suppose it's women's business." He grinned. "And I've got plenty to keep me busy and out of your hair."

Anna glanced over to where the second cabin was now getting its roofing installed. "That's looking good," she told him.

He strapped on his tool belt. "Want to get it weathered in. Just in case."

"Good idea. October is usually a fair month, but you never know."

"Tell Babette hello for me." He nodded and headed toward the cabins. Anna knew his plan was to get four of the cabins up and roofed and sided before the weather turned. Then he could finish the interiors during the winter. Eventually Shining Waters Inn would have a dozen cabins nestled along the river. Sometimes Anna almost had to pinch herself to see if this was real or just a lovely dream.

She hurried down to the dock where Babette's little cruiser was pulling in. Babette had one of the nicest boats on the river. Her first husband had been lucky in the gold mines, but he had died young, long before Anna was born.

"Alo!" Babette called out as Anna secured her boat.

"Welcome," Anna said as she waited.

Babette handed her a basket, then, holding on to Anna's free hand, carefully climbed out of the boat. She remained fairly nimble despite her years.

"What's this?" Anna asked as she peered into the cloth-covered basket.

"I hear your Lauren ees sick?"

"How did you hear that?" Of course, this was a silly question. News on the river traveled almost as fast as the current.

"Mrs. Thorne at the grocery store. She say Mrs. Danner tell her."

Anna nodded. "Yes, Dorothy probably mentioned it to her mother."

"Ees a secret?" Babette frowned. "You keep from old Babette?"

Anna smiled. "No, of course not. I keep nothing from you."

Babette pointed to the basket. "I bring goodies for Lauren. We will make her well again, Anna."

Anna glanced away. If only it were that easy.

"What ees matter?" Babette touched Anna's arm. "Ees eet serious? The illness?"

Anna nodded to the lawn chairs in front of the house. "Let's sit for a spell," she quietly said.

Without speaking, Babette sat down.

"Would you like some iced tea?" Anna offered as she set the basket down. "I can run up to the house and get you a glass."

Babette shook her head. "No, chéri. I only want to hear what you will now tell me. What ees matter with our Lauren?"

For the first time since hearing this news, Anna felt tears filling her eyes. She'd seen Lauren break down over and over, yet somehow Anna had managed to keep her own emotions in check. Now that was over.

"Tell Babette." She pressed a lace-trimmed handkerchief into Anna's hand. "Eet will be better, chéri."

So, with tears flowing, Anna poured out the whole story.

To Anna's relief, Babette seemed nonchalant about this news. "Eet happens, chéri," she said simply. "Bebes are sometimes a surprise, but always a blessing, no?"

Anna sighed. "Yes, I hope so."

"You no want a grand-bebe?"

She forced a smile. "Of course, I do," she assured her. "I would love a grandchild."

"Ooh, I must help with the bebe layette." She pursed her lips with a thoughtful look. "I have some lace and soft linen . . . .eet will make perfect christening gown!"

Now Anna felt nervous. How could she encourage Babette to make fine baby things for a child that might not . . . might not . . . ever be part of their family? And how would she explain that to Babette? This thought alone made her want to sob again. But, no, she needed to be strong. "Please, Babette," she said quietly. "Let's not speak of it anymore. I don't want Lauren to know that I told you."

"Oui, oui." Babette nodded. "I understand. My lips are closed."

"Now, should we take your basket up to the house and see if we can tempt Lauren's appetite? Lately she's been reluctant to eat much of anything." She explained about the morning sickness as they went up the stairs. "Mostly I'm afraid she's just feeling blue."

"Eet ees to be expected, no?"

"Yes, I suppose you're right. But I do worry."

Babette hummed cheerfully as they went into the house. In the kitchen she began to unpack her basket, setting items on the new laminated countertop that Clark had recently installed. Anna had decided on white because it looked clean and fresh and brightened the room much more than her mother's old dark-red linoleum. "Chicken soup with ginger," she explained as she handed the large jar to Anna. "And these ees fennel bread." She set a small loaf on the pine table. "Will calm her tummy." Now she took out a small flask. "Extract of crab apple." She patted her own stomach. "Also ees good for tummy."

"Are these things safe?" Anna asked quietly, "I mean for her condition?"

"Oui, oui. Your grandmamma, she tell me about zee crab apple, how to make eet in summer." Now she explained how much to give Lauren, then she removed a tin of chamomile as well as a small jar of lavender oil. "Put eet here." She touched Anna's temples and smiled. "Rub eet in gently. Eet will help."

Anna opened the small bottle and sniffed. "It smells lovely."

"We will make her well, chéri. You will see."

Anna hugged her. "Thank you, Babette."

Babette just waved her hand. "Ees nothing." Now she lowered her voice. "And your secret is safe." She picked up her basket. "Now I go to town. Anything you need me to bring to you?"

"I don't think so, but thanks."

Babette was barely gone when Lauren came shuffling out of the bedroom. With her unwashed, uncombed hair and pale face, she looked worse than ever. Her expression was one of pure hopelessness.

"You're up." Anna forced a cheerful note to her voice. "You just missed Babette."

Lauren said nothing, but simply flopped down on the brown leather couch in the living room. With a creased forehead, she fingered the corner of one of the pillows that Anna had covered in Indian blanket.

"How about a late breakfast?" Anna offered. "Babette brought some things to help with—"

"How does she know about me?" Lauren glared at her.

"Dorothy told her mother that you were sick and the word spread. Babette thought you had some sort of influenza." Anna held up the bread. "She made you some things to settle your tummy."

Lauren's expression returned to a pout. "I don't want to eat."

Anna decided to ignore this as she warmed the soup and sliced and toasted the bread. Spreading a little honey on the toast, like she used to do when Lauren was small, she arranged this meal on a tray and took it into the living room. "Babette is my dear friend," Anna told her as she set it on the coffee table. "For her sake, please, at least try to eat something."

Lauren said nothing and Anna went back to the kitchen, busying herself with tidying up and wishing she knew how to deal with this better. Part of her felt truly sorry for Lauren, another part of her just wanted to shake the silly girl. Even so, she knew that her only real recourse would be patience. Lots and lots of patience.

After awhile, Anna peeked out to see that Lauren was no longer in the living room; however, she had eaten everything on the tray. Feeling a small sense of victory, Anna picked up the tray and returned it to the kitchen. She was just rinsing the dishes when she heard Lauren's voice.

"It is not your problem!" she exclaimed vehemently. "And the sooner you get over it, the better off we'll both be!"

With a soggy dishrag in hand, Anna hurried out to see if her daughter had lost her senses. But halfway there, she realized that Lauren was speaking into the telephone.

"I'm sorry you feel that way," Lauren said in a snippy tone. "I had hoped that you'd want to help me."

Anna could tell by the quiver in Lauren's chin that she was about to break into tears, but all Anna could do was to stand there and watch as she wondered who was Lauren talking to.

"Fine!" Lauren snapped. "Have it your way. You always do!" Now she began to sob. "I don't want to talk to you anymore— I don't care!" She held out the phone to Anna now. "Here! You talk to the old witch!"

Anna's eyes grew wide as she took the receiver from Lauren, watching as her daughter streaked to her room and slammed the door. "Hello?"

"Anna? Is that you?"

Anna recognized her former mother-in-law's voice. "Yes, Eunice. It is."

"What in land's sake is going on out there?"

"Not too much." Anna braced herself. "The river is fairly quiet and the sun is—"

"I am *not* referring to the weather!"

"How are you, Eunice?"

"And I do not care to talk about my health, although after hearing what your daughter just told me, I feel I'm in need of an aspirin and a long nap. Is it true, Anna? Is Lauren—well, is she really pregnant?"

"Yes," Anna conceded. "The laboratory tests came back positive. It's true."

"It just figures that this would happen on your watch, Anna. You were always perfectly useless as a parent. Why Lauren wanted—"

"Excuse me." Anna sat down on the sofa, twisting the phone cord between her fingers. "Lauren did not become pregnant on my watch. Not that it matters particularly. What's important is that she *is* pregnant, Eunice. And I felt it was only right for her to let you know—"

"So that you could shame me?" Eunice demanded. "Or put the blame of this unwanted child on my doorstep? Because if you think you can—"

"That's not what I'm trying to do, Eunice. I only felt you should know."

"And if you think you're going to foist your pregnant daughter back on me, you are sadly mistaken, Anna. I am washing my hands of that girl."

"I'm sorry to hear that, Eunice. But, I didn't plan on sending Lauren back to you. I'm perfectly happy to keep her here with me."

"Do you know what she asked me to do, Anna?"

"She asked you to do something?"

"Yes. Do you have any idea of what kind of gall that daughter of yours has? I suspect she's reverting back to your family's savage ways. It's no wonder, living out there in the sticks the way you do. I shouldn't be surprised that she'd come up with such a barbaric idea."

Anna suppressed the urge to respond defensively. "What sort of idea?"

"Lauren actually asked me if I knew a doctor who could, well, you know . . ." she lowered her voice as if she thought someone might be listening to. "She wanted me to find a doctor who could get rid of the baby."

"Oh, dear." Anna cringed inwardly.

"Well, I told her in no uncertain terms that I most certainly did not!"

"Yes, well, I'm sorry Lauren brought that up." Anna was truly sorry.

"I suppose you might approve of such things, but I—"

"I do not approve."

"Well, at least we agree on one thing."

"Lauren has not been herself," Anna attempted to explain. "As you can imagine, she's very upset by all of this. I suspect she wasn't thinking clearly when she spoke to you on the phone. Her emotions seem to be a bit uneven."

"Still, that's no excuse, Anna. It will do no good to defend her on this. As my father used to say, she made her bed and now she can lie in it."

Anna said nothing.

"And if she expects anything from me, she is sadly mistaken."

"Yes, Eunice." Anna was trying to think of a graceful way to end this conversation.

"Although I would like to know what kind of responsibility young Donald Thomas is taking. You know, his mother, Ardelle, is a dear friend of mine, and she hasn't said a word about this to me."

"I suspect it's because she doesn't know about it."

"Surely Donald must know about Lauren's condition. What does he intend to do about it?"

"Those are questions for Lauren."

"Well then, get her back on the phone!"

Anna could still hear Lauren sobbing. "I'm afraid that might be impossible just now. Perhaps I can encourage her to call you later, after she's settled down some."

"Fine! But just so you know, I am severely disappointed. Not only in you this time, but I am deeply wounded by Lauren as well. I feel that your daughter has betrayed me, and I'm not even sure I can recover. When I think of all I've invested in that girl, all the bright hopes I've nurtured for her. Well, I am simply devastated. I shall be surprised if I don't need to call for Dr. Cybert before the day is done."

"Yes, well, perhaps an aspirin and a nap will put you back together," Anna said tightly.

"I seriously doubt it. Now, do like I say, Anna. Tell Lauren to call me as soon as possible. I must find out what to do about the Thomas family. Poor Ardelle. She will be devastated."

"Do take care," Anna said, hoping to end this conversation.

"And you tell Lauren to call me back—and I mean today, Anna!"

"I'll tell her." Anna hung up the phone with a solid clunk then let out a long exasperated sigh. Oh, she would keep her word and tell Lauren. But, she would not force Lauren to call Eunice back. In fact, if Lauren chose to completely ignore her grandmother, Anna would not mind in the least. Eunice had never been a healthy influence on Lauren anyway. For years she had overindulged her, spoiling her so badly that Anna felt it was useless to even attempt to parent her own child. But now this attitude of severe condemnation would only make matters worse. Eunice only ran hot or cold. Perhaps a break in that stressed relationship would do Lauren some real good.

Anna remembered some of the old strain that used to run between her own mother and Grandma Pearl. In some ways, it wasn't so different than this. Anna's mother had chosen to live like a white woman and disliked her mother's return to the old ways. Embarrassed by things like basket weaving or herb gathering, Anna's mother occasionally voiced her opinions to Grandma Pearl. Sometimes Grandma Pearl defended herself and an argument would ensue. But usually she just went off into the woods for a few days. Despite their differences, Anna believed that the two women loved each other. When it came to Eunice's true sentiments, however, Anna could never be sure.

5

"Hello, beautiful." Clark came up from behind Anna, wrapping his arms around her waist and pulling her close as she rinsed her hands at the oversized sink.

"Hello there, yourself," she said as she turned to face him, breathing in the fresh smell of the outdoors and what smelled like cedar shavings.

"How's our girl?" he asked quietly.

Running her fingers over his rough calloused hands, she gave him a quick update, lastly filling him in on Lauren's upsetting phone call.

"That woman." He grimly shook his head. "She's a real piece of work."

Anna nodded. "But I partially understand her—in a slightly twisted sort of way. Eunice's life was so entwined in Lauren's. I'm sure she feels a real sense of loss and shame and disappointment. In her own way, she does love Lauren. Or at least she did."

Clark shrugged. "Too bad she can't think of more constructive ways to show it."

"My only explanation of Eunice is that she is broken." Anna shook her head. "I don't know how or why, and I realize that people see her and think she has everything she could possibly want, but underneath the exterior of money and power lives a broken little girl."

"Who enjoys breaking others?" Clark made a half-smile.

"They say misery loves company."

"Well, I just came in to tell you something that I forgot to mention yesterday."

"What's that?"

"Mom called."

"Oh, how is she?" Anna warmed to think of her new mother-in-law. Hazel had been such a part of her life, right up until the wedding. In fact, Anna had been missing her recently.

"She said she was homesick."

Anna frowned. "But I thought she was home now."

"She is home. She said she was homesick for the river."

Anna laughed. "Well, did you tell her that her little cabin is vacant?"

"No." He shook his head. "Of course not."

"Why not?"

"For one thing, that would be for you to do, Anna. For another thing, Mom thinks we're still honeymooners. She even said as much."

Anna giggled. "Well, if we're honeymooners, what is my daughter doing here?"

He shrugged.

"I'm going to call your mother and tell her that she is more than welcome." Anna nodded firmly. "That is, if you don't mind."

"Not at all."

Anna went for the telephone now. "In fact, your mother might be just what we need around here," she said as she picked up the receiver.

"Tell her hello for me." Clark waved as he headed for the door.

Anna placed the long distance call then waited, wondering how much she should tell Hazel about Lauren's being here. "Hello?" Hazel said cheerily.

"Oh, it's so good to hear your voice," Anna said. "It's me, Anna."

They chatted amicably for a couple of minutes then Anna got to the point. "Clark said you were homesick for the river."

Hazel laughed. "Oh, you probably think I'm a silly old woman."

"Not at all," Anna declared. "In fact, I had been missing you." Now she explained about Lauren being with them. "And Clark and I would love to have you come back out. If you can, that is. Are you still working on your thesis?"

"I'm supposed to be doing my final edits right now, but I find myself getting quite distracted here at home. I'm always finding some way to sidetrack myself. Even if it's something as mundane as defrosting my freezer compartment—something I never do under normal circumstances. I know it's simply an avoidance technique on my part, but I cannot seem to escape it."

"Perhaps you'd be less distracted out here on the river?"

"You really wouldn't mind the extra company?"

"We would love it, Hazel!"

"Oh, you're such a dear, Anna. I'm so thankful that I found you that day on the river. Remember how you were out paddling in your canoe and I thought I'd seen a mirage?" She laughed heartily.

"It was one of the best days of my life," Anna told her.

"Well, I will gladly take you up on your offer, dear. I am ready to pack my bags this instant."

"Wonderful."

"Is tomorrow too soon?"

"Not a bit." They settled on a time to meet in town. Feeling surprisingly happy, Anna hung up. Confident that having Hazel here would help to lighten the atmosphere with Lauren, Anna went right to work gathering fresh linens for the cabin where Hazel would stay. It was the same cabin that Anna's grandmother had once inhabited. Of course there'd been much improvement since those days, but it was still a quaint little space. As Anna changed the sheets, she felt that her grandmother would be pleased to know that Hazel was coming back to visit. In many ways Hazel was a bit like Grandma Pearl. Strong and confident and very fiercely independent.

Clark opened the door and stuck his head in. "Does this mean that Mom is coming?"

"She is." Anna tossed the used linens in the wicker laundry basket. "Tomorrow."

His brows arched. "Tomorrow?"

She nodded. "I think your mom will be good for Lauren, Clark. I'm happy that she's coming."

He came all the way into the cabin now. "You know, Mom does have some experience in the way of, well, unwed pregnancies."

"Oh, that's right. I nearly forgot about that."

"I'm sure she'll have an opinion on the subject. That is, if you're comfortable with her knowing about Lauren."

"Hazel is family," Anna said firmly. "Of course she will have to know. Hopefully she will share some of her wisdom with Lauren."

Clark's brow creased. "But you need to remember, what was right for my mother might not be the best thing for Lauren."

Anna went closer to Clark, looking into his eyes. "I remember Hazel telling me how hard it was on you as a boy," she said gently. "Having no father, I mean."

He sighed. "Mom did the best she could. And I had my grandparents. But there's no denying that there was a certain stigma attached to our family. To be honest, it's not something I'd wish upon a child."

Anna frowned. "I feel sad that what would otherwise be such a happy occasion has become so clouded. It seems unfair."

He just nodded. "Children do suffer for adult choices, but fortunately they're somewhat resilient. Or so I like to think."

"It's interesting, isn't it? My childhood wasn't exactly idyllic either. There were times when I was picked on for being part Indian. But I don't think it hurt me too badly."

He gently touched her cheek. "I don't think it hurt you at all."

She smiled. "Really, it was my adulthood—enduring Eunice's bigotry and caring for Adam after the war—that took the biggest toll on me."

"And yet you're probably stronger as a result of those hard years."

"Maybe so." She smiled. "Anyway, I'm looking forward to your mom being here. I'm sure she'll help to brighten things up."

<hr />

Anna decided not to tell Lauren about Hazel's impending visit until Clark was on his way downriver to pick her up. She'd asked him to break the news to his mother before they came home. It seemed the easiest way to handle it. But now she had to inform Lauren that Hazel would soon be here.

"Clark is on his way to get his mother," she began carefully as she picked up Lauren's hairbrush.

"Hazel is coming here?" Lauren asked.

"Yes. She was missing the river and I invited her to come out." Anna began to brush out Lauren's tangled hair, just like she used to do when Lauren was a child.

"And I suppose you told her about me," Lauren grumbled.

"No, I only said you were visiting us for a spell."

"But you *will* tell her." Lauren narrowed her eyes.

"Honey, Hazel is Clark's mother, my mother-in-law. She's family and I love her very much. I see no reason she shouldn't know."

"*Fine.*" Lauren snatched the brush from Anna. "Maybe you'd like to place an advertisement in the local paper—tell the whole world that your daughter is—is in trouble." Now she threw the brush to the floor and fell across the bed and sobbed.

Anna picked up the hairbrush, sat down on the bed next to Lauren's heaving body, and continued to slowly brush her hair. "You know," she finally said after Lauren had quieted down. "You're not the first young woman to get pregnant outside of marriage."

Lauren made a grunt sound.

"In fact, it might come as a surprise to you, but Clark's mother has been through this exact same thing."

Lauren sat up, looking at Anna with puffy red eyes. "You're just saying that."

"No, I'm not, dear. It's true. Hazel became pregnant when she was in college."

Lauren blinked. "What did she do about it?"

Anna shrugged. "She had the baby. In fact, the baby grew up to be Clark."

"Really?"

Anna nodded. "So if you think Hazel is going to judge you about this, think again. Hazel is a bit like your grandmother in that she's a woman who speaks her mind, but she is also very kind and gracious." Anna continued to brush out the tangles, telling Lauren about how Hazel continued her college education and how her parents helped her to raise Clark. "It wasn't easy," she said, "but it was possible. And I know Hazel has absolutely no regrets about it now."

Lauren blew her nose on a handkerchief then looked at Anna with wistful eyes. "You know what I wish, Mom?"

"No."

"Well, I mean besides wishing that I wasn't pregnant?"

"What do you wish?"

"I wish that Donald would get on a big white horse and come galloping over here in a suit of shining armor and that he would get down on a knee and hold out a big diamond ring . . . ." She sighed. "And then he'd marry me and take me away and we would live happily ever after."

Anna made a forced smile. "Like a fairy tale."

Lauren nodded eagerly. "Do you think it could happen?"

Anna shrugged. "I thought you said Donald was very opposed to the idea of marriage and children."

"Of course he'd say that. I said the exact same thing to him. But circumstances have changed now. I'm thinking that I've been gone from school long enough that he will have to miss me. He will have to wonder. Don't you think he'd want to do the right thing, Mom?"

Anna made a genuine smile as she pushed a strand of unwashed hair away from Lauren's face. "Of course I think he would. Why wouldn't he?"

Lauren made a sad little smile. "I think I'll take a shower, Mom."

Anna tried not to look too relieved. "Oh, that's a wonderful idea, sweetie. Take a nice, long hot shower. You'll feel like a new person."

While Lauren showered, Anna fixed her a late lunch of a tuna sandwich and tomato soup. She felt surprisingly hopeful now, as if perhaps they'd turned a corner. And when Lauren emerged from her room, looking fresh and clean and dressed in tan woolen slacks and a butterscotch-colored sweater set, Anna felt certain that Lauren was making real progress.

"My pants are too tight," Lauren told Anna as she picked up the sandwich. "Do you think it's too soon for me to be getting fat? Do I need to get some maternity clothes?"

Anna laughed. "Well, it's only natural that you'll put on a few pounds at this stage. But I don't think you need maternity clothes quite yet. I'm sure we can let some things out for the time being."

Lauren was just finishing up when Hazel entered the house with a grocery sack in her arms. "Hello, hello," Hazel set the bag on the table. "Oh, my goodness, it is so good to be back!"

Anna rushed to hug her. "I'm so glad you're here."

"Clark, bless his heart, is taking my things to the cabin, but I just had to come up here and see you first." She patted Anna's cheeks. "You look well, my dear. Marriage must agree with you!"

"Thank you." Anna blushed. "I don't remember when I've been so happy."

"I had to clean out my fridge and decided to bring a few things to you." Now Hazel looked over to where Lauren was standing on the fringe of the kitchen with a worried expression. "And I am so very glad to see you, dear girl!" She bustled over and vigorously hugged Lauren then, holding her at arm's length she smiled. "Clark explained all about your situation, Lauren. And I just couldn't wait to tell you that it is going to be all right, darling. Trust me, my dear, you are going to be just fine."

Lauren blinked. "Yes, I, uh, I think so too."

Holding both of Lauren's hands in hers, Hazel directed her over to the couch. "Now, you and I are going to sit down right here. And we're going to have a nice long chat. Is that all right with you, dear?"

Lauren simply nodded and sat.

"Can I get you some tea?" Anna offered.

"Yes, dear. Tea would be lovely."

As Anna busied herself in the kitchen, she could hear Hazel talking quite openly to Lauren, assuring her that they lived in a new era. "Women no longer must settle for the role of housewife and mother," she told Lauren. "These days, women are making all sorts of achievements in the fields of science, literature, music . . . well, you name it and a woman is standing right alongside a man and doing it." Hazel laughed heartily. "Oh, there was a brief setback following the war. Our men came home and insisted the little women stay home and tend to the home fires. But women had already made their mark by then. Believe me, Lauren, a woman can do or be anything these days. Even if she is a mother."

Hazel continued espousing independent women and what they were capable of accomplishing, saying how it was possible to be a single mother and attend college and have a career. "But only if you're willing to work hard and make some sacrifices," she said firmly. "I don't want to paint the picture too brightly."

On one hand, Anna felt relieved for this reassurance. On the other hand, she felt quite concerned. Anna felt certain that Lauren was not as strong as Hazel. And she wasn't sure that Lauren would ever be. Besides being utterly spoiled by her grandmother during childhood, Lauren had always lacked motivation, and she'd always cared more about fashion and boys than her studies.

Just the same, Anna felt Hazel's pep talk couldn't hurt anything. And perhaps Anna had underestimated Lauren. If nothing else, it seemed that Lauren was finally getting away from that crazy talk about "getting rid of the baby." That in itself was worth a lot.

"Here you go," Anna said as she set the tea tray down in front of them.

"So you see"—Hazel poured the tea.—"anything is possible if you put your mind to it, Lauren."

Anna glanced at her daughter and was a bit surprised at Lauren's expression—a mixture of confusion and disbelief. "But what if all I want is to be a housewife and a mother?" she asked meekly. "Is anything wrong with that?"

"Well, uh, no . . . ." Hazel glanced uncomfortably at Anna. "I suppose not. If that's what you really want."

"That's right," Anna said to Lauren. "Being a mother and a wife is a very honorable thing to do. I think what Hazel is try-ing to say is that you don't have to settle for just that. I mean, if you want something more."

Lauren looked like she was on the verge of tears again. "But that's not good enough, is it?" She looked from Hazel to Anna.

"Of course it's good enough," Anna told her.

"No!" Lauren stood. "You both think I'm throwing away my life. You think I've messed up and am just settling now. But you don't know me. You don't know what I'm really like, what I really want." She burst into tears, turned, and ran back to her room, slamming the door loudly behind her.

"Oh, dear." Hazel shook her head. "That did not go as I had hoped."

Anna just sighed. "Her emotions have been a little unstable."

"Yes, of course. Pregnancy hormones do that to a woman." Hazel reached for her teacup. "She'll get better, Anna. Just give her time."

Anna filled her own teacup now. "Yes . . . I'm sure you're right, Hazel." Still, she didn't feel as confident as she sounded. More than ever, she felt that Lauren was a stranger to her. As much as she hated to think it, it seemed entirely possible that Lauren was more related to Eunice than to Anna.

6

Hazel had only been with them for a few days, but her optimism lightened everyone's spirits. Plus, she'd already made good progress on her thesis. During breakfast she read a portion of it aloud to them. It felt so authentic, almost as if Grandmother were speaking, that Anna grew teary. Later, as she carried a basket of dirty linens down the stairs, Anna thought about Grandmother and how she'd washed her clothes in the river. Anna just reached the laundry shed when she heard Henry's old boat chugging upriver toward them. They didn't expect any deliveries today, but Henry was clearly headed for their dock. She set down the willow basket and went down to see what had brought him their way.

Henry waved to her with a hard-to-read expression as she caught the rope and secured it to the dock. "Got a passenger on board for you." He jerked his thumb over his shoulder and she peered past him to see a woman in a navy suit with a veiled hat sitting primly behind him.

"*Eunice?*" Anna couldn't believe her eyes.

The older woman stood, and rocking precariously, she grabbed Henry's arm to steady herself. "Yes, of course, it's me. Who did you think it would be?"

"But what are you doing here?"

"Help me out of this smelly tub," she growled at Henry.

"Gladly, ma'am." He grabbed her elbow and led her up the steps as Anna hurried over and, giving Eunice a hand, helped her down onto the dock.

Eunice pulled her hand away with a scowl. "I am here for Lauren."

Anna blinked. "What do you mean?"

"I mean I came to take Lauren home with me."

"Does Lauren know about this?"

"She will as soon as I inform her."

"But I don't understand." Anna glanced up toward the house. Clark was coming down to the dock with a curious expression. Perhaps he could help her figure this out.

"What should I do with her stuff?" Henry asked Anna.

"What stuff?"

"That stuff," Henry pointed a gnarled finger at a small pile of luggage.

Anna looked back at Eunice. "What do you want Henry to do with your bags? Did you plan to stay here?"

"I planned to stay in a *hotel*." Eunice turned up her nose. "Is there such a thing in this backwater place?"

"Anna has a right nice inn," Henry said as Clark joined them on the dock.

"You're welcome to stay here, if you like," Anna told Eunice.

"Well, I don't know." Eunice looked like she'd just bitten into a lemon.

"We have plenty of room," Clark informed her.

Eunice adjusted her handbag on her arm, folding her gloved hands together in front of her. "I don't want to be an imposition."

"Like Henry said, this *is* an inn." He glanced uneasily at Anna. "Guests are always welcome. Although it is Anna's inn."

"It's *our* inn," Anna corrected.

He grinned at her.

"Wanna give me a hand with them bags, Clark?" Henry called out. "I still got me some deliveries to make 'fore the day's over."

"But you will return to transport my granddaughter and me?" Eunice asked urgently. "You haven't forgotten?"

"Like I already told you"—Henry handed Clark an overnight case—"all you do is give me a telephone call first thing in the morning, and I'll arrange to pick you up."

"But I intend to leave tomorrow," she told him with impatience. "I want you to plan on getting us tomorrow morning. Do you understand me?"

He frowned as he hoisted the last bag to Clark. "That's a mighty short stay, ma'am. 'Specially considering you brought all them bags with you."

"My luggage is no concern of yours," she retorted.

"Not now, it ain't." Henry tipped his hat to Anna then winked. "Looks like you've got your hands full, Anna."

"Thank you, Henry." She untied the rope and tossed it to him.

Henry put the boat in reverse and waved. "Let me know when you want me to come back for her," he called as he backed away.

"I said tomorrow!" Eunice shouted.

"I heard you," he shouted back.

Anna waved, then turned to Eunice. "May I show you to your room?"

Eunice stared at the house. "You really call this place an *inn*? It looks more like an old barn to me."

"It used to be a store," Anna explained as she led Eunice from the dock. "Our home was on the second floor and the store was below. But Clark helped me to remodel the old store space into several rooms. That's where you'll be staying."

"You're putting me in an old storeroom?" Eunice's nose was wrinkled as if she'd smelled something rotten.

"Like I said, we've done some improvements." Anna pointed to the smaller building. "Clark just finished the bathhouse last summer."

"You mean I have to go outside to use the restroom?"

Anna chuckled as she continued on the trail to the house. "Well, you would've had to use an outhouse before. But Clark wisely suggested a bathroom in this building too."

Clark pointed to the other building, in various stages of progress. "And right now I'm working on finishing up some more cabins."

"Those will be used for the inn too," Anna said proudly. She paused to admire some of the flowers she'd transplanted last spring. They looked so bright and cheerful in the late afternoon sun, putting on their last show of color for the season. "Someday we'll be able to host up to fifty people here." She glanced back at Clark and smiled. "Can you believe it?"

"So you honestly think people will actually pay good money to stay in this place?" Eunice shook her head.

"I haven't had many paying guests yet." Anna pressed her lips tightly together. She was determined not to react to Eunice's jabs. "But I believe that in time the guests will come."

"What on earth for?"

Anna exchanged glances with Clark as he lugged Eunice's bags up to the porch.

"A lot of people enjoy the natural beauty of the setting," he told Eunice. "The river is peaceful and the fishing is good. It's really a very attractive location."

"Humph." She shook her head. "Well, it's far too rustic for my taste. I recall Lauren telling me how you people didn't even have running water or electricity."

"We've made a lot of improvements." Anna opened the door to the suite. It was the largest of the three rooms downstairs and, like the rest of the rooms in the inn, it was decorated in lodge style with Native American blankets and rugs and rustic furnishings. "I'll put you in here, Eunice." Thankfully she had freshened the sheets since the last guests were here, back when they'd had a full house for their wedding. "There's the bathroom." She pointed to a door. "And the closet is here. Please, make yourself at home."

"Where is Lauren?"

"Upstairs." Anna stepped out of Clark's way as he sat the luggage by the door. "I'll tell her that you're here." She paused before she left. "Was Lauren expecting you?" Eunice's brow creased as she removed her hat. "How could she be expecting me? She never even called back." She shook her finger at Anna. "You promised that Lauren would return my call, *remember*? And, of course, I didn't have your phone number. So, what else could I do but come here myself? Traveling to the ends of the earth just to speak to my own granddaughter. *Really!*"

"Oh." Anna frowned. "I did ask Lauren to return your call, Eunice. I assumed that she had done so."

"Well, if she had returned my call, I wouldn't have been forced to come out here, now would I?" Eunice sighed dramatically as she peeled off her gloves and tossed them onto the dresser. "Heaven knows what this trip will do to my poor old bones. And the dampness of the river will play havoc with my arthritis. I have no doubt that it will keep me awake all night."

"Perhaps you'd like a little rest now," Anna suggested. "Dinner is at six-thirty."

"Yes. I do believe I could use a rest." She reached over and patted the bed. "Not that I imagine this bed will be any too comfortable. In the meantime, you tell Lauren that I want her to pack her bags and be ready to go home with me the first thing tomorrow morning. And I expect you to make sure that horrible river man comes to fetch me like he promised."

Clark gave Anna a sympathetic look. "If you need to leave in the morning," he told Eunice, "I'll be happy to take you in our boat—whenever you'd like to go."

"But I can't promise that Lauren will go with you," Anna said as she reached for the door.

"She'll go with me," Eunice snapped. "If she knows what's good for her, she will go. You do like I said. Tell her to be ready to travel in the morning."

Anna simply nodded. Then she and Clark stepped back out into the sunshine and just looked at each other. Anna didn't even have words for what had just transpired. In some ways it seemed like a very bad dream.

"It feels like the Wicked Witch of the West just arrived," he said quietly as he walked her over to the stairs.

Despite herself, Anna laughed. "At least she didn't destroy our house when she landed."

"Did you have any idea she was coming?"

"None at all." Anna shook her head. "Maybe it's a good thing. I'm sure I would've just worried if I'd known."

"Do you really think Lauren will go with her?"

"I honestly don't know."

He reached out and squeezed her hand. "Be strong."

She smiled. "It's a lot easier to be strong when I know you're nearby."

He tipped his head toward the cabin he was working on. "I'm just a holler away, darling."

Anna chuckled. "Well, if you hear me yelling, you better come running."

"Do you want me to inform Mom that we have a new guest?"

Anna grimaced. "I just hope that Eunice doesn't manage to insult your poor mother too."

"Oh, don't you worry about her. She can take care of herself."

"Yes, I expect she can."

"Anyway, I'll let her know. Knowing Mom, she might even have some trick up her sleeve for disarmament."

Anna thanked him then headed on up to speak to Lauren. She had no idea what Lauren's reaction would be to this new development, but at least she'd been having a relatively good day today. Since her initial encounter with Hazel, Lauren had been slowly warming to the idea that she might be able to do more with her life than just pine away in the hopes that Donald would turn into Prince Charming. Anna had even overheard Lauren telling Hazel that she might return to college someday. Not only that, but Lauren had actually made herself useful in the kitchen these last couple of days. And although it took a lot of nagging and prodding, Lauren had gotten up in time for breakfast today. Maybe next time she'd show up in something besides her bathrobe.

Anna paused at the top of the stairs and gazed out over the river. How was she going to break this news to Lauren? Just when she'd started to feel hopeful that Lauren was giving up her relentless pursuit of trying to reach Donald on the telephone. Anna could only imagine what their long distance bill would be since Lauren must've left that boy dozens of messages by now, begging him to return her calls at her mother's house. But, as far as Anna knew, Donald had yet to call back. Just the same, Lauren rarely ventured far from the telephone. Simply getting her to leave the house for a walk this morning had felt like a major victory. She hoped Eunice's presence wouldn't be a setback. Anna took in a deep breath and opened the door.

Lauren was curled up on the couch with a book in her lap and the telephone just inches from her elbow. "Good book?" Anna asked as she came over to join her.

She shrugged. "Hazel gave it to me. I guess it's kind of interesting. But there are a lot of words that I don't know."

"There's a dictionary on the bookshelf."

Lauren wrinkled her nose, reminding Anna of Eunice.

"I have a little surprise for you . . ." Anna forced a smile.

Lauren's blue eyes lit up. "*What?*"

"Someone is here to see you and—"

"*Donald!*" Lauren leaped to her feet, dumping the book onto the floor. "I can't believe it. Where is he—"

"No, sweetheart. I'm sorry. It's not Donald. It's your grandmother."

Lauren's smile disappeared and she sank back down onto the couch with a loud groan. "What's *she* doing here?"

"She says she's come to take you back with her."

Lauren scowled darkly. "Why would I want to go with *her*? She was so mean to me on the phone the other day. I don't want to see her. If she tries to talk to me, I will go to my room and never come out!"

Anna didn't know how to respond. Part of her wanted to agree with her daughter and put an end to Eunice's nonsense. But another part—probably the motherly part—knew she needed to encourage her to act more mature. "I can understand you not wanting to see your grandmother, Lauren. To be honest, I'm not that happy to see her myself. But she did come a long way to get here. The least you can do is hear what she has to say."

Lauren sighed. "I just wish Donald would call me back." She looked at the clock above the fireplace. "Maybe I should try his dorm again. He should be done with classes by now."

Anna just shrugged. "I'm going to start dinner."

As she went into the kitchen, she heard Lauren dialing the phone again. Soon she was speaking to someone—but as usual, it was not Donald. "Tell Donald this is extremely urgent," Lauren pleaded. "I have to speak to him as soon as possible. Tell him it's a matter of life and death! *I mean it!*"

Anna continued peeling potatoes, silently praying for Lauren to be strong—whether or not Donald ever came to the telephone . . . or to her aid.

"*Donald!*" Lauren exclaimed suddenly. "Why haven't you called me?"

Anna turned the water off and just stood there, anxiously waiting, but there was a long silence and she could only assume that Donald was speaking. However, she had no idea what he might be saying. She peered around the corner to see that Lauren's face looked distressed and slightly pale as she listened to the receiver.

"Don't you even want to know why I'm *not* there at school anymore?" Lauren finally asked in a small voice. "For all you know I could be dying, Donald. Don't you even care about me anymore?" Now there was another long pause.

"Donald, don't say that. I know you can't mean that! You can't be that cruel. You said you loved me before."

Anna felt sick as she backed into the kitchen, trying to refocus on peeling potatoes. What was Donald saying to her daughter? What kind of monster was this boy?

"But you said you loved me, Donald. More than once. And I've only been gone a couple of weeks. How could you change so much in such a short time?"

Anna set down her paring knife and leaned against the counter.

"But I *did* call you. Lots and lots of times. I left hundreds of messages and the guys said you'd gotten them, but you never returned my calls!"

Anna closed her eyes tightly. This was so hard to overhear. But she felt trapped in the kitchen just now.

"Fine, be like that, Donald Thomas. And just so you know—while you're taking out stupid old Cindy Payton—just so you are fully aware of what is what—*you are going to be a father!*" Lauren screamed into the telephone. "Yes, you heard me right, you no-good, cheating, two-timing liar. *I am pregnant*, Donald. I am having your stupid baby! Thank you very much! And if you think you can just go on with your merry little life while I sit here watching the world pass me by, you are sadly wrong, Donald Thomas. You are wrong, wrong, wrong!" This was followed with the crash of the receiver clattering down on the telephone and loud wails from Lauren.

Anna hurried out. "What's going on, honey?"

"Nothing, Mom. Nothing whatsoever." Lauren folded her arms across her front and scowled.

"Are you all right?"

"Oh, yeah, Mom. I'm just fine and dandy!" Then Lauren shrieked like a wounded animal and ran to her room, slamming the door so hard that the whole house seemed to rattle. Anna didn't know what to say or do. Wringing her hands together, she simply paced back and forth, silently praying for God to help them. She was just starting to feel her sense of serenity returning when the jangling telephone rattled her nerves.

Taking a deep breath, she politely said "hello" in the hope it might be an actual guest.

"*Lauren?*" demanded an angry voice.

"No. This is Lauren's mother. May I ask who is calling?"

"I—uh—this is Donald Thomas, ma'am. May I speak to Lauren?"

"I'm afraid Lauren is too upset to speak right now, Donald. Is there something I can help you with?"

"I—uh—I don't know. I just wanted to, uh, well . . . ."

"I don't know what you just said to Lauren, Donald, but it must've been very upsetting."

"Yeah, well, I'm upset too."

"I'm not surprised you're upset. I'm sure it's not easy to hear that you are going to become a father."

"So is it true?" He sounded more like a boy than a man now.

"Do you honestly believe this is something a girl makes up?"

"Maybe. If she's trying to catch a man. She might do something like that."

"Then, take it from me, Donald. Lauren is pregnant. She's been to the doctor. She's taken the tests. As they say in the movies, the rabbit died."

He let out a groan.

"And the next time you speak to my daughter, Donald, I suggest you use a tone that is respectful of the woman who is carrying your child."

"Yes, ma'am."

"Now I am not going to tell you what to do about this. That's something you and Lauren will have to figure out. But I will tell you this, son. It takes two to make a baby and, since you're older, I am holding you even more responsible for this than Lauren. Does that make sense?"

"Yes, ma'am."

"Good. Do you want me to see if Lauren feels up to speaking to you yet? Or do you need some time to carefully consider what you're going to say to her? Because I am not going to put up with any nonsense. This is a grown-up matter and I expect both you and Lauren to act like grown-ups. Is that clear?"

"Yes, that's clear."

"It's unfortunate how this all came about, but there is nothing you can do about it now—nothing besides taking responsibility and doing the right thing that is. Fighting and name-calling will do no good. And I plan to tell Lauren the same thing. But I expect you to take the high road, Donald. What Lauren has lost is going to cost her a whole lot more than it is costing you. For that, she deserves some sympathy from you. Do you understand what I'm saying?"

"I understand."

"Good."

"Tell Lauren that I'll call her back . . . um . . . later. Okay?"

"I'll do that."

Anna's hands were actually trembling when she hung up the phone. She couldn't believe that she'd actually spoken like that to Donald Thomas. But as she walked back into the kitchen, she was glad that she had and knew, if necessary, she would do it again.

7

I hear there's a new guest at Shining Waters Inn," Hazel said as she joined Anna in the kitchen. Dressed in her brown corduroy pants and a plaid wool jacket, Hazel's cheeks were ruddy. Her suede shoes had dampened toes, as if she'd just come in from a walk. "I thought perhaps you could use a hand."

Anna gave her a relieved smile as she set a small pitcher of fall flowers on the kitchen table. "I think I can use your moral support even more than your help." She pulled out a wooden chair. "Why don't you just make yourself comfortable and keep me company." While Hazel sat, Anna washed vegetables and quietly filled her in on the events of the afternoon.

"My, my . . . ." Hazel shook her head. "It sounds as if you've been through the wringer."

"It's Lauren I'm concerned for," Anna told her. "Donald seems intent on breaking her heart."

"So sad . . . and she seemed to be making such progress too."

"And now with Eunice here . . . well, I don't know what to expect."

"Do you think Lauren will go home with her grandmother?"

"I'd like to say no, but the truth is I suspect she will."

"Why is that? Lauren seems to like it here."

"I know. In fact, she's seemed more at home these past couple of days than I've ever seen her before. It gave me such hope."

"So why would she want to leave?"

"Her grandmother has methods for getting her way." Anna lowered her voice. "She sometimes uses her money . . . sometimes she simply applies pressure. But she has always been able to work Lauren."

Hazel looked disappointed.

"I know . . . it doesn't speak well of me, does it?"

"I'm not suggesting that."

"Well, it's how I feel. If I'd been a better mother—stronger, I mean. If I hadn't let Eunice rule over me all those years while Lauren was growing up, perhaps Lauren would be stronger now."

"I'm sure you did the best you could . . . under the circumstances. From what I've heard of Eunice, she is a force to be reckoned with." Hazel chuckled. "To be honest, I'm dying to meet this woman."

Anna wiped her hands on a towel and just shook her head. "I hope she doesn't say something to offend you, Hazel, but I'll warn you, it's a possibility."

"I'm a tough old bird. I suspect I can hold my own with her."

Anna glanced at the clock, deciding it was time to put the salmon into the oven. "At least Eunice always liked my cooking," she said as she closed the door. "I don't need to worry about that." She grinned at Hazel. "Although, mark my word, she will still complain about it."

"If she likes it, why does she complain?"

Anna shrugged. "I think that complaining gives Eunice pleasure."

Hazel looked confused. "But if she complains about the food, how can you be sure she likes it?"

"Watch her." Anna winked. "She'll clean her plate and ask for more."

Hazel broke into laughter.

"What's the joke?" Clark said as he came into the room, hanging his dusty felt hat by the door. His expression was curious as he peeled off his denim carpenter's jacket.

"Oh, nothing." Anna motioned to him. "But if you come in here, I'll fill you in on the latest developments." Then, as he munched on a carrot, she explained about Lauren and Donald.

Clark's blue eyes grew cloudy. "I'd like to wring that boy's neck."

"Get in line," she told him. "But at least I made myself pretty clear on the telephone. I told Donald in no uncertain terms that I expect him to act mature about this." She sighed. "I can't tell him exactly what he should do, other than to take some responsibility."

"If I were Lauren's father, I'd force Donald to do the right thing and marry her."

"Oh, Clark." Hazel frowned. "What good would that do?"

"Might do their child some good. Besides that, Lauren thinks she loves the boy. Maybe if he were man enough to marry her and take care of her, he'd grow into a better person."

Anna pressed her fingers to her lips now. "I think we should probably change the subject. What will be will be."

Clark chuckled. "You're starting to sound like Doris Day now."

She wrinkled her nose at him.

"Anyway, I'm going to clean up for dinner." He kissed her on the forehead. "Something smells mighty good."

Anna checked on the potatoes then turned to Hazel. "If you'd start setting the table, I think I'd like to go check on Lauren."

"The good china?"

"Of course," Anna assured her. "We have a new guest."

Hazel looked doubtful, but didn't argue.

Anna knocked on Lauren's door then let herself into the room. She expected to find Lauren in her bed, but instead, she was sitting by the window, looking out on the river with a very sad expression.

"Oh, Lauren." Anna came over and put her arms around her. "I'm so sorry about how Donald reacted to you today."

Lauren just shrugged.

"If it makes you feel any better, I had a nice long chat with him myself."

Lauren looked surprised. "You called him?"

"No, he called back. I set him straight on a few things."

"What?"

"Just that he needed to grow up and take some responsibility. And I told him to be more respectful of you too."

Lauren brightened a bit. "Thanks, Mom."

"I also told him that there would be no more blaming or name-calling." She stroked Lauren's hair. "On both ends."

Lauren just nodded. "He has a new girlfriend, Mom."

"Oh . . ."

"Cindy Payton. She's a stuck-up snob from Portland. She's in my sorority and she goes around acting as if she's better than everyone else. Just because her family is filthy rich. She's not even that good-looking. Honestly, I don't see how he can stand her."

Anna didn't know what to say.

"I feel so lost, Mom." Lauren looked up with watery eyes. "I don't know what to do. What should I do?"

"Right now, there's not much you can do besides what you're doing, sweetie. You need to take care of yourself. And it's almost time for dinner, so you need to eat. And, even though it seems dark at the moment, you need to believe that things will get brighter." Anna reminded Lauren of how difficult her life was when Lauren's dad came home from the war. "He was in such terrible shape, sweetie. And I had to take care of him, and you were still in diapers. And your grandmother treated me like a slave. Those were really hard times for me." She smiled. "But now I'm happier than I ever imagined possible."

"Yeah, but you're older, Mom. I'm still young. I don't want to live like you did for all those years."

Anna just nodded. "Can't say that I blame you. I don't want you to live like that either, sweetie. I just want you to remember that there's a light at the end of the tunnel. A silver lining in the black cloud. Things will get better. I know it."

"But now Grandmother's here." Lauren made a face. "And I don't think I can stand to see her. Do you think I could just eat my dinner in here? You could tell her that I'm not well."

"We could do that, but sooner or later you'll have to face her. Wouldn't it be easier to just get it over with?"

"I guess. It's been such a horrible day already; maybe it can't really get any worse."

Anna hoped that Lauren was right as she went back to garnishing the salmon with fresh sticks of rosemary. But, knowing Eunice, she knew that things probably could get worse. She was just taking the salmon out of the oven when Lauren emerged from her room. She'd taken the time to brush her hair and change into a fresh white blouse and had even put on some lipstick. "You look very pretty," Anna told her.

Lauren just rolled her eyes.

"Would you mind running downstairs to tell your grandmother that dinner is ready while I put the food on the table?"

"Might as well get this over with," Lauren said with a dour expression.

Before long everything was ready, but Lauren and Eunice were still missing. "Do you want me to go check on them?" Clark offered.

Anna was unsure. "Maybe they're talking."

"Let's give them a few more minutes," Hazel suggested.

Then, just as Anna became concerned that the food was getting cold, Lauren returned. "That woman!" she said as she slammed the front door.

"What's wrong?"

"She's impossible!" Lauren sat down at the table and growled.

"Well, is she coming to dinner?" Hazel asked.

"She wants you to take her dinner down to her," Lauren informed Anna.

"Oh, dear." Anna shook her head then told them to go ahead and start eating while she fixed a plate for Eunice. "No sense in everyone eating cold food."

"Hopefully Eunice won't think that she can have room service all the time," Clark teased as Anna set Eunice's dinner things on a tray. "You might want to set her straight on that, Anna."

"Good luck with that," Lauren quipped.

Anna tried not to feel too irritated as she carried the heavy tray down the stairs. On one hand, she should be relieved that Eunice wasn't going to spoil dinner for everyone. On the other hand, how selfish could one woman get?

"Here you go," Anna said as she set the tray on the dresser. "I hope it's still warm."

"Oh, don't worry about me," Eunice said in a pitiful tone. "I have no appetite anyway."

"Well, I'll just leave it in case you change your mind." Anna reached for the door.

"Wait," Eunice said in a slightly desperate tone.

"What is it?"

"I want you to tell Lauren that she *must* go home with me, Anna."

Anna just looked at her.

"Tell her she has no choice in the matter."

"But she does have a choice, Eunice. It's Lauren's decision."

"Yes, but you're her mother. You can make her—"

"I have no intention of making Lauren do anything."

Eunice narrowed her eyes. "No, of course not. You never did make your daughter do anything, did you? Why I thought you could help me now is beyond me. You were useless then, you are useless now." She waved her hand in a dismissive way. "Be gone with you!"

As she closed the door behind her, Anna remembered Clark's Wicked Witch of the West comment and couldn't help but smile. What made Eunice think she could come here and boss Anna around? And, definitely, there would be no more room service. If Eunice didn't want to come up for breakfast, the old woman could just go hungry.

8

Feeling a bit guilty for not being more concerned about the welfare of her "guest," Anna went down to check on Eunice before breakfast.

"Excuse me," Anna said when Eunice opened the door in a yellow bathrobe, "but I couldn't remember if I told you that breakfast is served at 8:30."

"Oh, yes," she said sleepily. "What time is it now?"

"8:15."

Eunice frowned. "You could've awakened me a bit earlier, Anna."

"You didn't ask to be awakened."

"Yes, well, anyway."

"If you don't make it up there by 8:30, I'll set something aside for you." Anna stepped in to remove the tray of empty dishes. "And did you still plan on leaving this morning? Clark wanted to know."

"Well, no, I don't think I'm ready to leave this morning."

Anna just nodded as she exited with the tray. She wasn't sure what to think now. If Eunice wasn't leaving this morning, how long did she plan to stay?

Hazel was helping Anna clean up the breakfast dishes when Eunice came up. "I've got a plate for you in the oven," Anna told Eunice after introducing the two women. "Would you like some coffee?"

"Please." Eunice sat down at the kitchen table, loudly clearing her throat. "I would have risen earlier except that I hardly slept a wink last night."

"I'm sorry to hear that." Anna exchanged glances with Hazel. "I tried to find the most comfortable beds possible."

"Yes, well, my bones are old." Eunice sadly shook her head as Anna set a plate in front of her.

"Mind if I join you?" Hazel asked as she brought over the coffee.

"Please, do." Eunice frowned down at her plate. "There's enough food here to feed a logger, Anna."

"Just eat as much as you like," Anna called.

"If you have trouble sleeping, you might want to try some of Anna's grandmother's natural remedies," Hazel told Eunice.

"Are you referring to Anna's Indian grandmother?" Eunice sounded horrified.

"Yes. I'm writing my doctoral thesis on Pearl. Did you know she was one of the last Native American healers of her time? A very wise woman indeed."

Eunice laughed. "You've got to be joking."

"I am most serious." Hazel began to tell Eunice about a fern that tasted like licorice and worked wonders on arthritis.

"If you think I'm foolish enough to eat some strange plant because of some old Indian mumbo-jumbo, you are sadly mistaken."

"Perhaps you're unaware that most of our modern medicine is extracted from natural sources," Hazel told her. Now she began listing off medicines and the plants they used to create them. "Aspirin was originally derived from *spiraea ulmaria*, otherwise known as meadowsweet, and yet aspirin is considered the wonder drug of this century. And meadowsweet is simply an innocent-looking little wildflower."

"I suppose you're going to tell me an Indian made this amazing discovery."

"All I am saying is that Native Americans were probably more evolved than us in the field of herbal medicine—quite likely there are many other things long since forgotten—it's a crying shame that so much was lost due to white man's ignorance."

"Oh, please! Are you suggesting Indians knew more than whites?"

"About some things, absolutely."

"Then tell me, why are the Indians nearly gone and we are still here?"

"Because the white man stole tribal land, broke their treaties, shared their lethal diseases, and practiced genocide not so much different than Hitler in Nazi Germany."

"Oh, pish-posh." Eunice waved her hand. "For an educated woman, you are certainly full of a lot of foolish notions."

"Lauren should be coming back soon," Anna said to Eunice, hoping to change the subject before the conversation grew any more heated. She didn't mind Hazel sharing her knowledge with Eunice, but she knew that Eunice was just words away from saying something truly regrettable.

"Coming back from where?" Eunice demanded. "Didn't you tell that girl I wanted to speak to her?"

"She took a walk," Anna said as she refilled Eunice's coffee cup. "The fresh air and exercise is good for her." Anna told Eunice a bit about Donald's disturbing phone conversation yesterday. "So you see . . . Lauren is still rather upset."

"I should imagine she'd be upset. What on earth is wrong with that boy anyway?"

"What is wrong is that he is just a boy," Hazel answered, "who needs to grow up."

"His mother is a good friend of mine," Eunice stated. "She raised him better than that."

"Does his mother know about this?" Anna asked.

Eunice looked uncomfortable. "Well, I considered telling her . . . but I just wasn't sure how to go about it. I thought that if I could bring Lauren back with me, we could go to see her together—and we could insist that Donald do the right thing."

"The right thing?" Anna shook her head. "How do we know what that is? Right now Donald is dating another girl. He acts as if he has no interest in Lauren. What good can come of forcing him to marry?"

"What good?" Eunice looked shocked. "A marriage will make this thing right . . . or as right as it can be. It won't eliminate all the shame, but babies are known to arrive early. The sooner we get those two kids married, the better it will be for everyone."

"But a marriage without love?" Anna frowned.

"Oh, you are one to talk," Eunice said sharply. "Where was the love in your marriage, Anna? And don't think you can fool me. I was there, remember?"

"You weren't there early on, not when Adam and I first met and married—"

"Married against my wishes!"

Anna ignored that. "At least Adam and I were in love," she said to Hazel. "But when times got tough, even that love wasn't enough . . . not after he came home from the war. For Lauren and Donald to marry . . . without love . . . it seems doomed from the start."

70

"Anna is right," Hazel agreed. "It would be better for Lauren to raise the child on her own than to subject it to a bad marriage."

"And I can help Lauren with the child if she likes," Anna said. "Clark and I have discussed it. We're willing to have them stay on with us for as long as they like."

"You expect Lauren and her child to live out here in the sticks with you?" Eunice set her coffee cup down with a loud clink. "Perhaps you want Lauren to raise her child like a little Indian? Maybe you'll take to eating plants for medicine?" She pointed to a basket on a shelf. "I expect you'll teach the child to weave baskets too." She laughed as if this was ridiculous.

"I would be proud to teach both Lauren and her child about her heritage." Anna stood. "Including basket weaving."

Eunice chortled even louder now, only stopping when Lauren came into the house. "Oh, Lauren, you are missing all the fun," Eunice called out in a snide tone. "Your mother plans to teach you to weave Indian baskets and turn your baby into a papoose. In no time, I expect to see you wearing moccasins and beads, dear. Can you imagine?"

"What?" Lauren looked at Anna in confusion.

"Oh, your grandmother is just being humorous." Anna felt an old familiar flush of anger and humiliation running through her as she went over to the sink. All the times that Eunice had made fun of her came rushing back—how had she endured those years? And did she have to continue to endure it, right here in her own home?

"I do not find any of that to be humorous," Hazel said stiffly. "In fact, I find it to be rather bad taste, Eunice. And I think you owe Anna an apology."

"You expect me to apologize?" Eunice sounded affronted.

"You have insulted your hostess," Hazel continued. "I'm not sure how you were raised, Eunice, but I was taught to be more respectful than that. Especially when staying as a guest in someone's home."

"Oh, don't be too shocked, Hazel." Lauren went over and put an arm around Anna. "Grandmother is always like that. But you're used to it, aren't you, Mom?"

Anna turned and looked at Lauren. "I suppose I am used to it, Lauren. In the same way that a dog that is regularly beaten becomes used to it. But it still hurts."

Lauren looked surprised. "Really?"

Anna just nodded and returned to rinsing dishes.

"Then I agree with Hazel, Grandmother. I think you owe my mother an apology."

"*Well!*" Eunice made a *harrumph* and Anna heard the sound of a chair scraping across the floor. "*Excuse* me!" The sound of footsteps was followed by the firm closing of the front door.

"Was that supposed to be an apology?" Hazel asked.

"Maybe for Grandmother it was," Lauren said.

Anna looked back at Lauren and smiled. "You know, sweetie, that is the first time you've ever stood up for me."

"Really?" Lauren looked sad. "I guess I never knew that it bothered you so much."

"You never knew?" Anna frowned.

"You always seemed so strong, Mom, like nothing could penetrate or hurt you."

Anna just shook her head. "I guess I put on a good act, then. But all those words, all those years . . . they hurt. Trust me— they hurt a lot. They still do."

Lauren seemed truly surprised. "I'm sorry, Mom. I really didn't know."

Anna reached out and hugged Lauren. "Maybe that's my fault . . . for keeping my feelings locked up all those years." She stroked Lauren's hair. "It seems like you've been feeling better this morning."

Lauren made a sad smile. "I do feel better. I guess the stuff Babette sent over really works."

"Did you have a good walk?"

"Yeah. It's really pretty out there, Mom. I even saw fish jumping in the river."

"Have you ever been fishing?" Hazel asked Lauren.

"Not really. I went with Donald once, but I never actually fished myself."

"Maybe you'd like to try it."

"Would I have to bait my own hook?" Lauren looked concerned.

Hazel chuckled. "I'll help you with it."

"Do you think I should, Mom?"

Anna nodded. "I think it's a wonderful idea."

"Why don't you come too?" Lauren suggested.

"Yes," Hazel agreed. "We'll do a girls' day. We'll take a picnic and really make a day of it."

Anna glanced out the window. "The weather is certainly enticing. But what about Eunice? I should probably stick around to make her some lunch."

"Why not let Clark handle that?" Hazel suggested.

"You think Clark would really want to fix Eunice's lunch?" Anna tried not to look shocked.

"He knows how to cook," Hazel assured her. "And I'll bet he'd agree that you deserve a day off, Anna."

"Yeah, Mom." Lauren nodded eagerly. "You're always working."

So Anna decided to just do it. But as she made a picnic lunch, she made extra provisions for Clark and Eunice. She was just finishing when Clark came in.

"I hear that I'm on KP for lunch." He leaned over and pecked her on the cheek.

She pointed to a plate of sandwiches. "I made extras."

He gave her a hurt expression. "What? You don't think I can cook?"

"I'm sure you can cook, darling. But I was making sandwiches anyway."

"Mom told me about Eunice's bad manners this morning." He put a strong hand on her shoulder, giving it a gentle squeeze. "I don't blame you for wanting to escape. Any idea when she's leaving?"

Anna straightened the collar on his plaid woolen shirt. "She didn't mention anything. I suppose she can always call Henry if she wants out of here today. We'll have the boat."

"If she wants out of here today, I'll even drive her, although she might not enjoy the bumpy ride and it will take longer." His blue eyes twinkled with mischief. "But at least we'll be rid of her."

"Somehow I have a feeling she's not ready to leave yet."

"Well, you girls have a fun day, and don't hurry back either."

She placed both hands on his cheeks now, feeling the beginning of stubble against her fingers. She looked intently into his face. "Do you know how much I appreciate you?"

He grinned. "Probably not as much as I appreciate you, darling." He leaned forward until his forehead touched hers. "And don't think it's easy for me seeing Eunice treating you like she does. For your sake I try to mind my manners, but my tongue is getting doggone bloody."

"*What?*"

"From biting it so much."

⊶∞⊷

Despite the span of their ages, Hazel, Anna, and Lauren actually did have a fun day. After getting over her initial squeamishness, Lauren even managed to put a worm on her own hook. And she squealed in delight when she landed the first catch of the day—a ten-inch trout. Between the three of them, they caught more than a dozen fish. Then, with their fish on ice, they tied the boat to a decrepit dock and enjoyed a picnic on an island. Afterwards they gathered blackberries and pickleweed and even explored an abandoned farmhouse that was reputed to be haunted. When they'd gone nearly to the river's end, they decided to stop in town for a bit. There they got an afternoon snack of ice cream and some additional ice to keep their fish cool.

"Oh, look what's playing at the theater," Lauren said as they walked with their cones. "*Some Like It Hot*."

"What's that?" Hazel asked.

"Just the funniest movie ever," Lauren told her. "I saw it last summer. You mean you never saw it?"

Hazel laughed. "I haven't been to a movie in ages."

"Nor have I," Anna admitted.

"Look, there's a matinee," Lauren exclaimed. "Let's go!"

"Right now?" Anna looked uncomfortably at Hazel.

"Why not?" Lauren said.

Anna didn't know what to say. On one hand, she was thankful that Lauren was having such a good time . . . on the other hand, what about Clark . . . and Eunice?

"I think we should do it," Hazel pronounced. "*Carpe diem!*"

"What?" Lauren tipped her head to one side.

"That means 'seize the day,'" Hazel explained. "Enjoy the moment."

"Yes." Lauren linked her arm into Anna's. "Let's do that."

"But we'll get home after dinnertime," Anna protested.

"Clark will handle it," Hazel assured her.

"But I—"

"Come on, Mom." Lauren tugged on her, and Hazel was already purchasing tickets. Giggling like she was a girl again, Anna gave in. Of course, it was a very silly movie, but Anna laughed so hard she had tears running down her cheeks.

"See?" Lauren said as they exited the theater. "Wasn't that fun?"

"Yes." Anna nodded then frowned to see that the sky was getting dark. "But I have to call Clark. Let's go to the grocery store and I'll use the payphone."

To Anna's relief, Clark seemed fairly unconcerned. "But I do appreciate your calling," he told her. "I told our guest about your outing and I noticed that she'd helped herself to food. There are plenty of dirty dishes in the sink. So I know she's not starving."

"Oh, good. How about you?"

"I'm enjoying the peace and quiet at the moment."

"So you don't even miss us?"

He chuckled. "Of course I miss you. But while you're in town, why not get yourselves some dinner? I already finished off the leftovers from last night."

So that was what they did. Lauren picked the Burger Shop and they all got hamburgers and milkshakes and continued to talk and laugh about the movie they'd just seen. "This was so much fun," Lauren told them as they got back into the boat. "It was like being with my friends."

"Well, I hope we *are* your friends." Hazel opened a storage bin and handed out blankets. "It's probably going to be cool out on the water."

"In some ways it was even better than being with my friends." Lauren wrapped the blanket around herself like a shawl. "Sometimes my friends can be a little mean," she admitted.

"That's because your friends are still young," Hazel explained. "Trust me, Lauren, women get better with age."

Anna started the engine and was soon steering the boat out into the center of the dark river. Lights from town reflected on the surface of the water, painting a scene that reminded her of an impressionist painting she'd admired in a library book once. Unless she was wrong, it was Van Gogh's *Starry Night*.

"Really?" Lauren sounded skeptical. "You honestly believe that women get better when they get older?"

"Well, some women do," Hazel clarified. "Not all of them, mind you."

The river was calm and quiet with no other boats in sight. The incoming tide helped propel the boat so that Anna could run the engine slow and easy. "Look at the moon just coming up." She pointed to the east. "It looks like it's going to be full."

"A hunter's moon," Hazel proclaimed. "Lovely."

"What's a hunter's moon?" Lauren asked.

"It's the full moon that follows the harvest moon. It's also called a beaver moon."

"Yes," Anna said. "I remember Grandma Pearl telling me that. She had a beaver moon story too."

"That's right," Hazel said. "Do you remember it?"

"I think I do."

"Tell us," Lauren urged her.

Anna thought hard, trying to recall exactly how it went.

"Didn't it start with Wolf howling at the moon?" Hazel suggested.

"That's right," Anna told her. "Maybe you should tell it." Then she explained to Lauren about how Hazel was including Grandma Pearl's story in her thesis.

"I'll help you if you like, but I'd like to hear your version, Anna."

Anna nodded. "The story begins with Wolf. Like Hazel said, Wolf was howling at the moon. Every night he'd howl and howl at the moon. But Moon didn't like it because it disturbed Moon's sleep."

Lauren snickered.

"So Moon made a deal with Beaver to make a trap to catch Wolf so that Moon could kill him. But Beaver tricked Moon, so Moon turned Beaver into a stone. Meanwhile Wolf continued howling at the moon. Next Moon told Fox to make a trap for Wolf. And since Fox saw what happened to Beaver, and because he didn't want to become a stone, Fox agreed. But before Fox finished making the trap, Wolf pushed the stone that was Beaver into the river and Beaver became Beaver again."

"Good for Wolf," Lauren said.

"But that night Fox's trap was finished and Wolf was captured. Moon came down and skinned Wolf and stretched his skin out to dry."

"Poor Wolf."

"But that's not the end. While Moon was sleeping, Wolf snuck out and stole his skin from the stretcher and Beaver helped him to sew it back on."

"That must've hurt." Lauren laughed.

"Moon was so mad that he disappeared completely. When he came back, Moon was so small that Wolf quit howling at him. But every time Moon got all big and full, Wolf would howl at him again. I think it was to remind Moon that he hadn't beaten Wolf."

Hazel laughed. "Well, that's not exactly like your grandmother's story, Anna. But I think I like it even better."

"And you really wrote these stories all down?" Lauren asked Hazel.

"Yes. And they may even be published in a book someday."

"My great-grandmother's stories?" Lauren sounded slightly impressed.

"Yes, her stories and lots of other things."

"That's nice," Lauren said. "I'd like to read some of the other stories someday."

Anna felt an unexpected rush of joy as she clutched the wheel of the boat. This whole day, and Lauren's words just now, felt like more than she'd dared to hope for. It seemed as if Lauren was finally growing up. Anna felt so elated that she could almost relate to Wolf's ecstasy and, for a moment, she considered howling at the moon too. But she kept her gaze forward as she navigated along, watching the black glossy surface of the river for any stray logs. Howling at the moon as she sunk the boat would be the wrong kind of ending for such a perfect day.

9

It wasn't until the next morning that Anna consciously thought about Lauren's "delicate condition." They'd had such an unexpected day yesterday, plus she'd finally connected to Lauren in a significant way. Consequently, she'd simply blotted the pregnancy from her mind. But as she made coffee, it was all she could think about. It had been so pleasant seeing Lauren having fun, letting her guard down, and just being a girl. Almost as if she too had forgotten about the unborn child growing within her.

For the fourth day in a row, Lauren hadn't woken with morning sickness. When Anna had peeked in on her, she was sleeping peacefully. That in itself was something to celebrate. However, the fact remained—Lauren *was* going to have a baby. Decisions would eventually need to be made, and Lauren would have to accept that she had a responsibility to her child. Anna knew that adoption was a valid option. Yet she longed for a grandchild. If she could have her way, she would encourage Lauren to keep the baby, to remain here, and to let she and Clark help in raising it. However, Anna knew it was not her decision to make. Lauren would have to decide what was best for her . . . and the child.

"Is that coffee ready?" Clark landed a kiss on her forehead then reached for a blueberry muffin.

"Almost."

He broke it in half and took a bite. "I noticed Eunice was up and at 'em already."

"Really? She's up?"

"She was out there walking, not too fast, but she made it to the dock and back." He grabbed a dishcloth and wiped some spilled coffee grounds into the sink, then popped the rest of the muffin in his mouth.

"Do you think she's getting ready to leave?" Anna asked hopefully.

Before he could answer, they heard the front door open and close. "Good morning," Eunice called out in a surprisingly cheerful tone.

"Good morning, Eunice." Anna wiped her hands on a towel then turned, making a stiff smile for her guest.

"I see you decided to come back." Eunice frowned as she joined them in the kitchen. "Did you bring Lauren back with you?"

"Of course." Anna removed an egg carton from the fridge. "She's still sleeping."

"Well, the way you and Hazel whisked her away did give me cause to wonder."

Anna cracked an egg into the ceramic bowl. "I don't see why. We simply went fishing and exploring the river a bit. Then we stopped in town and Lauren insisted we needed to see a film."

"You might've informed me of your activities."

"I asked Clark . . ." Anna glanced over to see him filling a coffee mug.

"I told you what was going on," Clark firmly said to Eunice. "Don't you remember?" With a creased brow, he took a sip of coffee.

She sniffed. "Well, all I can say about that is if this is how you plan to treat your guests, I can't imagine how your inn will be much of a success."

Anna pressed her lips together as she cracked another egg, whacking it so hard that shell fragments fell into the bowl.

Clark cleared his throat. "You mentioned your visit was going to be brief, Eunice. Do you need us to call Henry for transportation?"

"That won't be necessary."

Anna exchanged glances with Clark. He shook his head and excused himself to go check on something outside. She knew he was simply trying to escape Eunice. He probably was concerned he might say something regrettable, or maybe his tongue was sore again. "Would you care for some coffee, Eunice?"

"If it's not too much trouble." Eunice sat at the kitchen table, holding her head as if she thought she was queen. Perhaps she did think that. Anna filled a coffee cup, put it on a saucer, added the cream and sugar just like she knew Eunice preferred, and set it in front of her.

"Have you been able to convince Lauren that she should go home with me?" Eunice asked as she lifted her cup.

"No, I don't believe it's my place to convince Lauren of anything." Anna checked the bacon and returned to cracking eggs in a bowl.

"As her mother, you don't feel a responsibility to direct Lauren?"

"I can share my opinions with her, but, no, I don't think I should be directing her."

"Well, that's perfect nonsense." Eunice made a *tsk-tsk* noise. "Lauren is a child, Anna. She needs the adults in her life to guide her."

"I think she needs to listen to own her heart," Anna said quietly, "and figure out what is it that she really wants. Then I will support her in that decision."

"Really?" Eunice sounded doubtful. "You would support her in the decision to go to a doctor and have a procedure to get rid—"

"No," Anna said quickly. "I already made my position clear about that. And I think Lauren respects that."

"But you would support her in the decision to give the baby up?"

Anna came over to the kitchen table and looked into Eunice's eyes. "It wouldn't be my first choice for her or the baby, but, yes, I would back Lauren's decision if she decided that the baby would be better off with different parents." Anna felt a lump in her throat. "In fact, I think that would be a very selfless decision on Lauren's part . . . to allow her child the opportunity to be raised by a healthy, happy couple that wanted a child."

"Oh, pish-posh." Eunice set her cup down so firmly that Anna blinked. "That isn't being selfless, that's being a coward. And who's to say it would be best for the child?"

Anna studied Eunice with curiosity. "So, tell me, what is it you really believe that Lauren should do about this? Do you really want her to come home with you, to live under your roof as an unwed mother? You would proudly parade your grand-daughter and her fatherless child around town, Eunice? Is that what you're suggesting?"

"No, of course not. I would insist that Donald and Lauren marry, as quickly and quietly as possible."

"Really?" Anna lowered her voice, worried that Lauren might awaken and hear them discussing her future so casually, although she usually slept later than this. "I'm very curious as to how you would accomplish this impossible feat?"

Eunice laughed, or was it a cackle, but then just shook her head. "Oh, don't you worry about that, my dear. Where there's a will, there's a way."

Anna returned to fixing breakfast. She knew that Eunice was without scruples when it came to manipulating others to get her way. And, most likely, she would use her wealth and her influence in this matter. The sooner Lauren decided what she truly wanted, the happier Anna would be. Still, she didn't want to push or rush Lauren.

To Anna's relief, Lauren slept in during breakfast. And Hazel's cheerful chatter helped to keep their conversation from going down the wrong paths. Anna suspected that Clark had given Hazel a head's up about the friction building up between Eunice and herself.

"So, when are you going home?" Hazel asked Eunice as Anna cleared the table. "I heard the weather is going to get a little stormy this weekend."

"Oh, I'm not afraid of a little weather," Eunice said in a falsely cheerful tone.

"I hadn't heard that about the weather." Anna rinsed a plate and set it aside.

"Yes, I overheard someone in town saying that yesterday," Hazel said.

"You might want to consider that, Eunice," Anna told her. "If the weather turns nasty, it can be rather unpleasant traveling to town on the river or by road."

"I'm not worried about that."

Anna wanted to demand to know why Eunice was suddenly digging her heels in to remaining here, but knew that was too rude. "So am I to take it that you've decided you like Shining Waters Inn?" she asked.

Eunice laughed. "Your inn seems to be rather missing something, Anna. I mean guests—well, besides members of your family that is. Still, I don't see how you can call it an inn, or how you expect it to turn a profit."

"I happen to be a paying guest," Hazel told her.

"Oh no, you're not," Anna said. "You are our guest, Hazel."

"No, I most certainly am not," Hazel insisted. "If you think I plan to stay here and freeload off of you, I will have to pack my things and go home."

"But, Hazel—"

"No buts, Anna." Hazel firmly shook her head.

Anna didn't know what to say. "Well, I expect I will have to let Clark settle this matter with you."

Hazel grinned at her. "I expect you will."

Eunice was getting up now. "If you will excuse me."

"Yes, of course. But please, Eunice, you might want to consider how long you really want to stay here. Bad weather can really make a person feel trapped out here. I'd feel badly if you got cabin fever and were forced to travel during the middle of a storm."

"Do not concern yourself with me."

Anna sighed.

"Although I do have a suggestion for you, Anna."

"What is that?"

"If you really intend on running this, this *place*, as a business, you should put televisions in the rooms. Even the cheapest hotels have TV these days."

Anna grimaced. "Even if I had televisions in the rooms, there would be no reception out here, Eunice. Besides, that is not the purpose of this inn."

"The purpose?" Eunice frowned.

"My goal here is to create a peaceful environment where guests can participate in nature and experience the healing elements of the river and the sky and the trees, not sit around watching TV."

Eunice laughed loudly at this. "Well, now I have heard everything, Anna."

Anna watched Eunice go out the door, still chuckling to herself as if her clueless former daughter-in-law was very entertaining.

"Oh, Anna." Hazel let out a loud sigh. "How you put up with that woman is a complete mystery to me. I am controlling myself for your sake, but I'm telling you it is not easy. I'm not a violent person, but I find myself wishing I could wring her scrawny turkey neck."

Anna couldn't help but laugh at that.

"Is Grandmother gone?" Lauren asked cautiously as she emerged from her room. She was still in her bathrobe, and her blond curls resembled a rag mop.

"The coast is clear," Hazel called out.

"And I saved some breakfast for you," Anna told her.

Hazel stayed and visited for a bit then, excusing herself, explained she had work to do. With just Anna and Lauren left, the room seemed quiet.

"It's nice you've gotten your appetite back," Anna said as she refilled her coffee cup and sat down with Lauren.

"Yeah, I'll probably get fat as a pig now."

"Not if you eat sensibly and get a little exercise."

"I guess." Lauren frowned as she spread apple butter on her toast. "I wonder why Grandmother is still here."

"I was wondering the same thing myself."

"I mean, she's always made it clear that she hates this place. She complains about everything. I don't see why she doesn't just go home."

"I think it might be because she's still hoping to convince you to leave with her, Lauren."

Lauren wrinkled her nose. "Fat chance of that."

"I wonder if it would help if you communicated that to her."

"I thought I already did." Lauren reached for another piece of bacon.

"I know, but your grandmother is a stubborn woman. She thinks she'll talk you into it."

"I don't see how. I mean, if I have to go through this pregnancy, and it seems I don't really have much choice about that, then I certainly don't want to go back to Pine Ridge and have everyone staring at me as I get bigger and bigger. I can just imagine the old gossips talking behind my back and making fun of me. I just couldn't take that, Mom."

"Well, we are rather isolated out here," Anna admitted. "You used to dislike that part, but maybe now you can see there are some benefits to it as well."

Lauren nodded. "That's exactly what I'm thinking. In fact, I hope I can keep my whole pregnancy a big secret."

"A secret?"

"Yes." She nodded eagerly. "I've been making a plan. I'll stay out here with you. I'll tell my friends that I've got tuberculosis."

"Tuberculosis?" Anna stared at her daughter.

"Or something serious like that. I'll tell them that I have to be isolated until I get well. Then, after the baby is born next summer, I'll return to my old life. I might even go back to school."

"And . . . what about the baby?"

Lauren waved her hand. "I'll give it up, of course."

"Adoption."

"Yes. Maybe the doctor knows a family that would like it."

Anna nodded, trying to maintain a pleasant expression. "Yes, maybe so." She looked down into her empty coffee cup and told herself to keep quiet. This was Lauren's life . . . Lauren's decision . . . Anna had no right to question it.

10

For the rest of the day, Anna managed to conceal her real feelings about Lauren's decision to give the baby up for adoption. But after dinner, Clark invited her out for an evening stroll, and as they walked alongside the dark blue river, she let it all come pouring out.

"Let's check the progress on the cabin," he said as he guided her into the building he was currently working on. "More privacy in here."

"Thanks." She removed a handkerchief from her pocket and blew her nose. "It's silly to get so emotional over this."

"No, Anna, it's not silly at all." He turned on the overhead light and she looked around to see that the kitchenette was making real progress. The lower cabinets were nearly framed in and the rough plumbing was finished. "I think, all things considered, you're handling it very well."

"But I'm falling apart on the inside. It's so frustrating not being able to say or do a thing about it. I just have to bite my tongue."

He ran his hand over a cabinet door that was laid upon a sawhorse. "Sometimes that's all you can do, sweetheart. Just be quiet and ride it out."

"I keep telling myself that Lauren will have other children and that I'll get to be a grandmother some day."

He turned to look at her now. "Did you tell Lauren that you and I are willing to keep the child?" He touched her cheek. "You're still young enough to be the mother of a small child. We could raise the baby as our own."

She gave him a watery smile. "Thanks, I appreciate that. And I did tell Lauren that before . . . back when she just wanted to be rid of the whole pregnancy. She didn't like the idea then and I suspect she still won't. It's as if she wants to just pretend it never happened."

"I'm thankful my mother didn't do that."

"Even though it was hard on you as a child?"

"I wouldn't change anything."

"But your mother isn't . . . well, she's not like Lauren." Anna felt tears coming again. "I feel like such a failure, Clark."

"That's nonsense, Anna. You're the farthest thing from a failure. I've never known a woman as strong and good as you are."

"But with Lauren . . . I feel that I've failed her as a mother. Badly."

"You're wrong, Anna. Lauren might be a bit spoiled and immature, but I've noticed that she seems to be changing. I think you're a good influence on her." He sighed. "Speaking of influence, why do you think Eunice is staying on with us?"

"I haven't a clue. Lauren told her this afternoon that she has no intention of going home with her. Your mother pointed out, again, that it wasn't too late to beat the weather and make it out of here. And I even offered to drop everything and take her downriver. But she refused."

"I think the old girl is up to something."

"What do you mean?"

"I mean she's got this look in her eye. Did you notice it at dinner? Like the cat that ate the canary . . . like she's got something up her sleeve."

"What could it possibly be?"

"I have no idea, but I would wager that she's conniving over some kind of wicked plan." He rubbed his hand together, making an evil-sounding cackle.

Anna laughed. "You're probably right." She blew some sawdust off the top of the cabinet. "This place is looking really good. I can't wait until it's time to put on the finishing touches."

"These cabins are so homey, I wouldn't mind living in one of them myself."

"By yourself?" She lifted her brows.

He reached for her, pulling her close. "Not by myself."

"It would be cozy out here." She leaned her head against his shoulder.

"In fact, I'd even imagined Lauren and her child living in one of these cabins." He smoothed her hair. "I would've loved growing up in a place like this as a kid."

"I know I did."

The sound of someone knocking on the door made them both jump. Clark went to open it and there stood Lauren with an excited expression. "Sorry to bother you, but I saw the light on and hoped you were in here. You will not believe what's going on."

"Come in," Anna urged her. "Tell us what's up."

"Grandmother invited Ardelle to come here!"

"Ardelle?" Clark looked confused.

"Ardelle is Donald's mother," Anna explained. "She's a good friend of Eunice's."

"And she'll be here tomorrow," Lauren said with frightened eyes.

"Why?"

"Grandmother wouldn't tell me."

"Do you think she knows?"

"I have no idea." Lauren was pacing now, chewing on her thumbnail as she went back and forth next to a pile of lumber. "I know Donald wouldn't tell her. I'm sure he wouldn't want anyone to know."

"So if Donald's mother is coming here, is it just for a day visit?" Clark glanced at Anna. "Or do you think she plans to stay?"

"Well, she hasn't made a reservation," Anna pointed out.

"Neither did Eunice."

"That's true."

"Oh, Mom, what am I going to do?" Lauren looked on the verge of tears. "Why is Grandmother doing this?"

Anna went over and hugged Lauren. "I don't know, but whatever is going on, we'll just have to be strong."

"But I don't want to see her. I don't want her looking at me, thinking that I'm a bad girl."

"You're not a bad girl," Anna quietly told her.

"You know what I mean."

Clark looked uncomfortable and Anna tipped her head toward the door. He quietly let himself out.

"If your grandmother has told Ardelle about the baby, there's nothing we can do about it," Anna told her. "And if Ardelle treats you poorly, I will stand up to her, Lauren."

"Really?" Lauren sniffed.

"Of course I will. In fact, I'll warn Hazel about what's going to happen, and I know she will stand up for you as well. So will Clark. And, if either Ardelle or Eunice is unkind, I will call up Henry and ask him to pick them both up and transport them out of here."

"You'd do that?"

"I would. This is my inn and it's meant to be a place of peace and healing. Anyone who does not respect that is not welcome here." Anna looked around the cluttered room, trying to find a spot where they could sit. "Is your grandmother still in the house?"

"She went to bed." Lauren made a face. "I hate her."

"Oh, Lauren, you just feel like you hate her."

"I do hate her, Mom. She is evil. She's been mean to you for as long as I can remember. And now she's doing it to me too."

"She's mad at you because she can't force you to do what she wants, sweetie." Anna opened the door. "Let's go back to the house."

"I feel like running away," Lauren said as they walked through the darkened yard. "That would serve Grandmother right. Then she and Ardelle wouldn't be able to torture me. Maybe I'll hide out in one of the cabins. You wouldn't tell, would you?"

"I'm surprised that Eunice told you that Ardelle was coming," Anna said as they went up the steps. "She could've just surprised us, the way she did with her own arrival."

"I know why she told me," Lauren said as they went inside.

"Why?" Anna took off her jacket.

"So I would be sure to fix myself up. Grandmother told me that I was letting myself go and that it was no wonder Donald didn't want to marry me. Can you believe that?"

Anna sighed. "Unfortunately, I can."

"Anyway, I guess I better take a bath and do my hair."

"For Ardelle?"

"Well, I don't want her thinking that I've turned into a slob. She might tell Donald."

Anna wanted to question whether that even mattered, but decided to keep her thoughts to herself. Besides, it wouldn't hurt if Lauren took better care of herself. She used to be annoyingly fastidious in her appearance. Maybe she would find a happy medium now.

Anna could tell that they were all on pins and needles as they waited to hear Henry's boat come chugging up the river. Even Hazel seemed uneasy as she helped Anna clean up after lunch. "I cannot believe the nerve of that woman." She shook her head as she scrubbed the soup pot. "Inviting her friend here without even asking you first."

Anna sighed, placing a plate in the dishwasher. "I'm trying very hard not to feel vexed."

"Are you going to charge Ardelle for her room?"

"Oh, I couldn't."

"You could and you should, Anna. This is, after all, an inn."

"Yes, but Ardelle is . . . well, now that Lauren is pregnant, it's almost as if she's family." She handed the wet pot to Hazel then lowered her voice. "Although I have to admit that I'm slightly relieved that she won't actually become family. Ardelle is, well, she is a bit like Eunice."

"I was afraid of that."

"You see, Ardelle's mother was Eunice's best friend and when she passed on, back when Ardelle was a young bride, Eunice took her under her wing."

"Well, if Ardelle's got any kind of a conscience, she will offer to pay you for her room." Hazel chuckled as she dried the last pot. "In fact, I would love to see you present both her and Eunice with a big fat bill at the end of their stay. Nothing would bring me more pleasure."

Anna gazed out the window. "Looks like it's getting ready to rain."

"Good. I hope your unexpected guest gets thoroughly soaked."

Anna squinted down the river. "Is that a puff of smoke?" she asked. "Or just a low cloud?"

Hazel adjusted her glasses and leaned toward the window. "Looks like Henry's boat to me."

"Oh, my. Are we ready for this?"

"I wouldn't miss it."

Anna had decided to treat Ardelle like a real guest. She and Clark would greet the boat, welcome her, carry her bags, and settle her into one of the rooms downstairs. Hazel had suggested that Eunice might share her room with Ardelle. Naturally, Eunice declined.

It was just starting to rain when Henry's boat pulled in. Quick greetings were exchanged. Anna opened the umbrella she'd brought and, reaching for Ardelle's hand, helped her off the boat. "Thanks, Henry," she called out. "Let's get inside before it really starts to pour," she told Ardelle as Clark scrambled to grab her bags.

"I had no idea you lived so far from the beaten path," Ardelle said as they hurried through the rain.

"We are a bit out of the way," Anna admitted. "But we like it that way. And on a sunny day, it's really quite beautiful." She opened the door to the room she'd decided to offer Ardelle. "As you can see our accommodations are quite simple, but I hope you'll be comfortable." She showed her where the bathroom was and tried not to be offended by Ardelle's complete lack of appreciation.

"I realize it's more rustic than what you're used to . . ." Anna made a stiff smile. "But I hope you'll try to make yourself at home."

"I'm sure that outdoorsy people are perfectly comfortable here. Harry and his fishing buddies would probably like it."

"Oh, there you are!" exclaimed Eunice as she emerged from her room. She hugged Ardelle. "Mercy, did you get wet? It's raining cats and dogs out there."

"You didn't tell me that this place was so remote," Ardelle told Eunice. "I feel almost as if I've gone back in time."

"If you'll excuse me," Anna moved toward the door. "Eunice can tell you about when we have meals and such."

"Yes, of course, I'm sure you have other things to do." Ardelle made a dismissive wave. "Don't let us keep you."

Anna left the umbrella there for them, then hurried up the stairs, letting out a loud groan as she went into the house.

"That bad?" Hazel turned away from the fireplace.

"I will not let them get the best of me." Anna shook off the rain's dampness. "I will not."

"I took the liberty of making a fire."

"Thank you." Anna smiled. "You are truly a blessing, Hazel."

"Did Ardelle say anything to you?" Lauren asked as she joined them by the fireplace.

"You mean about you?" Anna held her hands out to get warm.

"Yes. Do you think she knows yet?"

Anna frowned. "I honestly don't know. Mostly she commented on how this is such a remote location."

"Not remote enough." Lauren scowled.

"Well, you look very pretty," Anna told her. Lauren had on her baby-blue sweater set and a plaid skirt in shades of pink and blue.

"Thanks." Lauren patted her hair. "I will not have Ardelle going back to Pine Ridge telling everyone how I've gone to the dogs."

Just then the front door opened and both women burst into the room. "My goodness!" cried Eunice. "It's a deluge out there."

Ardelle closed the umbrella, setting it by the door. "What do you do out here when the weather's so nasty?"

"The same kinds of things you do back in Pine Ridge." Anna pointed to a shelf. "There are books and puzzles and some games if—"

"Not yet," Eunice said. "First we all need to sit down and talk." She frowned at Hazel. "A family talk."

"Hazel is family," Anna said. "She's my mother-in-law."

"And my new grandmother," Lauren proclaimed. "Did you know she's getting her doctorate degree?"

"Would anyone like coffee or tea?" Anna offered.

"Not yet," Eunice commanded. "First I want us to sit down and talk."

Lauren fidgeted with her strand of pearls, glancing from one face to another and looking like she wanted to bolt.

"I've already told Ardelle the unfortunate news," Eunice said as they found seats in the living room.

"Naturally, I was shocked and disappointed," Ardelle said primly.

"As were we all," Eunice added. "But like I explained to Ardelle, these things happen. Even to the best of families. There's no need to be ashamed." She pointed to Lauren. "At least there's no need for us to be ashamed. As for you and Donald, well, that is another matter."

Lauren pressed her lips together, narrowing her eyes and folding her arms across her front. Meanwhile, Anna braced herself for the storm that was about to begin raging. She felt certain this one would rival the gale outside in its bluster and brute force.

11

Ardelle seemed to want to take the lead in this uncomfortable discussion. Anna watched silently as she stood and straightened the front of her charcoal gray suit jacket and, as if full of self-importance, began to pace back and forth in front of the fireplace. It almost seemed she was posturing, trying to get the upper hand. "I am fully aware that some girls get in this condition in order to snare themselves a husband," Ardelle paused to study Lauren carefully. "However, your grandmother has assured me that was not the situation with you. And I realize that Donald could have done worse." She shook her head. "Some of the girls that boy has brought home."

"It is a benefit that Ardelle and I are already good friends," Eunice pointed out. "That makes this so much easier."

Ardelle nodded eagerly. "Which is precisely why we've decided that we will handle everything for—"

"Excuse me," Anna interrupted, "but I'm feeling rather lost."

"Me too," Lauren said. "What are you talking about anyway?"

"Why, you and Donald, of course." Ardelle's brow creased. "Seeing how you and Donald are in dire need of help, Eunice and I have taken it upon ourselves to make some plans for your future."

"*Our* future?" Lauren tipped her head to one side. "What do you mean exactly?"

"First of all, you obviously must get married, quickly and quietly." Ardelle glanced at Eunice. "Right?"

"Exactly." Eunice pointed at Anna. "We will tell everyone that history has repeated itself and that Donald and Lauren eloped to Reno just like Lauren's parents did twenty years ago. Naturally, we'll make up a date, saying they were secretly married not long after Lauren began her first year of college."

"Of course, the baby may arrive a bit early," Ardelle added, "but people tend to overlook those things . . . especially over time."

"Donald will be employed at the mill," Eunice told Lauren. "I will see to it that he gets a fine job in management. You two will live at my house until you can afford a place of your own."

"And hopefully we will all live happily ever after." Ardelle laughed, but not with real mirth. She shook her finger at Lauren now. "And, perhaps in time, I will forgive you for making me such a young grandmother."

"But what about Donald?" Lauren asked with worried eyes. "He made it painfully clear that he has no intention of marrying me—ever."

"Oh, don't worry about him." Ardelle waved her hand. "I'll see to it that he marries you, Lauren."

"That's right," Eunice concurred. "We have ways of making that boy do as we say, don't we, Ardelle?" The two women chuckled as if this were a private joke.

"Then what about me?" Lauren stood up with balled fists. "What about what I want? Do you think you can force me to do what you want too? What if I refuse to marry that big baboon?"

"Why on earth would you do that?" Ardelle's voice grew stern.

"Because I have a choice in this matter." Lauren was backing away, and Anna knew that this conversation was over.

"But I thought you loved Donald." Eunice's brows drew together.

"I *used* to love him." Lauren's voice choked with emotion. "Now I hate him. I hate him, I hate him. I wish he were dead!"

"But you are carrying his child!" Ardelle's face was red with anger. "Doesn't that mean anything to you? Do not forget that child isn't just his and yours, Lauren. That's my grandchild, too, and it belongs to Eunice as well. You can't just make this decision based on your own childish feelings."

"You wanted to marry Donald before," Eunice pleaded with her. "Why should that have changed now?"

"I—uh—I don't know." Lauren turned and ran to her room, slamming the door.

"*Well!*" Eunice turned to Anna, looking at her as if she were somehow to blame for all this. "When I think of the work we've gone to, trying to help your ungrateful daughter, and this is the thanks we get. Well, I never!"

"Can you blame her?" Hazel stood, placing her hands on her hips. "You're treating Lauren like a child, as if she doesn't have a mind of her own, as if you think we're still living in the dark ages." She strode over to the front door. "Please excuse me, Anna. I'm afraid if I stay I will say something I *truly* regret." Hazel closed the door with a solid thud.

"I agree with Hazel," Anna told quietly them. "You can't force Donald and Lauren to marry simply for your own convenience."

"Then tell us," Ardelle said in a demeaning tone, "what would you suggest?"

"I suggest you let Donald and Lauren figure out their own lives. They were old enough to get into this predicament, and they are old enough to decide what to do about it. In the mean-time, I will stick by my daughter no matter what she chooses to do." Anna stood. "Now, if you will excuse me, I will check on her."

The autumn storm seemed to put a damper on everything and everyone. To Anna's relief, everyone seemed to stay in their rooms. It wasn't until dinnertime that the strange group recon-vened. As Anna set a heavy platter of roast beef, potatoes, and vegetables on the dining room table, she could see that Lauren had calmed down some, although she was still treating Ardelle and Eunice rather coolly. After grace was said, Clark, bless his heart, attempted to make pleasant conversation and even managed to get Ardelle to laugh a couple of times. Just the same, Anna was greatly relieved when the meal ended and she could escape to the kitchen to clean up.

"Before I excuse myself for the night," Ardelle said loudly in the living room, "I do have a small announcement to make."

With a dishtowel in hand, Anna returned to the living room to listen.

"I took it upon myself to invite Donald to come for a visit."

"You what?" Lauren exploded.

Ardelle nodded. "That's right. I felt that Donald should make an appearance, Lauren."

"You didn't even ask me!" Lauren shouted.

"No need to act like a juvenile," Eunice told her.

"I think it's a good idea to have Donald come out here," Clark said to Lauren.

She blinked. "You do?"

"Yes. For one thing, I would like to meet this young man. And, although I realize I'm only your stepfather, I would like to have a word with him."

"Why?" Lauren's eyes narrowed.

"I think he needs to be held accountable." Clark glanced at Ardelle. "I assume his own father might agree with me on this."

Ardelle just shrugged. Anna remembered Harry Thomas from her years in Pine Ridge. He'd always been a pushover. Ruled by his wife, he had never seemed to wield much influence over his rebellious son.

"Anyway, I think Donald might benefit from coming out here," Clark continued, focusing on Lauren. "You two need a chance to air your feelings and sort things out. Hopefully, without everyone else putting their oars in." He turned back to Ardelle and Eunice. "Don't you think so, too, ladies?"

To Anna's surprise, both women simply nodded. Whether it was because Clark was a man or because they were surprised he'd taken such an interest, Anna was thankful.

"Now, if you'll excuse me," Clark said, "I'll go downstairs and make a nice fire for Eunice and Ardelle to enjoy before they go to bed."

Anna sent him a grateful smile, and before long it was just Anna and Lauren in the kitchen. To Anna's surprise, Lauren had offered to help. "I'm so nervous," Lauren admitted as she scrubbed a pan. "I can't believe Donald is really coming here."

"Well, I agree with Clark," Anna said as she mixed some batter for tomorrow's breakfast. "I think it will be good for you and Donald to talk . . . undisturbed." She thought about the cabin that was getting close to completion. "In fact, I'll ask

Clark to put a couple of lawn chairs in the cabin so you two can have a private place to talk. It's a little messy in there, but Clark could make a fire in the fireplace and you could at least have a place to sit and be warm."

"Thanks, Mom." Lauren sighed. "But I'll be surprised if Donald is willing to talk. In fact, I'll be surprised if he even shows up." She frowned. "What kind of pressure do you think Ardelle and Grandmother are putting on him?"

"I don't know, but I assume it has to do with finances. If Ardelle cuts him off, he probably won't be able to continue in college. And perhaps the job your grandmother plans to offer him will be tempting." She shook her head. "Honestly, I don't know." Anna wanted to say that she hated to imagine the ways those two women might pressure Donald and Lauren . . . or what that kind of pressure might do to a young couple.

"I was thinking about you and Daddy," Lauren said quietly. "You were about my age when you married, and I was born about a year later, right?"

Anna nodded sadly. "But we *chose* to marry, Lauren. No one forced us. And even though we thought we were in love . . . well, I still feel we married too quickly. Your father didn't even tell Eunice until after the wedding. And, as you know, Eunice never really got over that."

"But if Dad hadn't come home from the war, well, you know . . . messed up . . . don't you think you could've had a happy marriage?" Lauren looked so hopeful.

Anna smiled. "Yes, I do think we could've been happy. But only if we'd gotten a house of our own, Lauren. Of course, that wasn't possible with the way things they were. Still, if by some chance you and Donald do decide to marry—and I'm not even suggesting that's the best choice for you—but *if* that happens, I hope you will not accept your grandmother's offer

103

to let you live in her house with her." Anna sighed. "I'm afraid that would be a huge mistake."

Lauren laughed, but her eyes were sad. "Well, it's highly unlikely that Donald will really want to marry me anyway. And I refuse to marry him unless it's really his choice and not just because his mommy is pushing him. I may be pregnant, but I still have my pride."

"Good for you." Anna hugged her. "And I am proud of you. I'm so glad you're facing this head on. It's nice to see."

"You mean finally?"

Anna smiled. "We all have our own journeys. Some take longer than others, but as long as we eventually arrive, it doesn't really matter."

Lauren nodded. "I like that."

It was during a break in the storm that Henry delivered Donald to them. Dressed in a letterman's jacket and blue jeans and loafers, he didn't look much different from when he was in high school. Except his expression was different. A strange combination of surliness and shame, Anna thought as she and Clark greeted him on the dock. Anna was relieved that Clark had insisted on joining her in this less-than-pleasant task. He carried the bulk of conversation, mostly small talk about the weather and the boat trip. Meanwhile Anna said as little as possible as they showed Donald to his room, right next to his mother's.

"Make yourself at home," she said stiffly, turning to go.

"I expect you're mad at me." Donald's voice was quiet.

She turned and looked evenly at him. "Not mad . . . but I am disappointed."

His blue eyes clouded as he shoved his hands in his pockets.

"Even so, I hope for the best for you, Donald. For both you and Lauren. And I hope you can figure out what is the best thing to do in your situation." She glanced at Clark. "And I don't necessarily agree with your mother or Eunice."

Donald looked surprised. "You don't?"

She shook her head. "I believe a marriage needs a strong foundation of love and commitment to work. Without that, I don't see the point."

Clark nodded. "That's my sentiment too. However, I do believe that whether or not you and Lauren marry, you still have a responsibility to your child. You are the child's father and that makes you legally, morally, and ethically responsible. I hope you will take this responsibility seriously. Both to your unborn child and to Lauren. Do you understand?"

Donald's eyes grew wider. "Yes, sir. I do, sir."

"Good." Clark explained about the cabin where Donald and Lauren could talk privately. He was barely finishing up when Ardelle and Eunice burst into the room.

"Oh, there you are," his mother said as she hugged Donald. "It's so good to see you."

"We want a word with you," Eunice said in a conniving tone.

"Yes," Ardelle smiled in a catty way. "In private, please."

Anna and Clark took the hint and excused themselves. "I'm so glad you got to speak to him first," she told Clark as they went upstairs.

"He doesn't seem like a bad kid," Clark said.

Anna chuckled. "I think you scared him a bit."

"Maybe he needs to be scared."

They went inside to see Lauren nervously pacing in the kitchen. "Was that him?" she asked with worried eyes.

"Yes, he's settling in," Anna explained. "Clark told him about the cabin where you can speak together in private."

"Is he there now?"

"No, he's talking with Eunice and Ardelle." Anna made an uneasy smile.

Lauren grabbed her coat. "I'm going over to the cabin now," she said quickly. "If Donald wants to speak to me, tell him I'm there."

"It should be nice and warm," Clark said.

With Lauren gone, Anna started pacing now. "I know I need to just let it be," she confessed to Clark, "but I feel so concerned . . . for both of them. This is such a big decision . . . what if they decide to marry for the wrong reason?"

Clark put his arms around her. "Unfortunately, that happens all the time, Anna. We can only hope for the best and be prepared for . . . well, whatever."

Within the hour it seemed that they were really getting "whatever." Lauren burst into the house, and with flushed cheeks and large blue eyes, she informed Anna and Clark that she and Donald were going to marry. "Oh, it won't be a big wedding like I've always dreamed of," she admitted. "But at least we'll be married. That's what counts."

"This is what you want?" Anna asked.

"It's what I've dreamed of, Mom." She patted her stomach. "We'll be a family. Donald and me and the baby." She let out a happy sigh. "We'll live happily ever after."

Anna had to bite her tongue.

Lauren explained that, like Eunice and Ardelle suggested, she and Donald would elope the following day. "The sooner the better." She giggled. "And now I have to pack."

"Do you need help?" Anna offered.

"Just make sure that Henry can pick us up tomorrow morning." Lauren did a happy little spin, just like she used to as a little girl. "We're all leaving in the morning," she explained. "Grandmother and Ardelle too. They'll go back to Pine Ridge, but Donald and I will drive straight to Reno." She giggled. "It'll be a long drive, but by tomorrow night, we will be legally married. And Grandmother gave Donald enough money for us to have a real honeymoon too."

The rest of the plan was for Ardelle and Grandmother to travel back to Pine Ridge, where they would do damage control by feeding the rumor mill with exactly what they wanted people to know. "They'll tell everyone that Donald and I were so in love that we eloped and quit school." Lauren laughed. "All's well that ends well, right?"

Anna simply nodded, watching as Lauren skipped blissfully to her room. "Oh, my." She turned to Clark. "Can you believe this?"

He made a sympathetic smile. "We can't live our children's lives for them."

"I just wish that our children didn't have to repeat our mistakes." The idea of Lauren and Donald living together under Eunice's roof concerned Anna more than she cared to admit, even to Clark.

By the next morning Anna felt sick about the whole thing, but keeping her emotions to herself, she bid her daughter farewell. "Please stay in touch," she told her for the umpteenth time. "And if you ever need anything, please, call me. You will always be welcome here. You know that."

With tears in her eyes, Lauren thanked her. "I don't know why I'm crying," she said, "I've never been so happy. Before midnight tonight, I will be Mrs. Donald Thomas, Mom! What could be better?"

Anna touched Lauren's cheek. "I wish you nothing but happiness, darling." And, just like that, all the unexpected "guests" were gone.

"My goodness," Hazel said as the three of them waved from the dock. "I feel like we've just survived a whirlwind."

Anna wasn't positive she'd really survived. "I have a lot of housework to do," she said quietly. "That should keep my mind off of things for a while."

"And I have a cabin to work on," Clark said as they walked down the path from the dock.

"And I have a thesis to finish," Hazel said as she turned toward her cabin. Then she paused and looked at Anna. "I remember a saying of your grandmother's . . ."

"What's that?"

"You probably remember it too. Pearl said we all have to paddle our own canoes."

Anna smiled. "I do remember it."

"And that's what Lauren is doing now, paddling her own canoe."

Anna nodded. "Yes, despite pressure, I do believe she made up her own mind about this." Anna glanced back at the river, looking up to see that the clouds were still thin and not full of rain. "In fact, I think that's exactly what I'm going to go do." She chuckled. "I am off to paddle my own canoe."

Clark grinned. "Good for you."

"That's right," Hazel told her. "Housework can always wait. But the weather and the river . . . now that's something you need to grab when you get the chance."

12

Seasons changed gently, almost imperceptibly on the river. Winter had occasional days that masqueraded as summer, and spring sometimes blew as cold and hard as winter. But eventually the trees budded, grasses greened, and foliage thickened . . . and finally the wild flowers began to bloom, and that's when Anna knew that summer was around the bend. How much she had looked forward to summer this year! Primarily because Lauren's baby was due in late June, but also because six of the new cabins were up and ready for guests, and, slowly but surely, the reservations were coming in.

"Anything in the mail?" she asked hopefully, as Clark came in for dinner.

"A card from Mom." He held up a postcard with pyramids on it. "Sounds like she's having a good time."

"I think your mother could have a good time anywhere." Anna read the back of the card and smiled. "Can you believe she rode a camel?"

He chuckled. "Doesn't surprise me in the least."

Anna shook her head as she handed him back the card. "But nothing else in the mail?"

"Just the utility bill. I put that on the desk."

She sighed.

"Why don't you just call her, Anna?"

"You know why." She turned back to the stove, checking on the marinara sauce, although it was fine.

"Because of Eunice," he answered for her. "But even if she does answer the phone, you can insist that you called to speak to Lauren."

"It's just not worth it, Clark. By the time I get Eunice to hand over the phone, that is, if she's even willing, I'm usually so miffed that I have a difficult time speaking a complete sentence to Lauren. And she's usually in a foul mood anyway. I just wish she liked writing better."

"At least she knows how you are doing," Clark sneaked a breadstick.

"Sometimes I wonder if she actually takes time to read my letters."

"Oh, sure she does." He pecked her on the cheek. "I'll go wash up."

As she sat the table, Anna wondered about how Lauren was really doing. She knew she was unhappy, but she couldn't tell if that was because of Eunice . . . or Donald. Most likely it was both. Poor Lauren. But Anna knew this was part of letting her daughter go. These were the lessons Lauren had to learn on her own.

"Hello to the house!" called a man's voice.

"Hello back at you." She peeked around the corner to see that Stan and Martha, two of her guests, were just coming in. "How was fishing?"

"Fabulous," Stan told her.

"Stan spent the last hour cleaning the trout," Martha said. "And I got them all wrapped and packed into the freezer."

"Convenient that you folks have the big locker freezer down there," Stan said as he thumbed through a hunting magazine from the coffee table.

"I keep telling Stan that you folks think of everything," Martha said as she came into the kitchen. "You spoil me so much that I'll never want to go to another fishing lodge."

"That's fine with me." Anna smiled.

Clark came in now, offering the middle-aged couple before-dinner drinks and making light conversation like usual. Before long the other guests trickled in, two brothers from Idaho and a youngish couple from Eugene. Tonight there were eight for dinner, but Anna had served as many as twelve before. Fortunately the cabins were equipped with kitchens, so if the inn was ever completely full some guests could be on their own for food. But at times like this, Anna didn't mind the extra company at the table. And the additional money came in handy when it was time to pay bills.

However, the best part was getting to meet so many new people, witnessing them interacting with each other, and hearing their reactions to the river and the inn. "I tried that lavender soap in the shower," said Shirley, the younger woman. "I thought it would smell like my grandmother, but it was actually really fresh and nice."

"My friend Babette makes that herself," Anna told her. "She says that lavender has a restorative, healing quality to it."

Shirley nodded. "I think it must. I felt completely refreshed after using it . . . and relaxed too."

"There must be something in the air here," Martha said. "I've slept better than ever these past few nights."

"It's because it's so quiet," her husband told her. "Lots more peaceful than home."

"That's true. But we have three teenagers at home," Martha explained. "My dear old mother is there with them now. I can't even imagine what kind of headache she must have . . . I don't want to know."

Stan laughed. "Maybe we should stay a few extra days, honey."

"I saw an enormous bird today," Shirley said suddenly. "Long legs and a long bill. Very majestic."

"Was it dark blue?" Anna asked.

"Bluish gray, I guess."

"That's the Great Blue Heron."

Now they started talking about the other birds and wildlife seen along the river and Anna offered Shirley a bird book as well as binoculars to borrow.

"And see, you thought you'd be bored here," Shirley's husband teased.

"Well, it seemed so remote . . . I wasn't sure."

"I knew she needed a break like this," he said. "She works for an insurance company and they just run her ragged."

"Well, this is really a special place," one of the brothers said. "I plan to become a regular here."

"So do I," the other brother added. "Next time, we'll be bringing our wives."

"Maybe even our kids," the other said. "This seems like a great place for kids."

"We've got the canoes," Anna pointed out. "And there's swimming in summer. And sometimes we have bonfires at night for roasting hotdogs and marshmallows."

"Your kids must love it," Shirley said. "I mean, if you have kids, that is."

Clark and Anna exchanged quick glances. "We do," he said. "A son who's about to graduate high school and a daughter with a baby on the way."

"Oh, a baby," gushed Martha. "You must be so excited." She frowned at Anna. "Although you look far too young to be a grandmother."

"Thank you." Anna smiled. "And you're right, I am excited. It's just weeks away now."

"Will you go to be with your daughter when she has the baby?" Martha asked.

"I'm not sure." Anna frowned.

"I've told her she has to go," Clark explained.

"But there's the inn," she said. "We'll have so many guests then."

"Babette has offered to help with the cooking."

"Oh, you must go be with your daughter," Martha insisted. "I don't know what I would've done without my mother with every one of my children. A girl really needs her mother when she has a baby."

Anna nodded. "Yes . . . I will do what I can." Fortunately, someone changed the subject, but Anna's mind was still stuck on Lauren—she so wanted to go and be with her when the baby was born. But how could she leave Clark minding the inn by himself? If only Lauren wanted to come here for the birth of her baby. However, Anna knew that was out of the question. All three of them—Eunice, Donald, and Lauren—had rejected that idea straight out. Anna understood their concerns regarding the remote location, but Dr. Robertson was known to make housecalls and, after all, he'd been the first doctor to see Lauren. Still, Anna knew that was not an option.

Later that evening, as she and Clark were getting ready for bed, she broached the subject again. "I know you say that you can handle the inn on your own," she said gently, "but I'm afraid you don't realize what all it entails. There's not just the food, and that's a big thing, but there's laundry, and the little

113

extras like soaps and fresh flowers in the room and, oh, a million other little things."

"Maybe we could give the guests who come that week an unexpected discount and explain the situation. No frills due to the missing hostess."

She laughed. "No frills such as no clean linens or meals?"

He frowned. "That might not fly."

"Really, as badly as I want to go, I don't see how it's possible."

He held up his hand. "I have an idea."

She paused from brushing her long hair. "And we cannot close the inn. Not this early in the game, Clark."

He nodded. "I realize that. But Mom will be home by then. She's done with her thesis and she'll want something to keep her busy. How about if she helps out here while you're gone?"

Anna frowned. "I don't want your sweet mother working her fingers to the bone."

"But she'd love it. And if you had some things pre-prepared, you know, like all the laundry done and folded, and the shopping and menus all planned out, maybe some sauces or casseroles in the freezer. We could have a bonfire night with hotdogs one evening, that's always easy enough. Babette would want to help too. And school should be out, so I can get Marshall over here as well. He's always willing to roll up his sleeves for you."

"I don't think it's practical to—"

"Hear me out, Anna. You could just plan on being gone a day or two for starters . . . and if things don't fall completely apart, and I don't think they will, you could stay a little longer if you like."

"Oh, Clark." She set down her hairbrush and went over to hug him. "Do you know you are the sweetest man ever?"

He grinned. "I'd like to think you think so."

"Well, I'll give your plan some thought. Besides, it wouldn't hurt to get ahead of the game by getting foods and things *pre-prepared*, as you say."

"Yes. Just be ready . . . and who knows." He leaned down and kissed her.

"Who knows . . . ?" she whispered back. Really, he was the sweetest man! What would she do without him?

13

For the next two weeks, Anna worked harder than ever. Her plan was to have the inn running so smoothly that if—and it was a big if—but *if* she decided to return to Pine Ridge for the birth of her first grandchild, it wouldn't be a great imposition on anyone. However, this was the first season that the inn had been host to this many guests and so many little things came up, situations she wasn't prepared for. Like when the Barnes family needed a first-aid kit, or the Taylors needed a crib. Fortunately she had good friends on the river. Not only that, but Clark's son was spending the summer with them. Anna called Marshall her "go-to man" and insisted that she was going to pay him for his help at the inn, although Clark suggested they simply put his money into a college account.

"You keep that crib for as long as you like," Mrs. Danner told her as they stood on the dock together. "Dorothy won't be having any more babies, and her girls are too young to need it anytime soon." She smiled in a knowing way. "Besides, you're going to have your own grandbaby soon, aren't you?"

"Lauren's due date is the end of the month," Anna said.

"Well, you just keep this as long as you need it, dear. It was simply gathering dust." She glanced up at the inn, where

Marshall was jogging down the path toward them. "Why, your place just keeps getting nicer and nicer, Anna." She shook her head. "Your parents would be so proud."

"Thank you." Anna felt a warm rush. "Please, tell Dorothy hello for me if you hear from her."

"She and the girls will be coming for a visit in August." She made a slight frown. "Too bad your inn is so full up with guests. I know they'd rather stay here than my little house. I wouldn't mind much either."

Anna laughed. "Well, you tell Dorothy that if I have room, I'll be happy to have them."

"Telephone for you," Marshall told Anna. "I'll get this crib over to the Taylors' for you."

Anna thanked him and waved to Mrs. Danner as she hurried back up to the house. The phone had been ringing more and more lately. She knew it was the result of an article Hazel had written about the river and the inn and Native American history. She'd sold the piece to a national travel magazine and now they were getting reservations far in advance. She'd shown Marshall how to book a reservation in her big black book, so perhaps this was something different. She picked up the phone, answering breathlessly.

"Mom!" cried Lauren. "It's time for the baby. I'm in the hospital, and I'm so scared. Can you come?"

Anna felt her heart pounding, and without even thinking, she said, "Yes. I'll come right away."

"Hurry, Mom! I want you to be here!"

Anna quickly calculated the absolute soonest she could make it there. It was too late in the day to catch the bus. That meant she'd need to drive. And although she now had her license and they'd purchased a station wagon for the inn, she still felt a little unsure. "I won't get there until after four," she said.

"Well, drive fast," Lauren commanded. "I really need you, Mom!"

"I'm coming," she promised. Then she dashed to her room where she threw a few things in an overnight bag and grabbed the box of things she and Babette had put together for the baby, then hurried back out to where Clark was fixing something in the shower house. "It's time," she told him between breaths. "Lauren wants me." She made a nervous smile. "She said she needs me, Clark. She *needs* me!"

"Of course she does." He smiled. "The car is all gassed up. The road out of here shouldn't be too bad since it hasn't rained for a few days. But if you want, I could drive you out and catch a ride back with Henry—"

She looked at his toolbox and the clogged sink. "No, you need to be here."

"How about Marshall, then?"

"No," she firmly told him. "I'll be fine. If I can't make it out of here, I shouldn't even be driving."

He grinned. "Just take it easy, okay? No speeding tickets."

As if her mother were still looking over her shoulder, Anna glanced around to be sure no one was looking, then kissed him. "I'll miss you, darling."

"You call me as soon as you get there. If you need anything, call. I can drive out if I need—"

"No," she said firmly. "You need to stay here and keep this place running."

"I'll call Babette and let her know," he said as she was leaving.

"You know where all my lists are," she reminded him.

"Don't worry," he called. "We'll be fine!"

As she got into the station wagon, she could barely believe she was doing this—not just leaving the inn, but driving all the way to Pine Ridge on her own. If anyone had told her just one year ago that she would be capable of such a thing, she would have laughed. So much had changed—mostly her!

As she drove, she felt thankful that driving was still new enough to her to be a challenge. It required her full attention and consequently didn't allow her to think too much about Lauren . . . or to worry. But each time a fretful thought came, she turned it into a prayer, reminding herself that soon she would meet her grandchild—her very first grandchild! And what a beautiful day to be born, she thought as she drove through a canopy of evergreen trees, golden sunlight filtering through. Surely this child would be a blessed one!

It was getting close to five by the time Anna pulled into the hospital parking lot. Not much had changed here since she'd given birth to Lauren twenty years ago. She hurried through the entrance, heading directly to the maternity ward, and pausing at the nurses' station to inquire about Lauren. "I'm her mother," she explained.

"Mrs. Thomas delivered at 1:47," the uniformed nurse told her.

"She's already had the baby?" Anna was surprised since her own labor had taken much longer than this.

"Yes, a baby girl." The nurse looked at her clipboard. "Seven pounds, eight ounces."

Anna giggled. "A girl, she had a girl!"

The nurse tipped her head down the hall. "The baby should be in the viewing window by now. And Mrs. Thomas is in room 206."

Anna thanked her then hurried to the window to get her first peek at her granddaughter. *A granddaughter,* she thought, *what could be better?* But when she reached the window, she saw that Eunice was already there, leaning forward with a disturbed-looking expression.

"Hello, Eunice," Anna said cheerfully. "Is anything wrong?"

Eunice frowned at Anna. "Haven't you seen the baby yet?"

"No, I just got here." Anna peered through the glass to see three bassinettes. "It must've been busy here," she said as she read the cards.

"That's her," Eunice pointed to the baby on the left.

Anna read the card aloud. "Thomas Baby Girl," then sighed to see a smooth-faced child, sleeping peacefully. "She's beautiful," Anna gushed. "And look at all that hair."

"Yes . . ." Eunice shook her head in a dismal way. "It's nearly black. She looks just like a little Indian."

Anna bristled at the jab. "She is absolutely beautiful," she said quietly. "Perfect."

"Yes, well, you would think that, wouldn't you?" Eunice made a *tsk-tsk* sound. "I'd thought with her two fair-haired, blue-eyed parents, the baby would've had a, well, a fairer complexion."

Anna pressed her lips together. She was not about to ruin this moment and she refused to let anyone else spoil it for her either. "I'm going to see Lauren now," she told Eunice.

"Prepare to get your head bitten off."

Anna ignored this as she headed for Lauren's room. "Hello, darling," she said quietly as she went into the sun-filled room.

Lauren gave Anna a pouty expression. "Oh, I see you finally made it."

"I came as fast as I could. In fact, I probably could've gotten a speeding ticket, I drove so fast."

"Why didn't anyone tell me how perfectly horrible it is to give birth to a baby?"

"Did you have a very hard time?"

"For a while, I thought I was absolutely going to die. Then the doctor gave me something to take the edge off. After that, it all got pretty blurry."

"Well, at least it's over now." Anna pushed a strand of hair off Lauren's forehead. "Good job, darling."

"Did you see the baby yet?"

"I did." Anna reached for Lauren's hand. "She is beautiful, Lauren. Perfectly lovely."

Lauren's frown returned. "Grandmother is calling her a *papoose*."

Anna took in a deep breath. "Well, if it's any comfort, she called you a papoose too . . . at first anyway."

Lauren blinked. "Really?"

"That's right." Anna sat down in the chair by her bed. "You were born with dark hair like that too. But then it fell out." She chuckled. "I was a little alarmed at first, but the doctor assured me that was normal. Eventually it was replaced with what looked like soft yellow duck down."

"Really? I looked like her, all dark like that?"

"The doctor had a name for that kind of hair. Prenatal, I believe."

"But you think her hair will really turn blond?" Lauren looked up with hopeful blue eyes.

"Well, I can't promise anything. I'm just saying that's how you started out, sweetheart. But, really, Lauren, would you love your child any less if her hair stayed dark like mine?"

Lauren looked down at her hands, fidgeting with her gold wedding band. "No, no . . . of course not." She looked up with a partial smile. "And, just for the record, I think you're pretty, Mom . . . for an older woman, that is."

Anna laughed. "Thanks . . . I think."

"But Eunice made such a fuss about Sarah that—"

"*Sarah?*" Anna asked. "That's her name."

"Yes. After Donald's grandmother."

"It's a lovely name."

"Sarah *Pearl*." Lauren made a smug smile.

"Oh, Lauren, that is so sweet of you."

Lauren wrinkled her nose. "I think I did it just to get Grandmother's goat. She was being such a pill about the baby's coloring. Good grief, you should've heard her going on and on about it. I finally told her to leave and not come back unless she could be civilized."

Anna patted Lauren's hand. "Good for you. Now, tell me, how are you feeling?"

"A little groggy."

"Maybe I should let you get some rest."

Lauren nodded sleepily. "But you're not going home yet, are you?"

"No, I'll stick around for a while. You rest up, sweetie. I'll see you later."

Anna couldn't wait to return to the baby window to gaze at her beautiful granddaughter, but when she got there not only was Eunice still staring, but Ardelle was with her. Polite greetings were exchanged then Ardelle held up a paper sack. "I just bought our little granddaughter the most adorable outfit." She reached in and removed a frilly pink dress with a matching bonnet. "Won't she look exquisite in it?"

"It's precious," Anna told her.

"And the bonnet will cover up *that hair*," Ardelle continued.

Anna just nodded.

"Look, she's opening her eyes," Eunice said quickly. "See how dark they are, Ardelle. I told you she looks like an Indian."

"Oh, all babies have dark-blue eyes when they're first born," Ardelle said casually. "Trust me, they'll turn as blue as Donald's before long. His are a darker blue too."

Anna took in a slow breath. "And if they don't turn blue?"

Ardelle laughed as she slid the lace-trimmed dress and bonnet back into the bag. "Oh, we'll love her anyway, won't we, Eunice?"

"Well, of course." Eunice gave Anna a tolerant look. "But it is possible her looks *will* change." She turned to Ardelle. "As I recall, Lauren looked a bit odd when she was first born, but she turned out to be rather pretty."

"Yes, babies can change a lot in the first few weeks."

"Please excuse me," Anna told them. Stepping away, she tried not to listen as the two women continued to speculate over the child's appearance and how she might or might not turn out, as if her looks alone would define her as a person. Anna had to control herself from making a real scene. Instead, she returned to the nurse's station and asked if it was possible to hold her granddaughter.

"You see, I live several hours from here, and I won't be able to see her too much."

"Of course." She motioned to a younger nurse, instructing her to help Anna to sterilize herself properly. Before long Anna was scrubbed and wearing a protective gown, waiting in a rocker as the nurse carefully picked the drowsy infant out of the bassinette, gently placing her in Anna's arms.

"She's so small," Anna whispered. "I'd nearly forgotten how tiny they are."

"And this was a good-sized one. We get some premature ones sometimes . . . and it's so sad."

"Hello, baby Sarah," Anna quietly said.

The baby's long, dark eyelashes fluttered against her cheeks then, and opening her eyes she blinked once then looked directly into Anna's face. "Hello, darling," Anna cooed at her. Sarah pulled a perfect little hand out of the tightly wrapped blanket, shoving it into her mouth and sucking noisily on it.

"Would you like to feed her?" the nurse asked. "It's time."

"Feed her?" Anna looked up in surprise as she remembered how she'd nursed her own baby. "How?"

"She's on the bottle, of course," the nurse explained. "I know that some of you grandmothers don't understand about using formula, but it's really much better for both the mother and child. A modern convenience of motherhood."

As Anna looked down at the small vulnerable face, she wasn't sure she agreed with this modern convenience but then remembered, like so many things regarding Lauren, it was not Anna's decision. "Oh, sweet Sarah." She gazed into the slate-blue eyes. They reminded her of deep pools along the river. "You are a beautiful little princess. A Siuslaw princess," she whispered. "The blood of your ancestors flows through you. I pray it's a blessing . . ." Anna sighed. How she would love a grandchild who understood the old ways, but what were the chances?

"You'll come to visit me on the river," she said quietly. "You'll learn to use a canoe and to how to fish and maybe you'll even weave a basket or two." She glanced up to see both Eunice and Ardelle peering around the corner of the viewing window, attempting to get a look at her and the baby. Their faces looked displeased, but Anna simply smiled at them, nodding down to the baby with happy pride.

"Here you go," the young nurse handed Anna a warmed bottle. "Do you know how to do this?"

Anna tried not to laugh. "I think I can figure it out."

The baby eagerly went for the bottle's nipple, and Anna watched as the hungry child sucked earnestly. "You have spirit," Anna told her. "You will grow up to be someone very special, Sarah Pearl. I just know it. You will be our little Siuslaw princess." She chuckled. "But we will keep this our secret for the time being." She reached down to stroke the dark wisps of hair. To her surprise, the texture was nothing like Lauren's newborn baby hair had been. Lauren's dark hair had felt fuzzy, similar to brushed cotton. Sarah's hair felt silky and smooth.

Chances were this hair was not going to turn blond after all. Anna couldn't believe how glad that made her.

"You will have to be very strong, Sarah Pearl," she whispered. "Not everyone will love you like I do. But you have your ancestors' blood, your great-great-grandmother's blood, and that will make you strong. I can feel your spirit, little one. You will be very strong." She leaned over and kissed the top of Sarah's head. "Be blessed, little Siuslaw princess. Be very, very blessed."

14

Anna used a hospital phone to place a collect call to Clark, quickly relaying to him that she was safely in Pine Ridge and about her granddaughter. "She's absolutely precious, Clark. I fell in love with her immediately."

"That's great. And there's nothing to worry about on the home front. Everyone is helping out, Babette fixed a great dinner of beef bourguignon."

"Now you're making me hungry."

"You haven't eaten yet?"

"No, I was spending time with Lauren and the baby."

"Do you know where you'll be staying tonight?"

She sighed. "Well, Eunice didn't offer any accommodations."

"That figures. But I don't want you staying with her anyway, Anna. Isn't there a hotel or inn in town?"

"Yes, but—"

"No buts. I want you to go to the best place, get the nicest room, and then buy yourself a wonderful dinner. Don't think about the money. Like I keep telling you, we're just fine. I want you to splurge, Anna."

She giggled. "Fine. I will splurge and I will celebrate the birth of my adorable granddaughter."

"That's the spirit." They talked a bit longer, then expressed their love and hung up. Anna glanced down the quiet corridor of the maternity ward, deciding to tell Lauren goodnight before she left. That is, if no one else was in there with her. Lauren had been quite busy with visitors—friends from school, and family members. By dinnertime her room had been filled with flowers. However, Anna hadn't seen Donald there yet. Perhaps he would be with her now.

But when she found Lauren, she was alone, and judging by her expression, unhappy. "I just came in to say goodnight," Anna said quietly as she came in.

"Oh?" Lauren looked up with a tired expression. "It is getting late, isn't it?"

Anna nodded. "Visiting hours are nearly over."

"And Donald hasn't even been here."

Anna tried not to seem surprised. "Not at all?"

"Well, sure, he was here earlier. He saw the baby and everything. But then he said he had to get back to work to take care of something." She looked at Anna with fearful eyes. "But I don't know if I should believe him."

"Why not, sweetheart?"

"Because he's such a liar."

Anna braced herself.

"I don't know what I'm going to do, Mom." Lauren had tears in her eyes now.

"I don't understand . . ." Anna sat down, waiting.

"Donald is a lousy husband, Mom."

"In what ways?"

"Every way."

"I assume he's providing for you, by working."

"Yeah, he works. But that's about the only thing he does right. If you can call it that. He's supposedly saving money for our house, but I have my doubts."

"Why do you have doubts?"

"For one thing, he drinks like a fish."

"Oh . . ." Anna frowned.

"He goes out almost every night, comes home late, and he doesn't seem to care a bit about me or the baby."

"Do you think that it was too much too soon for him?" Anna asked gently. "I mean getting married, going to work, having a child . . . all in such a short period of time . . . it seems a lot."

Lauren folded her arms across her front and scowled. "I didn't figure you'd stand up for him. My own mom."

"I'm sorry, Lauren. It's not that I'm choosing sides. I just know that for any marriage to work, you need to give and take. It's possible Donald is going through a rough spell. What did he think when he saw Sarah?"

Lauren shrugged.

"It might take him some time to adjust."

"Time, time . . . everything takes time." Lauren started to actually cry now. "But when do I get time? First I get big as a house and can't do anything fun. Now I'm going to be stuck taking care of a baby. Plus, I have to live under Grandmother's roof! You know what an old grouch she can be. And now that I'm not pregnant, she'll probably let Mabel go."

"Mabel?"

"Our housekeeper. Grandma said she only hired her to help out while I was pregnant."

"That was nice of her."

"But now she'll expect me to do everything." Lauren shook her head. "And that's just not fair."

Anna didn't know what to say. "Maybe you and Donald should think about finding a small house that you could rent."

"A small *rental* house?" Lauren looked like Anna was suggesting she go live in a tent.

"Just for a while." Now Anna told Lauren about how happy she and Adam were for a short time. "It was just the three of us, cozy and comfy in our little house. Housekeeping wasn't very difficult. It was truly one of the best times of my life, I mean before most recently. But then the war came along and Eunice insisted that you and I should move in with her." She sighed. "I never should've given in."

"So where did you and Dad live back then?"

"In one of the mill cottages over by—"

"Eew. You lived in one of those horrible shacks?"

"It was just past the depression, Lauren. And they were in better shape then, and—"

"No, thank you. I would rather live with Grandmother."

"I wasn't suggesting you needed to live in a mill cottage."

"I should hope not."

Anna reached over and took Lauren's hand. "Visiting hours are over and I can tell you need your rest. Try not to worry about these things right now. It's normal to feel overly emotional after giving birth . . . just give yourself a chance to rest and recover. All right?"

She just nodded. "I am sleepy."

"See you tomorrow, sweetie."

Anna felt sad and frustrated as she left the hospital. Sometimes Lauren seemed to be growing up and making progress and sometimes she seemed to be going backward. Anna hated to blame anyone, but she couldn't help but sense that Eunice's influence was overly strong.

Deciding to get a room at the Starlight Hotel, Anna pulled her car into the back parking lot. To her surprise, there was a car there that looked exactly like Lauren's baby-blue convertible, and to Anna's knowledge there was only one car like that in town, the one that Eunice bought for Lauren's sixteenth birthday several years ago. The car looked a little more worn now, but as Anna got her bag from the trunk, she checked the license plate to see that it was indeed Lauren's car.

Curious as to what this meant, Anna went on into the hotel and booked her room. Then, after dropping off her bag, she went back downstairs to the restaurant. There, as she was waiting to be seated at a table, she glanced into the smoky lounge and saw Donald seated at a small table with a pretty redhead sitting across from him. The two had their heads close together, drinks at hand, and cigarettes glowing in the dimly lit room. Anna took in a quick breath as she considered going in there and hitting him over the head with her handbag.

"Right this way," the hostess said pleasantly. "Unless you care to sit in the lounge?"

"No . . . no, thank you." Anna told her. "I don't care to sit in there." She followed the young woman to a corner table, feeling slightly shaken as she slid into a chair. What should she do? What should she do? Pretending to study the menu, all Anna could think was that she needed to go out there and confront her son-in-law. But how? What should she say? Soon the waitress returned, telling Anna about the special, something with chicken. "I'll have that," Anna told her. "And coffee." She glanced toward the lounge. "If you'll excuse me, I want to go say hello to someone in the lounge."

"No problem." The waitress smiled.

Steadying herself with a deep breath, and silently whispering a prayer, Anna made her way to the lounge. She was actually hoping she'd been mistaken. Perhaps it was simply someone who looked like Donald. And perhaps Lauren had gone into labor with her car parked out back . . . and it had been left there for someone to pick up later. But she quickly realized that, no, it was indeed Donald. And judging by the way the young woman was looking into his eyes, this was not just a casual encounter.

"Excuse me, Donald." Anna stood right next to his table. "I thought that was you."

He looked up with a shocked expression. "Mrs. Gunderson!"

"No, I'm not Mrs. Gunderson," she corrected him. "I'm Mrs. Richards now. Remember, I remarried." She looked directly at the young woman with a somber expression. "I just came from the hospital, where I've been with your wife, Donald. Lauren mentioned that you had been detained at work this afternoon. I see that isn't the situation now." She gave him a confused frown. "I would've assumed you'd want to spend your spare time with your wife and newborn baby."

"I, uh, I, well . . . visiting hours are over now."

"So that is why you are here, Donald? Because visiting hours are over?"

"Look, Mrs., uh, Mrs . . . ."

"*Richards*, Donald. Your mother-in-law's name is *Mrs. Richards*."

"Yeah, right." He looked flustered. "Well, you don't know everything about Lauren and me. Just because she's the one getting all the attention for having a baby doesn't mean that she's blameless in everything."

"You're right, I don't know everything, Donald. But I do know this—you are *married* to my daughter. You have a newborn baby. If this is your idea of being a good husband, I'm afraid your marriage is doomed. And if you have no interest in honoring your marriage vows, I suggest you make your position clear with Lauren. To go sneaking around like . . . *like this*—well, that is just lowdown rotten."

He just stared at her now.

"I am severely disappointed in you, Donald. If you were an honorable man, you would be severely disappointed in yourself as well." Anna felt angry tears stinging her eyes. "To think you are the father of that darling little baby girl, just hours old, and here you are." She turned to the woman. "Did you know about his baby? Sarah Pearl Thomas was born this afternoon—are you here to celebrate with the new father?"

The woman stood, quickly stepping away. "I gotta go."

"So do I," Anna told Donald. Then, fighting to hold back her fury and her tears, she turned away and hurried back into the restaurant where, with trembling knees, she sat down. With her eyes downward, she picked up her cup of coffee and, holding it with both hands to keep from spilling, she took a careful sip. Between sips she took in some slow, deep breaths . . . attempting to calm herself.

More than anything, Anna wished she'd tried harder to discourage Lauren from marrying Donald. Not that it made any difference now. "If wishes were fishes, we'd all have a fry," her father used to say. Really, there was no point in looking backward. Besides, she realized as her salad was placed in front of her, Lauren and Donald's marriage, even if it was a mockery, had allowed her granddaughter to be born into this world with no plans for adoption. Little Sarah Pearl had her place in this world, even if it seemed a slightly unstable place. That alone was worth a lot. So, as Anna slowly picked at her lemon chicken, she began to create a plan—a plan that might help to protect both Lauren and Sarah. Or so she hoped.

Anna called the law office in the morning. To her relief, Mr. Miller hadn't retired yet and sounded happy to meet with her. Feeling a sense of urgency and a sense of mission, she walked on over and was barely through the door when she began to pour out her troubles about Lauren and Donald and her granddaughter. "I knew that I could trust you," she said finally.

He nodded slowly, rubbing the bridge of his nose and adjusting his wire rimmed-glasses. "Certainly you can trust me. But I'm not sure how you want me to help."

"Well, I realize that I told you I didn't want anything from Eunice, regarding Adam's estate, I mean. But now I'm wondering if it's too late to change my mind on that."

He scooted his wide girth toward the desk and opened up the file folder in front of him. "Well, as I told you, some of the assets are frozen. And, despite your decision to back off from Mrs. Gunderson last time we talked . . ." He chuckled. "Well, I've just been letting sleeping dogs lie, so to speak."

"I'm not asking about this for myself," she explained. "But if there is anything left of Adam's estate, I would be so relieved to know that it could be used for Lauren and Sarah. I'm so worried that Lauren might find herself as a single mother and I don't want her to feel beholden to Eunice. On the same token, I don't want her to feel forced to come and live with me, although I would love it."

"You would?" His white eyebrows drew together as he smoothed his narrow tie.

She nodded eagerly. "Yes, most definitely." She described the situation of the inn and the cabins. "So we really have plenty of room. The only problem is that Shining Waters is so remote . . . and Lauren is accustomed to a social life. I know how important that is to her."

"Shining Waters sounds like a very nice spot to me." He jotted the name down. "In fact, I might like to come visit sometime. How's the fishing?"

She smiled. "It's great. And you'd be most welcome there."

"Now, as to Lauren and the child. I'd suggest we set up a trust fund. Especially if you have any concerns about Donald."

"Yes, a trust fund for Lauren and Sarah would be wonderful. I'd like Sarah's money to be protected too." She paused. "I mean . . . even from Lauren."

He nodded. "Don't worry, I get your drift." He wrote something else down. "And just so you won't be worrying about my age and retirement and all, I've hired an associate. My sister's son is going to be joining me in the fall. Laurence is young, but he graduated from Stanford with honors."

He pulled out a legal pad and began to go over some numbers and dates with her and finally he promised to have some papers sent for her signature. "Probably not for a couple of weeks," he told her as he stood to see her to the door. "I'm glad you came back. I never liked the idea of Mrs. Gunderson beating you like that."

"I was just eager to be out from under her," Anna explained. "Sometimes there are things in life that are worth more than money."

He reached for the doorknob. "I agree. But I'm still glad you're doing this . . . for Lauren and Sarah's sake. I don't think you'll be sorry."

"So what shall I tell Lauren now?"

"You just tell her that whenever she's ready—or if things really disintegrate in her marriage—you tell her to come and see me and that I'll help her out." He opened the door and led her out into the lobby.

"Thank you so much, Mr. Miller." Anna reached over to shake his hand.

"And I plan to take a vacation as soon as Laurence, that's my nephew, gets settled in. You think you'll have a room available in October?"

"I'll make sure we do. In fact, you can probably have a whole cabin if you like."

He grinned as he opened the front door. "Whatever you think is best."

"October is one of the most beautiful times on the river."

"Looking forward to it."

Anna decided to walk to the hospital from the law office. It was only six blocks and it gave her a chance to clear her head and to think. Walking past the city park, in the shade of a row of pine trees, she could hear the whirring of a lawnmower somewhere. She glanced over to the play area, wondering if Sarah would play on that slide or dig in that sandbox. Would Sarah's life in Pine Ridge be happy and carefree? Or would her parents' marriage problems ruin everything?

Anna had no idea what, or how much, she would say to Lauren about her encounter with Donald last night. Just the same, she felt certain that she couldn't simply sweep it under the rug. However, when she noticed Lauren's convertible in the hospital parking lot, she felt unsure. At least Donald was here today. That was something.

Anna tried to act natural when she found Donald at Lauren's bedside. Standing in the shadows of the doorway, she watched the scene unfolding. They would make a nice snap-shot, although Anna cared little for cameras. The handsome doting husband leaning over his pretty wife as she cradled the baby in her arms was quintessentially sweet. Then the baby let out a loud wail, and the magic was broken. "I don't know what to do with her," Lauren complained loudly to Donald. "She shouldn't be hungry. Do you want to hold her?"

"I don't know how to hold a baby," he protested as Lauren held Sarah out for him to take.

"Well, it's time you learned."

Worried the baby, caught in the lurch, might fall to the ground, Anna stepped up. "Hello there," she said casually, "how about if I hold her?" She shot Donald a quick warning look as she reached for the howling baby. "There, there, little Sarah," she shushed gently as she rocked the sweet bundle in her arms, "it'll be all right."

"Don't you think Donald should be willing to learn how to hold his own child?" Lauren asked loudly.

Anna nodded. Then, continuing to shush her granddaughter while the new parents argued about whose job it was to care for the baby, Anna made her way to the door.

"You're the one who wanted the baby," Donald was saying as Anna left the room. She carried the baby down the hallway, quietly talking, shushing, and rocking. By the time she reached the nursery, Sarah had settled down.

"Why did you bring her back?" the young nurse, who'd helped with the feeding yesterday, asked. "This is mothering time."

"Mothering time?"

"The babies are supposed to be with the mothers."

"Oh." Anna looked around the empty nursery. "But the father was there and, they, well, they were having a little disagreement."

"So . . . ?"

"And the baby was crying."

The young nurse just shook her head. "The sooner they get used to it, the better off they'll all be." She pointed to the door. "Please, take the baby back to her mother."

Anna sighed. "I suppose I see your point." Feeling like Sarah's traitor, Anna slowly walked her back to Lauren's room. At least the baby was calmed down now. "I'm back," she said quietly. "I took Sarah for a little walk, but the nurse told me to bring her back to you."

"These nurses are so stupid with their silly rules," Lauren said as Anna handed her back the baby. "I was just telling Donald that I want to be let out of here."

"And I told you that's up to the doctor." Donald seemed to be focusing all his attention on Lauren now, trying to avoid any eye contact with Anna.

"It's impossible to get any sleep in here," Lauren complained. "They wake you up constantly. Really, I'd get better rest at home in my own bed."

"Except that you'd have to take care of the baby then," Anna said gently.

"How hard can that be?"

"Harder than you expect," Anna told her. "But don't worry, it won't take long for you to get into some routines."

"Why don't you come home with me and help me with the baby, Mom?" Lauren's hopeful expression reminded Anna of when she was little. "And you can help me to convince Dr. Stangler that I'll be better off at home. *Please?*"

Donald reached over and patted Lauren on the top of her head. "I'll let you and your mother work these details out. I need to get back to work." But as he was leaving, Anna excused herself as well, promising to come right back, then she followed Donald down the hall, calling out to him.

He turned with a worried expression, but waited. "Are you going to bawl me out again?" he asked. "Right here in the hospital?"

"I didn't bawl you out, Donald. I caught you doing something you know good and well you shouldn't be doing. I simply called you on it."

"Well, I'm sorry about that." He shoved his hands into his pants pockets. "I know there's no real good excuse, but Lauren and me have been having our problems. She's not the easiest person in the world to live with, you know. Take it from me, a guy can only take so much."

Anna locked eyes with him. "That may be so, Donald. But if you really love Lauren and if you believe in your marriage, I think you'll find a better way to deal with your problems."

"Like what?"

Anna thought hard. "Maybe you should go to church."

He looked like he'd bitten into a sour pickle. "To *church*?"

"Yes. That's what Lauren's dad and I had planned to do after he returned from the war. We had decided we'd take Lauren to church every Sunday."

"I don't remember Lauren ever saying anything about going to church."

"Because it never happened. By the time Adam came home, he was too ill to go anywhere."

"Oh . . ." Donald looked down at his feet.

"You see, Donald, Lauren grew up without a father and it would be very, very sad if she had to raise her child without a husband. Tell me, is that what you really want?"

"No, of course not." He looked back at her. "It's just that I don't want to spend my whole life being miserable. And Eunice is not exactly a walk in the park either. She's always sticking her nose where it doesn't belong."

"Then find a place where you and Lauren can live on your own. Surely you can afford a small house or apartment."

He looked skeptical. "I don't know . . . ."

"Well, it might be what saves your marriage. In fact, if you honestly can't work a small rental into your budget, maybe I can help—"

"I don't want your help." He looked at his watch. "Really, I need to get to work."

She put her hand on his arm. "I had planned to tell Lauren everything . . . what I saw last night. Now I'm not so sure that's the best thing. Tell me, Donald, do you honestly want to make your marriage work?"

"I told you I do."

"Then I won't mention this to Lauren . . . not yet, anyway. But I promise you, if I ever find out that you're doing something like this again, I will definitely tell her everything I know."

He just nodded.

"And I want you to start looking for a place for you and Lauren to live on your own—*today*."

"But I've got work—"

"I'm telling you, Donald, either you look for a place or I will. There's no shame in living in a rental for a while. You can save up to buy something bigger later."

"Fine." His brow creased. "I saw a for rent sign on a duplex not far from the mill. I'll call them about it."

"Perfect." She smiled. "I'll tell Lauren the good news."

"Thanks." He actually seemed slightly relieved. "I guess you could be right. Having our own place might help some."

"I'm sure it will. I realized too late that I spent far too many years under Eunice's roof. It's not a healthy place for a young family."

She watched as her son-in-law walked away. She had never been terribly fond of Donald, but maybe he just needed some good encouragement. She really hoped that this might be a turning point for the young man. Sometimes it took something negative, like getting caught and being forced to face reality, to make a person wake up and turn a corner . . . sometimes it took a whole lot more.

15

By the end of the day it was all settled. Donald had rented the duplex and Lauren and the baby would be released from the hospital the following day.

"I can't see that this is a good thing," Eunice said as she and the two grandmothers stood in front of the viewing window, gazing at baby Sarah. "Those kids will be poor as church mice on their own."

"Then maybe you need to give Donald a raise," Anna said quietly.

Ardelle chuckled. "I have to agree with Anna on that, Eunice."

"Humph." Eunice removed a glove from her handbag.

"Why *don't* you give him a raise?" Ardelle demanded.

"Because he makes exactly what the last man in his position made."

"Yes, and poor old Rex Collins probably hadn't had a raise in decades." Ardelle shook her head. "He probably makes more in retirement than he did at the mill."

"I pay my men fairly." Eunice tugged a glove on.

"But if Donald doesn't even earn enough to rent a duplex, it can't possibly be a fair family wage?" Anna persisted.

"Are you going to tell me how to run my business now?" Eunice narrowed her eyes at Anna.

"Maybe Donald can find some other form of work," Ardelle said in a tight voice, "I'm sure there's someone in this town who will pay him fairly."

"Fine, fine. I'll give him a raise." Eunice shook a finger at Anna, as if she alone were to blame. "But mark my word, no good will come from this folly. Lauren doesn't know the first thing about housekeeping, not to mention caring for a baby. I predict that within the first week, the girl will fall completely apart. And do not expect me to pick up the pieces!"

"Lauren will learn," Anna told her.

"Don't be so sure." Now Eunice made a sly smile. "That girl is used to being pampered and spoiled. She likes it that way."

Ardelle laughed. "Well, now who doesn't want to be spoiled, Eunice? But I'm sure Anna is right, Lauren can learn to manage her household. It will be good for her."

Anna almost thought that, given enough time, she might actually begin to like Ardelle. "Maybe you can help her a little," Anna suggested to Ardelle. "I'll stay as long as I can and I'll help however I can, but after I go, perhaps you could drop in occasionally and give her some housekeeping pointers or help with the baby."

"Yes." Ardelle nodded eagerly. "I'd be glad to do that."

<hr>

Visiting hours would end soon. The shadows on the walls were getting longer, but Anna had lingered on, hoping to bolster Lauren's spirits and to encourage her that living in a duplex wouldn't be as bad as she was predicting. "It'll be your very own place," Anna said cheerfully. "You can decorate it however you like. Maybe you'll want to sew curtains."

"You know I can't sew."

"But I taught you enough that you could make a simple curtain, Lauren. All you do is sew straight—"

"Yes, perhaps I can weave the cloth myself too."

"Well, maybe I'll have time to make some. And, if you like, I can help you get a few things to set it up. I learned how to shop secondhand stores while getting the inn ready and—"

"Secondhand stores?" Lauren frowned. "I don't want a house filled with used junk, Mom. I mean that's fine for your inn, but I don't like old things."

"Well, however we do it, I'm sure we can make your house homey and comfy and sweet, Lauren. And once you're settled in, I'm sure you'll see how lovely it is to be on your own."

Lauren looked unconvinced. "I just wish that you'd come to live with us at Grandmother's, Mom, and that you'd help me with Sarah. Why can't you do that for a while?"

Anna had already answered this question . . . several times. "You know I would love to help you and the baby. And my offer still stands—if you want to come live at the river, I'll do all that I can to help. That is my home now, sweetie. And you will always be welcome there. You and Donald could have your own cabin and—"

"You know I don't want to live there, Mom. It's a nice place to visit. And I really did start to like the river, but it's too remote."

"Maybe you and Sarah could just stay with me, just for a little while," Anna suggested. "I could help with Sarah and teach you some things, like sewing and housekeeping."

"I don't know . . ."

"And Babette could teach you about French cooking. She's such an excellent cook."

Lauren looked slightly interested.

"It would be a chance for you to get your feet under you, so to speak. You could build up your confidence as a wife and a mother." Anna felt more and more that this might be the perfect solution. "Besides that, it would give Donald time to get things settled in the duplex. Perhaps he'd get some furnishings, or maybe he'd like to paint the baby's room."

Lauren's mouth twisted to one side, as if she was seriously considering this.

Anna patted Lauren's shoulder. "How about if you think on this, sweetie?"

"It does sound kind of good, Mom. And the idea of me being on my own, trying to take care of Sarah and Donald . . . well, it's overwhelming." She started to tear up now.

"You're tired, Lauren. You need to rest. If you get released tomorrow, it will be a busy day."

"But you'll go with me to stay at Grandmother's, won't you? Just for a while?"

"Yes, if your grandmother doesn't mind, I'll stick around to help out a bit." She kissed Lauren's cheek. "Good night, sweetie. Maybe you'll get more sleep tonight than last night."

"I doubt it."

Anna left, pausing to use the lobby phone to place another collect call to Clark. Again, he reassured her that things were under control. However, she felt she heard a tiny edge in his voice as he told her to stay as long as she needed. "You're sure?" she asked.

"Yes, really, we're fine. Marshall is even learning to cook. Between Mom and Babette, he might turn into a master chef." He laughed.

"If I thought Lauren was going to be okay, I'd come home right now," she confessed. "As it is . . . well, it's a long story and these phone calls won't be cheap."

"You just do what you need to do, Anna, and come home as soon as you feel it's right. Of course I miss you. But see to Lauren and the baby. They need you."

As she hung up she suspected that Clark, in his own way, needed her too. But at least he understood how desperately needy Lauren was. Just the same, she wasn't sure that anyone, short of God Almighty, would ever be able to meet all of her daughter's needs.

∽∞∽

Anna spent the next day getting Lauren and Sarah settled into Eunice's big house. Naturally, Eunice was no help. In fact, she seemed determined to make them as miserable as possible. To start with, she wasn't even home and had locked all the doors and Lauren didn't have a key with her, but Anna remembered an old hiding place and, to her a relief, a key was still there. But when they got inside, both the baby and Lauren were starting to fuss.

"I can't believe Grandmother let Mabel go," Lauren complained as Anna carried the baby up the stairs. "I know she did it just to spite me."

Anna didn't say anything.

"Here's the baby's room." Lauren opened the door to what had previously been a guest room, but was now a fairly attractive nursery. "Grandmother insisted on blue for the walls. She was certain that Sarah was going to be a boy and wanted her to be named Adam, after Dad."

"Well, you're not a boy, are you?" Anna said as she laid Sarah on the changing table. "Come learn how to change a diaper, Lauren."

"I'm tired," Lauren said. "Can't I learn later?"

"There's no time like now." Anna sniffed at the baby. "And you better get some wash rags too. Get them wet, too, warm water."

Lauren reluctantly left, returning with several washcloths then watched as Anna went through the steps, explaining each one.

"Ugh," Lauren plugged her nose as Anna peeled off the diaper. "That's disgusting."

"You'll get over it," Anna said as she held out the soiled diaper.

"I don't want to touch it!" Lauren jumped back.

"Lauren," Anna said sternly, "take it now."

"No, Mom!" Lauren shrieked. "That's nasty. I refuse."

Anna just stared at her daughter. "Lauren, you have to—"

"No, no, no!" Lauren cried as she ran from the nursery.

"Oh, dear." Anna kept one hand on the startled baby as she set the diaper aside. "Your mama has a lot to learn, little Sarah."

Soon Sarah was all cleaned up and tucked into her crib, but Anna knew that it would be feeding time before long. She found Lauren in her room, sitting in a chair with a slightly glazed expression. "I wish I'd stayed in the hospital now."

"Well, it's too late for that." Anna frowned. "I'm going to get the baby things from the car. We'll need to make her some bottles."

Lauren just nodded.

"You need to come downstairs," Anna told her. "So you can learn how to make the bottles."

"This is too hard," Lauren mumbled as she followed Anna back down.

Anna had read about how to make the baby's formula, but it was still new to her. However, she figured it couldn't be any harder than canning preserves. "You put a pan of water on to boil," she told Lauren. "You can boil water, can't you?"

Lauren rolled her eyes.

"I'll get the stuff from the car."

Anna paused outside to look up at the sky. She remembered how, so many years ago, she used to do this very thing. She'd be homesick for the river and she'd go outside and just stare at the sky, trying to imagine it was her river. "God help us," she prayed.

They were just finishing up the last bottle when Sarah's loud wails echoed down the stairs. "I'll go and check on her while you warm this," Anna told Lauren.

"How do I warm it?"

"Just put it in that hot water." Anna pointed to the pan. "Until it's body temperature. You can do that, can't you?"

Lauren narrowed her eyes. "I'm not an imbecile, Mom."

"No." Anna turned away. "You are not. Bring it up to the nursery when it's warm." Now she hurried to fetch Sarah out of her crib, sat down with her, and tried to soothe her from crying. "Your mama's coming, little one," she said, "be patient . . . be very, very patient."

Lauren eventually came up and Anna handed her the baby. "I know you know how to feed her," she said. "I'm going to get your diaper pail set up and then we'll make a plan for how you are going to change diapers, Lauren."

By the end of the day Anna felt certain that Lauren was not ready to set up housekeeping and care for her own baby. Not for the first time, Anna marveled at how she'd managed to raise such a helpless daughter. Still, she told herself, Lauren could learn. She would have to.

After a rather hostile dinner, which Anna prepared, and where Eunice played the wounded benefactress, Donald the sulking husband, and Lauren the weary mother who excused herself early, Anna realized that she needed to speak out. "I think it would be best if Lauren and Sarah went home with me for a spell," she announced.

"Whatever for?" Eunice demanded.

"Because Lauren needs help with the baby and I can help her, but I need to go home and see to the inn as well."

"But you were the one who thought Lauren and Donald needed a place of their own." Eunice narrowed her eyes. "What became of that little plan?"

"That's right," Donald said. "I went ahead and put money down on that duplex. I told the guy we'd be moving in this weekend."

"And you should move in, Donald." Anna nodded. "And while Lauren is with me, learning some housekeeping skills and getting more comfortable being a mother, you'll have time to get your house together so that she and Sarah will have a nice place to come home to."

"I guess that makes sense." Donald reached for another biscuit. "Hopefully you'll teach Lauren to cook too."

"That's part of my plan."

"Well, I think that's utter nonsense." Eunice laid her napkin on the table. "First you say Lauren needs her own place, now you say she must go home with you. I suspect your true plan is to keep Lauren and Sarah there with you indefinitely."

"I plan nothing of the sort." Anna set down her coffee cup. "Even if I did, we all know that Lauren is a strong-minded young woman. No one can force her to do anything she doesn't want to do."

"Even so." Eunice stood. "I think you are acting very wishy-washy, Anna. It seems you can't even make up your own mind."

Anna decided to ignore that remark, turning her attention back to Donald. "I figured it would take you some time to get the duplex set up. You'll want to get the baby's room ready. I think Lauren is hoping you'll paint it pink. And I'm sure you'll need some furnishings and linens and kitchen things. Perhaps your mother . . . or maybe even Eunice . . . will be able to give you a hand getting it all set up."

"Humph." Leaving her plate on the table, Eunice started to depart. "It was my understanding that no one needed my help anymore, Anna. Surely you're not changing your tune about that as well."

"I'll leave that between you and Donald." Anna got up and, picking up her own place setting, went to the kitchen, where she silently counted to ten. How was it that, after all these years, Eunice was still able to get under her skin?

16

Lauren's second day at home was no better than the first, but Anna was determined not to let Lauren push off all her motherly chores onto her. She'd even dug out a pair of rubber gloves for Lauren to wear while rinsing out diapers in the toilet. "I feel like I'm being tortured," Lauren moaned as she gingerly held a dripping diaper over the toilet.

"Now you need to wring it out," Anna said. "Before you put it in the diaper pail with the bleach solution."

"This is so nasty. I feel like I'm going to throw up."

"Just hurry and put it in the diaper pail." Anna waited with the lid in her hand.

"Ugh." Lauren dropped the soggy diaper in the pail then peeled off the rubber gloves. "These detestable gloves are disgusting."

"Then don't use them." Anna put the lid back on the pail and washed her hands.

"That's even more disgusting."

"Like I said, hands are easy to clean, Lauren." Anna dried her own hands.

"Excuse me," Eunice stuck her hand in the bathroom. "I can see you're having a lovely time in here, but would it be possible to speak to my granddaughter?"

Lauren looked surprised. "Sure."

"Alone?" Eunice glared at Anna as if she were some kind of international spy.

"Don't mind me. I'm going to go pack up some more of the baby things," Anna told them. "We want to leave as early as possible tomorrow morning, and I'd like to have the station wagon mostly loaded by the time we go to bed."

Anna tiptoed into Lauren's room where she'd already started boxing up the things that she felt the baby would absolutely need. Fortunately, she already had the crib that Dorothy's mom had loaned her. She had called Clark last night—not collect either, which seemed only fair since Eunice had so freely used the inn's phone. Plus, she'd not only cooked last night's dinner but cleaned up afterwards. As a result, she took her time to tell Clark about the plans for bringing Lauren home. And he agreed to have the cabin closest to the house all set up for Lauren and Sarah.

"That's close enough for me to be able to help her, but not so close that she'll expect me to play nanny," Anna told him. "I want Lauren to become somewhat independent."

It wasn't until the next day, when Anna, Lauren, and the baby were well on their way that Anna discovered what Eunice's mysterious private conversation with Lauren was about. "She was trying to bribe me to stay with her," Lauren admitted.

"What sort of bribe was she using?"

"She promised to get Mabel back."

"Oh . . ."

"But I reminded her that Mabel had already made it clear that she didn't like babies. So, really, what was the point?"

Anna just nodded, keeping her eyes focused on the road. She was well aware of her inexperience and that her driving skills weren't as good as she wished they were . . . and that today she was carrying very precious passengers. She had considered asking Lauren to drive, but knew that she was sometimes a bit reckless behind the wheel.

"Then Grandmother even offered to hire a nanny as well."

"That must've been tempting."

"It actually was. But then I thought about what it'd be like to be stuck living with Grandmother and Mabel and a nanny and Donald and the baby . . ." She sighed loudly. "And it just sounded like a three-ring circus."

"It could be a little crazy."

"And I kept thinking about what you'd said about Donald and me and the baby living in our own little house, with me taking care of things. Kind of like those old reruns of the *I Love Lucy* show. Lucy and Ricky live in that tiny apartment with Little Ricky and yet they seem so happy. And I realized that Grandmother wants to keep me her little girl, you know, always under her thumb."

"That's probably not far from the truth."

"And I decided that I don't want that, Mom. I want to be in charge of my own life."

Anna smiled. "You don't know how happy it makes me feel to hear that, darling."

———ornament———

The trip home took a couple hours longer than the trip out had taken. But with numerous stops to tend to the baby and Lauren, it was mid-afternoon by the time Anna parked the car in town. "Clark is meeting us with the boat," she explained. "It's faster than the back road, not to mention smoother." She glanced up at the sky. "And it's a perfect day for the river. But let's bundle Sarah up just the same."

Anna held the baby as Clark guided the boat up the river. Lauren, to Anna's delight, seemed to be happy just to sit and look at the scenery, occasionally commenting on how beautiful everything was. "I forgot how pretty it is here, Mom," she said happily.

Anna smiled. It was the first time Lauren had sounded happy in days.

As the boat made its way up the Siuslaw, Anna talked quietly to the baby, telling her about the river, about the fish and the birds, about how one day Sarah would paddle her own canoe around the shining waters. "Just like a real Siuslaw princess," she promised as the inn came into sight.

"All those cabins," Lauren said to Clark. "How on earth did you manage to finish them all?"

"Marshall came out during spring vacation and gave me a hand," he said as he slowed the boat.

"Everything looks so nice," Lauren told Anna. "The flowers blooming, the picnic tables—and you even got more boats. It's like a real resort."

Anna laughed. "And you used to think it was the *last* resort."

"You ladies go in and get settled," Clark said as he tied the boat to the dock then gave them each a hand getting out. "Marshall and I will get all this stuff unloaded."

They were just going up the dock when Babette and Hazel came down to meet them. "Allo, allo," Babette called out.

"Welcome home," Hazel said heartily. Then both the older women oohed and aahed over the baby.

"She ees so beautiful," Babette gushed. "She ees so much like Anna when she was a petite bebe."

Lauren nodded as she looked down at her baby, still in Anna's arms. "Everyone thinks she takes after Mom."

"Eet ees a good thing," Babette told her.

"A very good thing." Hazel put her arm around Anna's shoulders and squeezed her. "We're so glad you're back."

"And I have saved lunch for you," Babette said. "If you are hungry."

"I'm starving," Lauren told her. "And Mom says you're going to teach me how to cook French food."

"I am pleased to teach you." Babette grabbed Lauren's hand, swinging it as they walked to the house. "Just the way I teach your mama."

Anna smiled as she and Hazel followed them up to the house. "Here we are," she said to Sarah. "Home sweet home."

Thanks to Hazel and Babette, and even Marshall, the first several days went relatively smoothly. With her helpful volunteers, Anna was able to spend a lot of time with Lauren and Sarah. She took Lauren through all the steps of caring for her baby. She taught her to bathe Sarah and how to change diapers without rubber gloves. She made sure Lauren was able to sterilize the baby bottles and do the formula on her own. She showed her how to use the washer and dryer, explaining that Lauren needed to be responsible for her and Sarah's laundry. Anna even helped Lauren make a simple daily chores list. As far as Anna could see, they were off to a good start.

Consequently, Anna encouraged her helpers to return to their regular routines, assuring them that Lauren was no longer in need of so much help. And Anna had been glad to return to her routines. A few things had gone undone in her absence, not big things, but some of the little niceties that Anna enjoyed providing for the guests. She was beginning to feel caught up and even had time to work in the garden, but halfway through the second week, it became clear that Lauren was still dragging her heels along the road to motherhood.

"It's not that I don't want to help you," Anna told Lauren for the second time. "It's just that you need to learn to do it yourself."

"But how am I supposed to both do my laundry *and* watch the baby?"

Anna suppressed the urge to laugh. "The machines do most of the work, Lauren, and Sarah is perfectly safe in her baby seat. It's not hard to keep an eye on her and do the laundry at the same time." She resisted the urge to tell Lauren about how it used to be, back in the good old days when Anna did the laundry in a decrepit wringer washer, hung it on the line to dry, cared for her own fussy baby, nursed her ailing husband, and cooked and cleaned for an entire household.

"So I have to drag everything over to the laundry room and Sarah too?"

"It's part of being a mother." She continued stirring the egg salad mixture. "You have to choose how to manage your time. For instance, you can do things like the laundry while Sarah is napping or—"

"When Sarah is napping, I need to take a nap too," Lauren insisted.

"That's your decision. The point is, you have to figure it out."

"Fine! I'll just drag your baby granddaughter to the laundry room and if she gets accidentally put into the dryer with the towels, don't blame me."

"Oh, Lauren!" Anna frowned. "Don't say such things."

"But why can't I just leave her up here with you?"

Anna held up her hands. "Because I just started fixing lunch. The guests expect it to be ready in the next half hour. After that I need to freshen up linens in the rooms, and then there's the—"

"I don't know why I even came out here." Lauren snatched up Sarah from the floor where she'd just settled her on a blanket.

Anna didn't know what to say. She knew that she wasn't asking Lauren to do anything too hard, but the idea of Sarah getting hurt because of Lauren's angry carelessness was unsettling.

"Okay, Lauren," she gave in. "Leave Sarah with me. But just until you get a couple of loads started in the washer. Then you come straight back here and get her."

"Yeah, yeah." Lauren handed Sarah over to Anna. She was barely out the door when Anna's nose told her that Sarah was in a need of a diaper change. Naturally, all the changing things were in Lauren's cabin. Anna had suggested that Lauren use a diaper bag or leave a set of baby things up here, but so far that hadn't happened.

Anna considered improvising with a tea towel for a diaper, but then realized it would all be much easier if she simply went down to the cabin. Lunch might be a few minutes late, but she doubted that anyone would complain. On sunny days like this, she made bag lunches that the guests picked up at their leisure. Most of them liked to eat out at the picnic tables or on the river.

"Come on, Princess Sarah," Anna said as she headed out. "Time to freshen you up."

"Is lunch out yet?" Marshall asked as they met on the stairs. "The Brewsters want me to take them out fishing and we were going to take it—"

"It's not quite ready," she explained. "I'm running a little behind."

"Want me to help? I know how to make sandwiches and stuff."

She quickly explained about Sarah, and the egg salad she was just getting ready to spread onto bread. "Would you mind?"

"No problem."

"You are a good man, Marshall Richards." She smiled gratefully at him then continued on her way. Sometimes she wondered how it was that Marshall, two years younger than Lauren, had matured so much sooner. Oh, he'd gone through a rough spell a year ago. But then he'd straightened up. And now he seemed more grown up than ever. If she didn't appreciate him so much, she might actually feel envious.

"Here we are at your house," she said to Sarah as she went into the cabin that Lauren was calling home. But she'd barely gone through the door, when she let out a gasp. "What on earth?" She looked around the completely disheveled room in horror. The last time she'd seen it, all was clean and sweet and inviting. Now there were clothes and baby things everywhere. No beds were made. A pile of dirty, stinking diapers were over in a corner of the kitchenette. The counter was cluttered with dirty dishes and beauty products and the sink was filled with dirty baby bottles. It was sickening. Anna was so angry she felt tears come to her eyes. How was it possible that her own daughter, in less than a week, was living in absolute squalor?

Anna dug around to find what she needed to change Sarah's diaper. She moved a pile of smutty looking paperbacks from Lauren's bed to make a place to set a changing pad and lie Sarah down. As she began to peel away the baby's clothes, she reminded herself that Lauren didn't really spend too much time down in the cabin. Lauren liked to be in the house or outside with Anna. Naturally, Anna welcomed her company and she always assumed that Lauren had already tended to her own housekeeping.

"Your mama needs to grow up," she told Sarah as she unpinned the diaper. Then as she began to clean Sarah's bottom, the baby started to wail as if in pain. That's when Anna realized that poor Sarah had a severe case of diaper rash. Anna had told Lauren, more than once, how to properly clean the baby to prevent this. Obviously, like with so many other things, Lauren was not listening.

Anna quickly peeled off Sarah's clothing, noticing that she also had a rash under her arms. "When was the last time you had a bath?" she asked the crying baby. Wrapping her in a blanket, and wedging her safely in a corner of the bed, Anna went to the bathroom and began filling the baby bathtub they'd brought from Pine Ridge.

As she gently bathed her granddaughter, she couldn't remember when she'd felt so thoroughly outraged. As she washed Sarah's dark hair, she told herself she would not lose her temper with Lauren. That would do no good. On the same token, she would not back down either.

She was just getting Sarah dressed, in the only clean thing she could find, a soft cotton kimono, when she heard the door open. Bracing herself, she looked up to see Lauren peeking in the cabin. "So here you are."

"Sarah needed a diaper change," Anna said evenly.

"You could've waited for me to come back."

"Never mind about that." Anna sat down on the messy bed. "We need to talk."

"But you need to make lunch," Lauren reached for the baby, taking in her arms without even seeming to notice that she was freshly bathed.

"Marshall is helping with it."

"So now you're going to lecture me?"

"I'd rather you explain . . ." Anna waved her hand around the messy room, "this to me."

"What's to explain? I'm not like you. I'm a bad housekeeper."

"No, you're not a bad housekeeper. I've seen you, Lauren. You know how to pick things up. You are simply lazy."

"Fine. I'm lazy." Lauren jutted out her lower lip.

"I'm not trying to hurt your feelings. I'm just very, very concerned."

"I don't see why. It's not like you have to live here. Besides, I was going to clean it up."

"When?"

"After I did the laundry. I figured I'd just put everything away at once. No big deal."

"It's not the mess in here that concerns me most, Lauren. Oh, some parts of it worry me. I do not like seeing Sarah's baby bottles like that in the sink. Every one of them needs to be thoroughly washed now, with soap and water, then boiled for several minutes. You might even need a bleach solution to rinse them in." Anna got up and opened the small refrigerator and looked in. "And it looks like you don't even have a bottle ready for her next feeding. What did you intend to do about that?"

"I'll just quickly wash one out."

"And sterilize it too?"

Lauren glanced away.

"Lauren, do you understand that Sarah is completely dependent on you? Her survival is in your hands. What if she gets sick because you do something wrong with her formula? Would that concern you?"

"Of course it would."

"And when I changed her, she had a nasty case of diaper rash. And I could tell she hadn't been bathed in days."

Lauren looked up with angry eyes. "I can't believe you're going on like this, Mom. You're part Indian. How do you think your people raised their children?"

Anna was too stunned to answer.

"Think about it, Mom. They didn't sterilize their baby bottles."

"No, they breastfed their babies, Lauren. But it's too late for you to do that."

Lauren made a face. "And do you think they did laundry and changed diapers and bathed their babies every single day?"

Anna thought hard about this. "To be honest, I don't really know the answers to those questions. But I know someone who does." Anna reached for the baby and Lauren didn't resist. "Now, come with me."

"Huh? Where? What are you—"

"Come on, Lauren!" With the baby in arms, Anna led the way, marching over to Hazel's cabin. As she rapped on the door, she hoped that she was in.

"Oh, hello." Hazel gave them a quizzical look.

"Lauren wants to raise her baby the way her native ancestors did, Hazel." She glanced back at her daughter. "Or, at least she thinks she does. However, I'm not sure how that's done. So I thought you might like to help educate her."

"Well, certainly." Hazel grinned. "Where do we begin?"

"Back at Lauren's cabin," Anna said. "If you don't mind."

Lauren looked fit to be tied as Anna led their little entourage back to Lauren's hovel, throwing open the door. "Come on in, Hazel. And let Lauren tell you all about her theories on child rearing." She handed the baby back to Lauren. "If you'll excuse me, I need to go finish fixing lunch now." She paused to pick up an unwashed baby bottle. "You can pick this up in my kitchen, Lauren. It will be sterilized and ready for formula." She glared at her daughter. "That is, unless you intend to feed Sarah the old-fashioned way, the way your ancestors did."

Hazel laughed heartily.

Anna tossed Hazel an apologetic look as she closed the door. Walking back to the house, Anna had no idea what she was going to do about Lauren. She even doubted that levelheaded Hazel would be able to talk sense into her clueless daughter. It hurt to admit this, but it might've been better if the baby had been given up for adoption. She frowned at the crusty baby bottle in her hand. Really, did Lauren even want little Sarah Pearl?

17

To Anna's relief and surprise, Lauren attempted to turn over a new leaf in the following days. And thanks to the wisdom of Hazel and Babette, Lauren had a small village of older women looking after her, instructing her, gently encouraging her, and sometimes scolding. Anna wondered if this might not be similar to how it was a hundred years ago, back before the "moving man," as Grandma Pearl called the white man, took over. However, unlike Anna's ancestors, little Sarah wore diapers, continued to be bathed daily, and was fed formula in sterilized bottles.

"I'm exhausted," Lauren announced as she came into the kitchen where Anna was just starting to work on dinner.

"Being a mommy is hard work." Anna paused to smile at Sarah, who was nearly asleep in her mother's arms.

"You're telling me."

"Looks like you and Sarah might be able to catch a little nap before dinnertime."

"I'm trying to keep her awake." Lauren jiggled the baby now. "Hazel said she might start sleeping the night if I don't let her nap too much during the day."

Anna continued to chop carrots. She wasn't sure that theory would really work, but she wasn't sure it wouldn't either.

"Donald is supposed to call me at five o'clock," Lauren said as she sat down on the kitchen stool.

"How is he doing?" Anna kept her eyes on her knife. She knew that Lauren had called him several times during the past few days.

"Okay . . . I guess. I think he wants me to come home."

"Oh . . ." Anna slowly nodded. "What do you want, Lauren?"

"I don't know . . . . I mean I want to be with Donald. But I'm just not sure I'm ready. What do you think I should do, Mom?"

Anna sighed, laid down the knife, and turned to face her daughter. "I'm not sure, Lauren. But I do think you should listen to your heart."

"How do you do that?" Lauren licked her finger then used it to clean something from Sarah's cheek.

"It's not easy. But it helps if you get really quiet. Sometimes I go out in my canoe . . . in the morning."

"Uh-huh."

"And then I just wait, trying to listen to that quiet inner voice. I can't always hear it, but when I do, I like to think it's God's spirit whispering to me."

"Do you really think God can tell me what to do?"

"I think so. If you're willing to listen."

"Maybe I should take the canoe out and try it."

"Anytime you want to, Lauren. And if I'm not busy, I'm happy to watch Sarah for you."

Just then the phone rang. "That's probably Donald. Can you watch her now?"

Anna glanced at the clock as she reached for the baby. "Sure. But can you try to keep the call short?"

"Yeah." Lauren took off and, as she'd been doing lately, answered the extension in Anna and Clark's bedroom. Anna wasn't thrilled about this, but she knew Lauren needed her privacy when speaking to Donald.

"What do *you* want?" Anna asked Sarah. "Would you like to go home to your daddy? Or would you like to remain here on the river with all these people who love you?" Anna knew that if she could make this decision, she would have Lauren and Sarah stay with them indefinitely. However, it was not her choice. Lauren had to paddle her own canoe . . . and some-day Sarah would have to do the same. Anna kissed the top of Sarah's head. "I pray your mommy makes the best choice, my little princess. I pray that you are as cherished and loved, valued more than a precious pearl."

With the baby cradled in one arm, Anna attempted to do some of the dinner preparations, removing things from the refrigerator, setting out the utensils and ingredients she needed, filling a pot with water.

"Mom!" cried Lauren. "I'm going home!"

Anna forced a smile to her lips, trying not to bristle at Lauren's use of the word *home*. Naturally, Lauren would think of Pine Ridge as her home; she had spent most of her life there.

"Donald is driving over here to pick Sarah and me up on Saturday. I told him he can spend the night and we can drive home on Sunday. Isn't that great?"

Anna handed Sarah back to her. "If that's what you want, sweetie."

"Or course it's what I want. Donald is my husband. He's Sarah's daddy. And he's coming to get us!" Lauren was danc-ing around the kitchen, rocking Sarah in her arms. "Daddy is coming, Daddy is coming," she sang to the baby.

"I'm glad you're happy," Anna said as she turned her attention back to dinner preparations. "But I need to get these vegetables cooking."

"Donald said the duplex is all set up for us," Lauren continued. "And he even painted Sarah's room pink, Mom. Just like I wanted."

Anna turned, this time giving her a genuine smile. "That's wonderful." Perhaps both Donald and Lauren really were finally maturing. Sarah deserved an adult set of parents.

"He said Grandmother was in a perfect snit when he picked up the baby furniture. She acted like it belonged to her. But Donald had Jimmy and a couple of his friends with pickups helping him and they moved it right out." She laughed. "And then they picked up the bedroom furniture and all our things and Grandmother threatened to call the police."

"Oh, my!" Anna grimaced.

"But she was just bluffing." Lauren rolled her eyes. "I don't know why she's such an ogre."

"She has a need to be in control," Anna said as she poured some chopped vegetables into the boiling water. "Although I'm not sure why it's such an obsession."

"Well, she can't control me," Lauren declared. "Or Donald."

"I hope you'll still try to remain friendly with her," Anna said cautiously. "In her own way, I know she loves you, Lauren."

"She has some strange ways of showing it."

"I know."

"I won't go out of my way to be friendly to her," Lauren said as she plucked a stray carrot wheel from the countertop and popped it into her mouth. "But if she's nice to me, I'll be nice to her."

Anna just nodded. Sarah was starting to fuss now, but Lauren seemed slightly oblivious. "Do you think she should have a bottle before dinnertime?"

"Yeah, maybe so." Lauren took a roll from a breadbasket. "See you later."

The kitchen seemed extra quiet with Lauren and Sarah gone. A part of Anna appreciated the peace, but another part of her felt very sad. She would miss them more than she wanted to admit to anyone.

The next two days passed sweetly and sadly. Anna spent as much time as she could with Lauren and Sarah, savoring every moment. Although Anna didn't voice her emotions, Clark was very understanding. Hazel and Babette even helped out so Anna had more time to devote to Lauren and the baby. On Saturday morning Hazel offered to watch the baby while Anna took Lauren out for a walk.

"I want you to know," Anna said as they sat on a handhewn log bench by the river, "that Clark and I will always be here for you and Sarah. If you need anything, you know you can call us, Lauren, no matter what it is. Do you understand?"

She nodded in a slightly absent sort of way. "Thanks, Mom."

"Now, I have something very important to tell you." Anna paused. "I need you to listen carefully."

"Sure." Lauren turned to look at her.

"Mr. Joseph P. Miller is my attorney in Pine Ridge."

"I thought he was Grandmother's lawyer."

"He used to be. But he's the one who helped me to figure some things out with your dad's estate. Remember what happened last summer?"

"Oh, yeah. Grandmother was pretty mad."

"Well, your father had left a considerable amount of money to me . . . money that your grandmother, well, she sort of used and invested some of it."

"So that's what the fight was about?"

"It wasn't really a fight, Lauren. At least not in my mind. But at the time I told Mr. Miller to put it on hold. Actually, Clark communicated with him for me. You know Clark went to law school."

"I didn't know that."

"Yes, but he loves building. Anyway, back to Mr. Miller." Now she explained about her most recent conversation with him. "And I told him the time might come when you need some money, Lauren. I don't mean for having fun with or buying luxuries—and Mr. Miller knows that. But I mean if things get rough for you . . . if for any reason you ever find yourself supporting Sarah on your own and—"

"Oh, that'll never happen."

"I hope it never does, sweetie, but I know what it's like when it does. I know firsthand how hard it was to be dependent on your grandmother for all those years. I still regret it, Lauren. I think you and I have both paid a high price for her, uh, assistance."

Lauren sighed. "So what are you saying?"

"I'm saying if you should ever need financial help, go to Mr. Miller, Lauren. Or to his nephew who will be working there too. And, of course, you can call us too. Never think that you're all alone and on your own."

Lauren nodded. "Okay."

"And I hope we can stay in touch," Anna said quietly. "I'll probably keep writing you letters. It's an old habit." She told Lauren how she and her mother used to write so regularly.

"But I'm a terrible letter writer."

"I know. But even if you could just write a postcard. Or if you could send a photo of Sarah. I would appreciate it so much, sweetie."

"I'll try. And I'll call you on the phone sometimes, too, if Donald doesn't mind, that is."

"Reverse the charges," Anna suggested. "Just keep in mind what time of day it is and whether or not I'll be too busy to talk." She touched Lauren's cheek. "I wish I could keep you here with me," she confessed. "I wish you and Sarah Pearl could stay on the river always. But I do understand."

"You know, Mom, I really do love this river too. I never thought that I'd feel that way. But being here this summer has been different. Don't get me wrong, it's been really hard too. And I know that I was a brat for a while. But I've really liked having you and Hazel and Babette around to help me with Sarah and stuff. I'm going to miss all of you."

"Well, you'll have Ardelle to help you. And, if you play your cards right, maybe Grandmother too. Just don't let her reel you in."

Lauren laughed. "Oh, don't worry. I know how to handle the old lady."

Anna hoped so.

Lauren reached over to hug Anna now. "Thanks for every-thing you've done for me, Mom. And I promise I'll bring Sarah out to visit you whenever I can."

"Really?" Anna blinked tears from her eyes. "I would love that. And, if it helps, I'd gladly pay for your bus fare."

"I want Sarah to experience this place, too, I mean when she gets older."

"I'm so happy to hear that, Lauren."

Lauren stood now. "Speaking of Sarah, I should go finish making her bottles. I got them all sterilized, but I still need to make the formula. And I want to get the cabin all sparkly clean before Donald arrives." She grinned. "I want to impress him with my fancy housekeeping skills."

"Good for you." Anna reached for Lauren's hand, holding it in hers as they walked back to the inn. "I'm very proud of you, Lauren. You have really done a great job these past couple of weeks."

With all her heart, Anna hoped her daughter would continue this maturation process. And she hoped that Donald had changed as well. Almost as much as that, she hoped Donald would fully appreciate Lauren's progress and that their marriage would become strong as a result. Really, hope was all Anna had right now . . . hope and prayers.

18

Life seemed to settle into a quieter routine with Lauren and Sarah gone. Even so, Anna missed them. Still, she told herself, it was for their best. Donald and Lauren and Sarah could become a family now. To her surprise and delight, a postcard came from Lauren about two weeks after they'd left. Anna had already written her twice.

Dear Mom,

I'm trying hard to be a good wife and mom, but it is NOT easy. Donald isn't exactly Mr. PERFECT either. Sometimes I feel like I have TWO children. I haven't spoken to Grandmother yet, and Ardelle is more of a pain than anything else. I wish you would move back to Pine Ridge and help me, but I know you won't do that. Do you think Hazel would come?

Love and kisses,

Lauren

Anna sighed as she slipped the postcard into her desk drawer and reached for a clean sheet of stationary. The inn was quiet now. Even Clark had gone to bed. But it was in the evening, like this, that she was able to think and to write.

Dear Lauren,

I was so pleased to hear from you. We are all well. The weather has been more like winter than spring this week. So far the guests are not complaining too much. The forecast is for sunshine to return by the last week of July. I certainly hope so. I would like to hear about how our little Sarah is doing. Has she gained some weight? Is she sleeping through the night yet? How do you like your new little house? Have you made any curtains yet?

Anna paused, remembering when Lauren was a baby and how she'd sewn blue-and-white gingham curtains for the kitchen window. She'd found a little blue pitcher the same color as the fabric and she used to fill it with wildflowers and place it on the windowsill. She wanted to encourage Lauren to do something like that, but stopped herself. She realized that she and her daughter were two different people. Instead, she wrote about the pair of baby moccasins that she'd meant to send home for Sarah to wear, asking if Lauren would appreciate it. Then she told about the progress Clark was making on the next set of cabins and how Marshall had been helping the electrician and thought perhaps he'd like to become an electrician himself. She wrote about all the comings and goings of the inn, filling three pages, before she finally stopped. She knew she wouldn't get anywhere near that much information from Lauren, but she could hope.

Anna gave the dying fire a poke, watching as the red sparks flew up the dark chimney. Clark had felt it was a cool enough evening for a fire. Anna looked around the comfortable living room and smiled. So homey, so inviting. Just being in this room made her smile. She just wished that her daughter would figure out how to make a home for her little family—and how to become comfortable in it.

Anna tried not to nurse too many regrets, but if there was one thing she could go back and change about her life, she would undo her choice of letting Eunice run their lives. It had hurt Lauren far more than Anna had ever realized. Still, there was no point in dwelling on the past. At least Lauren seemed determined to distance herself from her grandmother now.

Summer days were filled with guests, picnics, fishing expeditions, river tours, and beach trips, and before Anna knew it, September was upon them, Marshall had returned to school, and only half the rooms were filled with guests.

"Do we need to be concerned?" she asked Clark one evening in late September. It was only about eight, but thanks to the chilly weather, all the guests had already called it a night.

"Not at all," he assured her. "I keep telling you that, honey."

She snuggled a little closer to him on the sofa. "I know, but after a lifetime of worrying about money, it's hard to believe I don't need to fret about it now."

He gave her a squeeze. "The reason I started doing the books was so you wouldn't worry. But if it would make you feel better, take a look at our finances and you'll see that we are doing just fine."

Anna knew this was partly because Clark had combined his own accounts with hers. At first she objected to this, worried that his money might be unfairly pulled into the inn. But he assured her that they were a team now, what was his was hers, and hers was his. "I'm the one who comes out ahead," he'd teased. "All you get is my money, but I get to participate in this amazing business venture."

"I don't want to look at the books," she told him. "I just want to know that if the inn isn't full of guests this winter, we won't go hungry."

He laughed. "I assure you, we will not go hungry. For one thing, I've seen all the preserves you ladies have been putting up lately. Besides that, if we ever did run out of funds, which I don't think is likely, I could simply go out and contract to build some houses."

"Or you could practice law."

He groaned. "That would require some work on my part. I'd have to study up and take the exams."

"You wouldn't want to do that?"

"Maybe someday." He flexed his arm muscle for her with a grin. "When I need to rely on my brain instead of my brawn."

She laughed.

"How about you? What if you get too old to run this inn? What then?"

She thought hard. "Do you think I'll ever get *that* old?"

"No," he told her. "Never."

"I see how your mother and Babette keep going and it gives me lots of hope. I'm not sure how old Babette is—it's her deep, dark secret—but I know she must be at least eighty, maybe ninety."

"You must be joking."

Anna shook her head. "I remember hearing she was older than my father. I couldn't believe it at the time, but I think it's true."

"She does not look a day over seventy."

"It's all those wonderful beauty products she's always concocting."

"That reminds me." He pointed to the notebook on her desk. "I had Mrs. Fischer write down the lavender products she wanted to buy. We were out of a couple of things."

"I'll let Babette know."

"What will you do if, well, if Babette gets too old to keep providing the inn with her lavender goodies?"

"She's already given me her recipes and this winter she plans to teach me how to make them. You know, some of them she learned from my grandmother."

"There really is a heritage of traditions here, isn't there?"

"I'd like to think so." She closed her eyes and leaned her head back. "You know what I wish more than anything, Clark?"

"What?"

"I wish that Lauren and Sarah would be able to continue these traditions. I wish that they'd come to love the river as much as I do."

He sighed. "That's a big wish. At least where Lauren is concerned. She doesn't seem to have quite the same temperament as her mother. But who knows, maybe it will skip a generation and Sarah will turn out to be just like you."

Anna smiled. "Speaking of them, it's been weeks since I've heard from Lauren. It's not that I'm worried exactly, but I've been thinking I should call her."

"What's stopping you?"

She shrugged.

"Is it too late?"

She looked at the clock to see that it wasn't quite 8:30. "I don't know."

"Surely they'd still be up. They're young."

"Young people with a baby."

"Lauren always liked staying up later than this." He stood, going over to the bookshelf. "Why not give it a try? I have a book I've been itching to start. I don't mind."

Anna stood too. "All right, I will." She went into the bedroom so that Clark could read in the living room without being disturbed, and placed the call.

"Hello?" Lauren's voice sounded on the verge of anger.

"It's me, darling," Anna said. "I hope I'm not calling too late."

"No, it's not too late," Lauren said sharply. "I just thought maybe it was my no-good husband."

Anna braced herself. "Is something wrong?"

"Just Donald. He's acting like a big baby. Honestly, Mom, I'm not kidding when I say it feels like I have two children."

Anna sat down on the chair by the window, looking out over the dusky river. "What's going on?"

Now Lauren began to go on about how Donald came and went as he pleased, how he expected her to cook and clean and pick up his dirty socks. "Just because he goes off to the mill to work. To work? I've been to his office. All he does is sit there all day, talking on the phone or writing stuff down. That's work? I slave away here, washing dishes and floors and doing laundry at the Laundro-mat, because we do not have our own washer and dryer, and taking care of Sarah. And yet, he expects me to treat him like king of the castle when he comes home. Who made those rules, Mom?"

Anna tried not to laugh. "I'm not sure, Lauren, but it does seem to be the way a lot of people think." She was thankful Clark was not like that, not that she planned to mention it to Lauren.

"Well, people should start thinking differently. Really, Mom, I work my fingers to the bone and does Donald appreciate it? No, he just complains that the meat is tough, that there are dirty dishes in the sink, or that Sarah is crying. Well, she's a baby and that's what she does!"

"How is Sarah?" Anna hoped to change to a happier subject.

"She's teething. At least that's what Ardelle says. I'm not so sure. But she is fussy, fussy, fussy. Speaking of Ardelle, she is turning out to be as bad as Grandmother."

"How so?" Anna took in a deep breath, leaning back and trying to relax.

"She is always telling me what to do, how to do it, and that I'm not doing it well enough."

"Oh . . ."

Now Lauren was starting to cry. "Why does everyone think I'm such a failure, Mom? It's like all they can do is find fault. And how do they think that makes me feel?"

"Not very good."

"Yeah. I mean when I was with you, I knew I wasn't doing my best sometimes, but you and the other women didn't make fun of me. You never treated me rudely or called me names."

"Well, I hope not." Anna wondered if that's what Ardelle was doing.

"You guys showed me how to do better."

"And you did do better, Lauren."

"Well, according to Ardelle, I am perfectly hopeless."

"I'm sorry."

Lauren sniffed loudly. "What am I going to do, Mom?"

"I . . . I don't know." Anna tried to think. "Is there one area in particular that you're struggling with?"

"According to Ardelle and Donald, I don't do anything right. Tonight Donald and I got into a big fight because dinner wasn't ready."

"What did you fix?"

"A roast. I didn't get it into the oven until after five. But how was I supposed to know it would take more than *three* hours to cook? I still don't think it's even done yet."

"Well, it will be good leftovers for tomorrow."

"You mean if I don't throw it at Donald as soon as he comes home."

"Remember, Lauren, you're a mommy now. You have to act like one."

"I'm sick of it, Mom. Really, I am. I wonder where you go to quit this job."

"You're having a bad day, Lauren. You should take the roast out of the oven, go and have a nice hot bath and—"

"A bath? This duplex does not even have a real bathtub, Mom. It has a shower. That's it."

"Oh, well . . . just take a nice shower and go to—"

"A shower is not going to fix this, Mom!"

Anna didn't know what to say.

"Really, I want to throw in the towel. I want out of this. I want to be a carefree college coed again. I was robbed of all that and I want it back!" She groaned loudly.

"What about Sarah?"

"What about her?"

"If you could get your life back, as a college coed, what would you do with Sarah?"

"I don't know."

"Don't you love her?"

"Of course I love her. She is the *only* reason I'm doing all this, Mom. If it weren't for Sarah and the fact that she needs a daddy, I would get on a bus going somewhere far, far from here. And sometimes I honestly think she might be better off if we both just left him for good."

"Really?"

"Yes! Donald doesn't give a rip about how I suffer, trying to make this dump into a home. He's mostly gone anyway. What's the point?"

"Then maybe you do need to consider doing it on your own," Anna said calmly. "Do you really think you could be a single mother, Lauren? I did it. Clark's mother did it. But it's not for everyone."

There was a long pause now. "I don't know, Mom . . . I mean, I guess I really do love Donald . . . despite all his faults, and there are plenty of them. I'm probably making this seem worse than it is. But sometimes when I see him coming home in his suit and tie, well, I sort of forget how mad I am at him."

"Then I suppose you're going to just have to try harder, Lauren."

"Maybe so . . . ."

"I wish we lived closer, sweetie. I wish I could come give you a hand."

"Me too." She sniffed loudly.

"Things are slowing down at the inn . . . maybe I could come for a little visit."

"Really?"

"Let me talk to Clark about it."

"Oh, Mom, if you could do that—oh, it would make all the difference in the world. I know it would! This place is tiny, but I could put a cot in Sarah's room. If you wouldn't mind."

"I wouldn't mind at all."

"Oh, please, don't just think about it. Please, do it!"

"I'll let you know. In the meantime, don't forget to take the roast out of the oven."

"Right. I better go get it now. I think I smell smoke."

"I love you, Lauren. Give Sarah a kiss for me." As Anna she hung up the phone, she hoped that the roast wasn't burning. Poor Lauren. Sometimes she was really her own worst enemy.

Anna and Clark discussed a visit, looked at the reservations book, and finally found a patch of three days during the first week of October when no guests were booked. "Why don't you go then?" he suggested. "That's just over a week away."

"You wouldn't mind?"

"Not a bit. Maybe I'll even go with you."

"But there wouldn't be room in their tiny duplex."

"We'll stay in a hotel."

She smiled. "Yes, that would be better."

"And mother can keep an eye on things here."

"I'll call Lauren in the morning and tell her the good news." She hugged him. "I can't wait to see Sarah!"

"And your daughter?"

She chuckled. "Of course I want to see Lauren too. It's just that she's a bit more difficult than the baby."

He nodded. "I must agree with you on that."

Anna knew that no matter how difficult Lauren could be, no matter how selfish or immature, she would always be her daughter and Anna would never give up on her. But for Lauren's own sake, she wished she'd grow up.

19

Lauren sounded very relieved to hear her mother was planning a trip to Pine Ridge. "But can't you come any sooner?" she pleaded.

"I wish I could come today," Anna told her. "But we have a commitment to our guests."

"So you're more committed to your guests than your own daughter?"

"Of course not. But I can't just leave them here on their own."

Naturally Lauren didn't understand this, and Anna realized it was pointless to try to explain it further. "If I could do it differently, I would."

"Okay . . . I guess I can make it through another week," Lauren said unhappily.

"I'm going to bring you all kinds of goodies," Anna promised. "I've got applesauce and green beans and peaches and jams. And Babette's made some dresses for Sarah, as well as some soaps and things for you. It will be like Christmas in October!"

"Okay." Lauren still sounded glum.

"Do your best, sweetie. If you get frustrated, put Sarah in her stroller and go for a walk, enjoy the fall foliage. And before you know it, I'll be there."

Lauren made a few more gloomy comments and Anna told her it was time to start fixing lunch. After she hung up Anna shook her head and wondered if someday Lauren would wake up, come to her senses, and realize all the goodness that was in her life.

For Anna the days passed quickly and soon she and Clark were on their way to Pine Ridge. "Do you remember the last time I drove you over these mountains?" he asked.

She smiled. "Yes, I was so nervous."

"It feels like a long time ago. So much has changed."

She nodded. "Lauren is so frustrated . . . I just hope I can be of help."

"If you can't help her, I don't know who can."

"She said that she feels like she has two children—Sarah and Donald."

He chuckled.

"I remember feeling like that too." She sighed, twisting the handkerchief that was in her lap. "When Adam came home from the war, he was a lot like a child."

"You mean because of his physical injuries?"

"Partly. He needed a lot of help doing things. His mind was like a child in some ways too. Not that his brain was damaged, per se. But his spirit was . . . well, it seemed that it was destroyed."

"War did that to a lot of men."

"And when I think back on it, the way he acted—somewhat selfishly and childishly—it reminds me a little of how Lauren acts sometimes. Not always . . . but sometimes."

"She is Adam's daughter."

"It's strange, isn't it? She never really knew her father. Not really. And yet she may be more like him than she is like me . . . even though she's known me all her life." She shook her head. "But, to be fair, she never really knew the real me. She saw a shadow of me, an intimidated me, the poor little woman me . . . the pitiful creature that Eunice walked all over." She felt a bit teary. "I was such a poor example to Lauren, Clark. Sometimes I feel completely to blame for all her problems."

"I've told you before, you can't blame yourself for the way you raised Lauren, Anna, not any more than you can blame yourself for what happened to Adam." He reached over and patted her hand. "I know you, and I can't believe you weren't doing the best you could under some very hard circumstances."

She nodded. "I know that's true. But it's hard not to feel guilty." She turned and looked at him. "Do you think all mothers feel guilty?"

He made a half-smile. "Except for the ones who make their husbands feel guilty."

She knew that his ex-wife had some games she still played. "Maybe so, but you don't have anything to feel guilty about when it comes to Marshall, Clark. He's a good boy."

He barely nodded. "Thank God."

She held her head higher. "Well, I'm going to think the best for Lauren. I believe she can be a strong person. And I'll do all I can these next few days to encourage her. I plan to help her establish some routines. I suspect that her housekeeping has slipped into some lazy habits. I'm sure that's aggravating to Donald. I don't want to place all the blame on Lauren, but I do think she has the power to set the tone for their home. It can be a happy place that functions somewhat smoothly . . . or it can be a miserable place where chaos reigns. Which would you rather come home to?"

"What do you think?"

"My point exactly. Somehow I want to convey that to her. Do you think it's possible?"

"Someday Lauren is going to figure out how strong you are, Anna, how you've always been strong. And I think she'll want to be like you."

Anna rehearsed some of the things she planned to say to Lauren as they drove. She was making all sorts of plans in her head. How she would take Sarah for a walk in the stroller while Lauren enjoyed some free time. How they would do some meal planning together and how Anna would help her to shop. They would stock her pantry with the kinds of items needed to prepare simple meals. She would organize the baby's room so that Lauren could find what she needed easily. Three days would pass quickly, but Anna would do everything possible to make Lauren's life smoother and easier before she left.

She felt a familiar sense of nervousness as Clark drove the station wagon into town. However, she reminded herself she was no longer that poor Anna Gunderson, Eunice Gunderson's pathetic excuse of a daughter-in-law. She was now Anna Richards, Clark's wife and co-owner of a lovely inn on the Siuslaw River. She held her head a little higher as he turned onto Sixth Street. "There it is," she told him as she peered down the street. "The yellow duplex on the right."

"Looks like someone is moving," he said as he pulled in front of the house where a small paneled truck was backed into the driveway. "You sure this is the right place?"

"Maybe it's the neighbors," she said as she got out. But as she went up to the house, she noticed the two moving men carrying what looked like Sarah's white crib out to the truck. "Lauren?" she called out as she went into a living room that looked like it might've survived a small hurricane. "Hello?"

"Mom?" Lauren appeared with a box in her hands. "What are you doing here?"

"I told you I was coming today." Anna frowned at the disheveled house. "What's going on here?"

"Sarah and I are moving out."

"Where is Sarah?" Anna peered over to where some boxes were stacked.

"Don't worry, Mom. I didn't pack her."

"But where are you moving? And what about Donald? And when did all this happen?"

"Donald doesn't know we're moving."

"Doesn't know?"

Lauren shook her head with a mischievous expression. "When he gets home, we'll be gone."

"But where are you going? And where is Sarah?"

"We're moving to Grandmother's. That's where Sarah is right now."

Anna blinked. "With Eunice?"

"Well, she's with Lou."

"Lou?"

"Lou, the nanny."

Anna frowned. "The nanny?"

"I can't explain it all right now, Mom. I have to get our stuff out of here before Donald comes home and blows his stack." Lauren waved to the moving men, pointing to a room. "Get the bedroom things out of that room too. Everything except for the pile of stuff in the closet. Then I think we're done."

Anna stepped out of their way. "Are you sure this is the best thing to do?" she asked Lauren.

"I'm sick of Donald's games," Lauren said.

"You don't love him anymore?"

She shrugged as she picked up a box of baby things. "I don't know. But I figure this will get his attention—once and for all."

"And what do you think he'll do?"

"Here." She handed the box to Anna. "Put this by the door."

Anna carried the box to the front door where Clark was standing with a quizzical expression. "What's going on?"

Anna quickly explained, as best she could, then handed him the box. "I think this goes in the moving van." She went back to Lauren. "I'm just confused," she began. "What gave you the idea to do this? You knew I was coming, right? I was going to help you. I wanted to help get this place—"

"Grandmother brought me to my senses," Lauren said as she put jars of baby food in a box. "She came over here and told me that I was living like poor white trash." Lauren looked directly at Anna. "And I had to admit, she was right."

"But you—"

"And Grandmother told me that if I would come home and start living like a respectable young woman, she would treat me like one." Lauren handed the box to Anna. "And that sounded good to me."

"So you are giving up on your marriage?"

Lauren shrugged. "Maybe for a while."

"For a while might turn into forever, Lauren."

"Not according to Grandmother."

Anna frowned. "How so?"

"Donald works for Grandmother. She plans to bring him to his senses too."

"Oh . . ."

"And she's hired this lovely woman named Lou to be Sarah's nanny. That's where Sarah is right now. This woman has taken care of all kinds of kids and she even wears a white apron. Then there's Mabel to keep house and do the cooking. And Grandmother said she'll let me join the country club now. And I'll be in her bridge club, and I can have my friends over for parties and things." She sighed happily. "Oh, Mom, it all sounds like heaven to me."

Anna didn't know how to respond. She simply carried the box of baby food out, handing it again to Clark. "I'm afraid we came too late."

He gave her a sympathetic look.

"Lauren's made up her mind. She's going to live with Eunice. Sarah is there now. With her nanny." Anna swallowed against the lump in her throat.

"Well, we better go over there and see her."

"To Eunice's?"

"She is your granddaughter, Anna." He looked over to where Lauren was coming to the door with a box in her hands. "You don't mind if your mother goes over to see Sarah, do you?"

"No, of course, not." Lauren handed him the box. "Want to put this in the van for me? I'm about ready to go to home myself. I'll meet you."

Anna just nodded. "See you there."

Clark put his arm around Anna as they walked to the car. "You are going to be all right, sweetheart," he whispered in her ear. "Be strong."

She simply nodded as he opened her car door, helping her in. Then as she sat down, she felt a few tears sneaking down her cheeks, and she dug out her handkerchief, quickly catching them as Clark slid into the driver's seat. "I feel like Eunice just won, Clark."

"Was it really a war?"

"No, of course, not. But there has always been a battle going on—between Eunice and me—fighting over Lauren. Now it seems that Eunice, with her power and her money and her willingness to allow Lauren to be less than her best, has finally won."

"Maybe she's won this battle, Anna. But I don't believe she's won the whole war. Lauren has you as an example. Eventually she's going to figure things out. But maybe it's going to take some time."

Anna considered this. "Maybe you're right. But it feels painful just the same. I had hoped for so much more for Lauren."

"You know what your grandmother would say, Anna."

She took in a long deep breath and slowly let it out. "That Lauren must paddle her own canoe."

"And right now, Lauren is just taking the easy route, going downstream with the flow of the water."

"That's true enough. But the easy route can easily wind up in rapids or a waterfall."

He nodded. "And maybe that will be her wake-up call. In the meantime, it doesn't seem there's much you can do." He was pulling up to the big house now, sending an old feeling of unhappiness rushing through Anna.

"Poor Sarah," she whispered.

"She's only a baby right now," he reminded her. "Things can change."

"That's true." She looked at the upper windows, fixing her eyes on the south facing window that had been Sarah's nursery. "And she will have a nanny," she told him as he helped her out of the car. "It's a comfort to know she will be properly cared for and supervised." She didn't want to point out how haphazard Lauren's care could sometimes be. "So at least she'll be safe and healthy . . . right?"

"Right." He reached for her hand. "And you get to see her now, Anna. You should be happy about that."

She smiled at him as they went up to the front door. "Yes. I am happy about that—that and so many, many things."

"For instance, we now have an unexpected three-day vacation to spend together." His blue eyes twinkled merrily.

"That's right," she said. "We do."

"And I plan to see that we both enjoy it thoroughly."

She chuckled. "I will be reminding myself of this pleasant possibility while I do my best to act civilly to Sarah's great-grandmother."

However, it wasn't easy to bite her tongue and mind her manners as Eunice administered her usual jabs. Obviously gloating over her success at enticing Lauren back into her lair, Eunice was in top form at making Anna feel small. She even tried to prevent her from seeing Sarah.

"I'm sure the nanny has just put her down for a nap," Eunice said sternly.

"Then what is that I hear?" Anna tilted her head toward the staircase.

"Sounds like she's awake to me." Clark made a forced smile. "Why don't you run on up and check, Anna."

"We are trying to get the baby on a schedule," Eunice called out as Anna headed up the stairs. "Please, respect this!"

Anna didn't answer as she hurried toward the sound of Sarah's crying, which seemed to be coming from one of the guest rooms.

"Excuse me," she said to the stout middle-aged woman standing by the window. "Is my granddaughter in here?"

The woman looked surprised, but simply pointed over to where a makeshift nursery had been set up. Sarah was lying in the center of the big bed, kicking her legs and crying. "Oh, sweet girl." Anna picked up the baby and instantly began rocking her, attempting to soothe her.

"I was trying to get her to sleep," the woman explained. "Her bed hasn't arrived yet and I don't think she's used to this room."

"Yes, you're probably right," Anna said gently to her. "And I'm sorry to interrupt, but I haven't seen Sarah for months and I'm not in town for long. I hope you don't mind if I rock her a bit."

The woman just shrugged. "Mrs. Gunderson suggested that I shouldn't coddle her too much. She doesn't want her to get spoiled."

Anna didn't miss the irony of that as she sat down in the rocker, still talking softly to Sarah, trying to get her to settle down. "I don't think it's possible to spoil a baby," she said quietly. "They are babies for such a short time."

"I always felt a happy baby was a healthy baby." The nanny came closer now, looking over Anna's shoulder as Sarah began settling down.

"I agree with you completely." Anna smiled at her. "It's been a long time since Eunice has mothered a baby. And I recall that when Lauren was an infant, Eunice didn't have much patience . . . especially when Lauren would cry. So perhaps you'd be wise to keep Sarah contented. That way both the baby and the great-grandmother will be happy."

The nanny nodded. "I think you're right."

"It sounds like the movers are coming." Anna tipped her head toward the still open door. "Maybe you'd like to supervise the setting up of the nursery. I can sit with Sarah."

"Thank you, I'll do that."

Anna let out a relieved sigh as the nanny left. "Oh, little Sarah," she said quietly. "Your life is changing again. But you will be resilient, little one. You will be strong like the fir trees that bend with the wind. And when you get a little older, you will come and visit me on the river again." Anna continued talking softly to her, watching as the baby's dark eyes studied her with an intelligent expression, and until the long eyelashes finally fluttered against her still-flushed cheeks. Even though she was breathing evenly and fast asleep, Anna continued to rock her, enjoying the warmth of the small body in her arms.

It was hard to put Sarah down on the bed. But as Anna gently arranged the pillows around like a makeshift crib in case

Sarah decided to roll, she knew that Clark had already been more than patient, and who knew what Eunice was putting him through? She leaned over and kissed the warm cheek. "Be blessed, little Siuslaw princess." She tiptoed from the room and quietly closed the door. Peeking in the nursery, she noticed that the blue paint had been changed to pink, and the movers, with the nanny directing, were getting the furnishings in place.

"There you are." Lauren had an armload of clothes, using her foot to push open the door to her room. "Grandmother was just asking if you were ever coming back down."

"Sarah's asleep now," Anna told her.

"I'm trying to get moved in," Lauren explained.

Anna just nodded as she followed her into the room. "I think that Clark and I will be on our way soon."

"Sorry about the misunderstanding." Lauren tossed the heap of clothes toward the closet.

"I just hope that you won't be sorry about leaving Donald like this."

Lauren laughed. "Are you kidding? Already, I almost feel like I'm on vacation. And my girlfriends are coming by this evening. Honestly, Mom, this is going to be like heaven."

Anna went over and hugged her daughter. "Maybe you'll have more time to stay in touch now."

Lauren made a sheepish smile. "Yeah, I'll bet I will."

"Take care, sweetie." Anna turned and left the room. Following the sound of voices, she found Clark and Eunice in the kitchen.

"What on earth is *this*?" Eunice demanded as Clark set the heavy wooden crate on the kitchen table.

"Those are some preserves I put up for Lauren," Anna explained as she joined them. "I thought Sarah might be ready for apple sauce and—"

"Heaven forbid!" Eunice picked up a shiny jar of recently canned green beans and scowled. "Don't you know that these home-canned foods contain botulism? Are you trying to kill us?"

With a stern expression Clark removed the jar from Eunice's hand. "Perhaps it would be better if we took these back to the inn with us. We enjoy them immensely there, as do our guests. No one has expired yet."

Anna shot him a grateful look. "Thank you for your hospitality to Lauren and my granddaughter," she told Eunice. "It looks as if your nanny knows what she's doing. I'm sure Sarah is in good hands. Now if you will excuse us."

Eunice looked surprised, but merely nodded as Clark and Anna made a quick exit. Anna felt certain that Lauren would be sorry about this decision . . . eventually. But, for the time being, there seemed little to be done about it.

20

Anna felt relieved to leave Pine Ridge behind them. She was disappointed that things hadn't turned out as she'd hoped, and she was concerned about the state of her daughter's marriage. Still, she knew those things were out of her control.

"The nanny did seem nice," she told Clark as he turned onto the highway.

"Well, that's something to be thankful for."

"And, really, all things considered, this move might be in Sarah's best interest."

He simply nodded.

"I'm sorry," she told him. "I don't mean to go on about it."

"That's okay," he said. "Maybe you need to reassure yourself."

"No." She shook her head. "I need to let it go."

"Then I'll change the subject." Now he told her about how he'd hoped to take her to see Crater Lake. "I know it's not far from here."

"What a lovely idea!"

"Yes, except that when I asked the moving guys for directions, they told me that the park was closed for the season."

"Oh, that's too bad."

"We'll have to go some other time. Then I remembered another national park in Oregon. And *that* is where we are going." He grinned. "Ever been to Oregon Caves?"

She blinked. "You're taking me to a cave?"

"So it seems. Are you amenable to that?" He chuckled.

"You can take me wherever you like, darling. Whether you take me to a cave or a tipi or a hole in the ground, I trust you implicitly."

"I would've loved to have gone to Crater Lake," he told her. "I saw it once as a boy and it's truly amazing."

"I've always wanted to see it too."

"You mean you've never been?"

"I know, it seems sad, especially considering that Pine Ridge isn't that far from it. But, well, you know how my adult life went."

"Did your parents ever take you on vacation as a child?"

"The store kept them from traveling much. I suppose it sort of anchored us to the river."

"Well, living on the river feels a lot like a vacation in itself."

"It's funny, we've only been gone for a day, and I already miss it."

"We can go back if you like." He looked slightly disappointed.

"Not on your life, Clark. I want to see your cave."

He threw his head back and laughed. "Okay then, I'll take you to my cave."

"You know, I remember a time when my father wanted to take a vacation one summer," she said now. "He wanted to take us down to see the redwood trees in California. And Babette had even offered to watch the store."

"Oh, yes, the redwood forest is certainly worth seeing."

"But Mother wouldn't hear of it. She said it was the busy season."

"Your mother sounds like she was a strong woman."

"I suppose she was strong in some ways . . . but in some ways I think she was weakened by fear. She was always worried about so many things."

"Like what?"

"Oh, money was always a big one. But, to be fair, it was the Depression. I suppose everyone had money worries. But she also worried that I was going to get hurt or drown in the river."

"Like your older brother?"

She nodded. "Yes, I suppose that was a valid concern. Mother fretted about a lot of things, sometimes insignificant things that seemed silly to me. But you know what I think was her underlying biggest concern?"

"What?"

"Knowing she was an Indian. She never really said it, but I'm sure that bothered her more than anything. In fact, it might've been the root of all her worries."

"That seems odd, considering how her mother seemed to return to her roots."

"They really were opposites. As different as night and day in some ways."

"Kind of like you and Lauren?"

"I suppose. And yet Lauren is nothing like my mother." Now she told him about what a hard worker her mother was.

"Kind of like you?"

She laughed. "No, I would look lazy next to my mother. She never stopped moving. Unless she was asleep. She was either cooking or cleaning or knitting or sewing or mending or . . ." She sighed. "Just thinking about it makes me tired. It was as if she didn't know how to just *be*. I don't believe I ever saw her

193

just sitting and doing nothing. She thought that when I took my canoe out it was idleness. I tried to get her to try it and we actually got into a fight." She shook her head. "But I was a teenager and we fought about a lot of things."

"I cannot imagine you fighting with anyone, sweetheart."

"Oh, you should've known me then. I could be rather feisty. I suppose living under Eunice's roof took a lot of that out of me."

"Well, I'll bet you'd get feisty if you thought someone was going to hurt Lauren or Sarah."

She nodded. "You bet I would. In fact, I suppose I have. But, for the most part, I prefer peace."

"I'm glad you do."

"You know that's what seemed missing from my mother, Clark. It's as if she never could find peace. At least not when I was around. Now that I think about it, there came a point in her letters when she started to sound more peaceful. Maybe she found it and I just never knew." She rolled the window down a bit. "I still miss her at times. It's wonderful being in her home, though. It makes me feel as if both she and my grandmother are near me. But I do wish I'd gone back to visit her more often while Lauren was growing up. That was a big mistake. In fact, if I'd gone home more, maybe things would've turned out differently for Lauren."

"But you had Adam to care for," he reminded her. "That must've made it difficult to do much of anything."

"It was a lot like living in prison. A prison with no bars, but a prison just the same. Poor Adam, it wasn't his fault." She turned and looked at Clark. She knew he had war stories of his own. She'd heard many of them. "I suppose that's just one more reason I hate war so much . . . because I believe that peacemaking is so vitally important. Both for a country and for individuals."

"Blessed are the peacemakers. They shall be called children of God."

"That's from the Bible, isn't it?"

"It is."

"Peacemakers shall be called children of God . . ." She considered those words. "You know, my people, the Siuslaw people . . . they were considered a very peaceful tribe. Do you think they would be called children of God?"

"I think so."

She nodded. "I like that." Out the window, the trees were a lovely blur of gold tones and russets and greens and reds. A perfect afternoon for a long drive. Despite the regretful earlier portion of her day, Anna had high hopes that spending the rest of it with Clark, even if they did end up in a dank, dark cave, sounded promising.

The sky was just growing violet and dusky by the time Clark pulled into the Oregon Caves National Park. "What a beautiful building," she said as he parked in front of a tall building. "Is this our final destination?"

"This is the château," he said as he opened her door and helped her out.

"We're not staying in a cave?"

He laughed. "Not tonight, darling."

The lobby of the château was an absolute delight. "Oh, Clark," she exclaimed, "this is charming!" With its rustic logs, handhewn staircase, and quaint furnishing, it reminded her of what she was trying to accomplish at Shining Waters, although the château was much grander. "I love it," she told him as he led her to a seating area.

"You wait here while I see if I can get us a room. I didn't have a chance to make a reservation."

She nodded eagerly as she sank into a comfy leather sofa by the stone fireplace. Tempted to cross her fingers, in the hopes they'd get a room, she smiled at an older woman seated across from her.

"Just arriving?" the woman asked.

"Yes. It's my first time here."

"So, tell me, what do you think of the place?" The woman studied Anna closely.

"I think it's perfectly wonderful," Anna told her. "Just marvelous."

The woman smiled. "Well, that is good to hear. So many of the younger generation don't appreciate this place. They think it's too old-fashioned and out of style."

"I disagree." Anna looked up at the open-beamed ceilings. "I love this sort of style. I just hope that we can get a room. We didn't make a reservation."

"Oh, you'll be fine," the woman assured her. "They're not that busy."

Feeling more comfortable, Anna told the woman a bit about her own inn. "It's not nearly as big and wonderful as this place, of course, but it is rustic." She smiled nervously. She didn't usually open up to people like this.

"Where is your inn located?"

Anna explained.

"Do you have a business card or brochure?"

"No, we're still so new. I haven't had a chance. This was our first season really."

"And did you have many guests?"

"Considering how new we are, I think we did all right." Now she explained about the magazine article her mother-in-law wrote.

"Oh, I believe I saw that story." The woman reached for her handbag and, opening it, removed a card and handed it to Anna. "I'm Margaret O'Neil. I'm working on a book about lodges of the west. Perhaps I should pay yours a visit."

"Really?" Anna blinked then, remembering her manners, introduced herself. "I would love you to visit us, but we're such a small inn. I'd feel bad if you were disappointed." She explained about the cabins and their capacity.

"This château only has twenty-three rooms."

"Is that all? It looks much larger."

Now Clark came over to join them and Anna introduced him to Margaret, explaining about her book and her thoughts about coming to their inn.

"We would love to have you come stay with us," he told her. "I'm sure you'd find Shining Waters to be a very appealing place. My wife has a real knack for hospitality."

Anna blushed. "I just want guests to feel at home."

"The sign of a good innkeeper." Now she took out a note-book and asked for the name and phone number.

Anna told her, waiting as she wrote it down.

"Shining Waters?" Margaret put her notebook and pen back in her purse. "What does that mean?"

Now Anna explained her Siuslaw roots and how her grand-mother used to call it that. "The river can sparkle like diamonds at certain times of the day," she explained, "when the tide is coming in and the current of the river meets it, especially in the afternoon. Shining Waters just seemed the right name."

"It's a lovely name and delightful story." Margaret stood now. "Well, I don't want to keep you kids." She paused to shake their hands. "I do hope you enjoy your visit here."

"And if you find time to make it out our way, I would love for you to stay with us," Anna said. "As our guest, of course."

Anna turned to Clark as Margaret walked away. "Can you believe that? I just happen to sit next to a woman who's writing a book about lodges of the west. What a coincidence."

He grinned. "Maybe it's not a coincidence, dear."

She smiled back. "Maybe it's not."

"I happen to think God has his hand on us. I think he directs our paths far more than we realize. When I think back to some of the messes I've made in my life—a broken marriage, a son who was rebelling—I wouldn't have believed it could turn out like this for us. I give God the credit."

She nodded. "And although this day looked like it was going to be a disaster a few hours ago, I love the way it's turning out. Thank you."

He handed her a key. "You go on up to our room and I'll fetch our bags. Then, I don't know about you, but I'm starving. They'll still be serving dinner for about an hour."

Anna's feet felt light as she went up the stairs. This was all so unexpected—and so fun—it reminded her of being a child at Christmas. Really, all things considered, today had turned out to be a perfect day!

21

Anna experienced mixed feelings when she first learned that Donald and Lauren had gotten back together. For one thing, it seemed to have happened far too quickly. Lauren had only been with Eunice for a week before Donald was somehow enticed, more likely pressured, to move back in with them. Now, according to Lauren, Eunice had just hired an architect to design a smaller, more modern house. "It'll be built out back," Lauren explained over the telephone. "Somewhere out past the swimming pool."

"There's plenty of room on the estate for it," Anna said. She remembered how often she'd dreamed of Eunice doing something like that for her and Lauren . . . long ago.

"So Grandmother will live in the new house," Lauren continued. "And she has promised that as long as Donald and I remain married, we can have the run of this house." She laughed. "At least Grandmother didn't stipulate 'happily married.'"

"Are you happy?"

"Oh, *Mom*." Lauren sounded exactly the same as when she was fourteen.

Anna looked out the rain-speckled window toward the gunmetal gray river. It was mid-November and stormy out. As a result, the inn had only three guests this week. "So, tell me, how is little Sarah Pearl?"

"She's fine."

"Is she crawling yet?"

"I don't think so."

"You don't think so?"

"Well, it's not like I spend every breathing moment with her, Mom. She does have her nanny, you know."

"Yes . . . I know."

"Anyway, Grandmother says her house should be ready by the end of next summer. Can you imagine, Mom? Donald and me with this whole big house all to ourselves?"

"You mean Donald and you and Sarah."

"Well, yes, of course."

"And the housekeeper and the nanny? I imagine they will continue with you as well?"

"They better. Otherwise Grandmother will be living here all by her little lonesome."

Anna considered questioning this but thought better of it. Instead she asked about the upcoming holidays. "Clark and I would love it if you could come visit us," she told her. "Either for Thanksgiving or Christmas. I would love to see you . . . and Sarah."

"I'd love to see you, too, Mom."

"Really? You think you might come?"

"I'll ask Donald about it."

"We'll close the inn," Anna promised. "Not that we'd be too busy anyway. But if you kids could come, we'd make it all about you and the baby. It could be such fun."

"Yeah. And it would give us a break from Grandmother." Lauren made a dramatic groan. "Honestly, it won't be one day too soon when she gets moved into the mother-in-law house."

"Mother-in-law house?"

"Yeah, Mom, that's what they call it."

Anna considered pointing out that Eunice was not Lauren's mother-in-law and that she would still own all the property.

"Speaking of Grandmother, it's almost time for our bridge club. Honestly, when Grandmother first told me about that I was over the moon. I mean who wouldn't rather play cards and eat goodies than change diapers and sterilize baby bottles? But these old ladies are starting to wear thin on me. One of these days, maybe after Grandmother gets all settled in her new house, I will have to send the old bags packing." She laughed. "But for now I need to go and make sure that Mabel has the sandwiches fixed properly. Last time she actually left the crusts on. Can you imagine?" She sighed loudly.

"Then I won't keep you, dear. Do give Sarah my love. And don't forget to talk to Donald about the holidays. We'd really love to have you."

Lauren promised, but as Anna hung up, she wondered how likely it was that they'd actually come. Except that Lauren had mentioned that it would be an escape from Eunice. That alone might motivate them to come. Anna could only hope.

Just days before Thanksgiving, and after Anna had already ordered their food, Lauren called to say that Donald couldn't get the time off to come. Then Christmas came . . . and the only thing Anna got from Lauren was more excuses. Fortunately Clark and she had already invited Marshall and Hazel and Babette and several others from the river. And, really, they had a lovely time. Even though Anna did miss Sarah and wished that Lauren might've thought to send a photo of her granddaughter. Anna had sent a large box of gifts for Lauren and Donald—mostly for Sarah. Certainly, they were homemade gifts, but they'd been sewn and carved and baked with love. Anna hadn't really expected Lauren to write a thank-you note, but a phone call might've been nice.

So it went for the next several months, but as summer drew near, Anna decided to try again. This time she invited Lauren to bring Sarah out for her first birthday. "We'll have a big party for her," she said with enthusiasm, going into all the details of a June celebration. Again, Lauren promised to think about it, but June rolled around and when Anna called Lauren to find out if they were coming, once again she was disappointed.

"Grandmother has already gone to so much trouble," Lauren explained. "She's sent out invitations and hired a clown and a pony." She made an exasperated sigh. "As if Sarah will even know what to do with a clown or a pony. But you know Grandmother, she gets her mind set and there's no turning her back."

"Sarah seems rather young for a pony."

"It's only here for the day, Mom."

"And how are the plans for the mother-in-law house coming?"

"They seem to be stuck. I'm not sure what it is this time. But nothing is happening. I told Grandmother she should hire Clark to come out here and build it. I saw how fast he got those cabins up."

"Well, those were just rustic little cabins, Lauren."

"Yes, that's what Grandmother said too."

"Besides, Clark is busy helping with the inn. He couldn't possibly spend that much time in Pine Ridge." Anna wanted to add that it would only be over her dead body, but controlled herself. "I'm sorry we'll miss Sarah's birthday, Lauren. But perhaps you and she would still come for a visit. Anytime this summer. You know we'd love to have you."

"I'll think about it."

"Yes, I'm sure you will." Anna felt like this conversation was turning into a broken record. Yet, because of her love for Sarah and her daughter, she refused to give up.

During the first four years of Sarah's life, Anna could count the amount of times she actually saw her granddaughter on one hand. And each time had only occurred because of Anna's willingness to make it happen and trekking to Pine Ridge. Besides the few weeks when Sarah was a newborn, Lauren had never kept her promise to return to the river for a visit. Not once. Oh, she always had excuses. Some, like when Sarah got the measles at Easter, were believable. Others were simply excuses.

It wasn't until Sarah's fifth birthday was approaching that Anna thought that perhaps this would be the year. Lauren called one evening in early June, bitterly complaining that her entire life had been turned completely upsidedown.

"What's going on?" Anna asked as she sat down on the sofa. Fortunately, it was nearly nine and the guests had all turned in.

"The building project has turned into a nightmare."

"You mean the mother-in-law house?" Anna knew that Eunice had managed to postpone the building of the additional house for years. Not that this surprised her much. But last winter, according to Lauren, Eunice agreed to start the process after Donald threatened to quit the mill, leave town, and possibly take Lauren and Sarah with him. Apparently that had gotten her attention.

"Yes. Grandmother and I were having such fun picking out new things for her little house that I got to thinking it would be a kick to spruce up this place too. You know how rundown things are around here. And there are such lovely new kinds of carpets and floorings and modern light fixtures and just all sorts of things these days—so many fun colors to choose from.

Even for appliances. I've decided to have the whole kitchen redone in avocado. Have you see avocado yet, Mom?"

"Well, I've eaten an avocado." Anna wasn't quite sure what Lauren meant. Was she planning on using avocados to decorate her kitchen?

Lauren laughed. "It's a color, Mom. Keep up with the times. Anyway it's just yummy and all the appliances and the floor and even the countertops will be avocado."

Anna imagined a sea of dark green. "Goodness, that's a lot of avocado."

"Grandmother is doing her little kitchen in harvest gold. I told her it wasn't fair that I was getting stuck with the old-fashioned junk when she was getting everything all brand new. So, of course, I was able to talk her into it. But, oh my, what a headache!"

"Why is it a headache?"

"Because we thought it would be smart to have the workers do both her house and my house at the same time. Now everything is all torn up in here, plus Grandmother's house isn't nearly finished and everything is a perfect mess. And on top of all that, I was forced to let Sarah's nanny go. I am beside myself!"

"Why did you let the nanny go?"

"Grandmother said that if I got new carpet and appliances and everything, I'd have to give up the nanny. You know, because of money. At the time, it sounded like a good deal to me. I mean Sarah is almost five. How much trouble can a five-year-old be?" She groaned. "I had no idea."

"So why don't you bring Sarah out here to visit me?" Anna suggested. "You can escape the chaos at your house. If you stay long enough, we could celebrate her fifth birthday. It would be loads of fun. And, compared to how you're living, it might feel like a real vacation."

"I *need* a vacation."

"Then come, Lauren. We had a gorgeous day here today. Sarah would have such fun. There are some other children here to play with. Clark put up a nice play area with swings and slides and things." As usual, she listed all the other fun things they could do. "And I'll bet Sarah has never even seen the beach yet."

"That's true."

"*Then come!*" Anna insisted.

"Okay." Lauren said this with the kind of conviction that made Anna believe she might actually do it. "I'd love to escape this mess, Mom. We'll come. Is tomorrow too soon?"

Anna was not terribly surprised when Lauren didn't come as soon as the next day, but she was pleased when Lauren called to say they would arrive in Florence on Tuesday afternoon. Thanks to publicity from Hazel's travel magazine articles and Margaret's book about western lodges, the Shining Waters Inn had gotten so busy that Anna had taken to hiring her old friend Dorothy's teenaged daughters, Jill and Joanna, during the busy season. The first summer the girls had only been fourteen and sixteen and somewhat insecure. This year they were eighteen and twenty and practically ran the housekeeping part of the business all by themselves. Dorothy always seemed glad to get rid of her girls during the summers, plus they were earning college money, and Anna didn't know what she'd do without their help. It was the perfect setup for everyone. Besides, it meant that Dorothy came to visit Anna more often since Dorothy really didn't last too long without her girls.

"I'm going to pick up my daughter and granddaughter," Anna told Joanna as they were cleaning up after fixing lunch.

"I'll bring back the grocery order as well. Is there anything else you need?"

"I don't think so." Joanna checked the menu roster. "Well, unless you want to get some crabs for tomorrow night. Henry forgot to bring those out yesterday."

Anna wrote it down. "I'll pick up a few more things I think kids might like to eat too," she told Joanna. "You know, it's been almost a year since I've seen Sarah. I can hardly wait."

"It's about time they made it out here." Joanna set a large mixing bowl on the counter. "I'm looking forward to meeting them both."

As she scrubbed the kitchen table, Anna still found it hard to believe that Lauren hadn't been out here since Sarah was an infant. This visit was well overdue.

"Feel free to take off whenever you like," Joanna said cheerfully. "I've got it under control here."

Anna set the dishcloth by the sink. "I know you do. And I greatly appreciate it."

As Anna went to the dock and untied her boat, a new model that Clark had surprised her with last spring, she marveled at how the inn continued to grow and improve . . . and yet the important things remained the same. More than anything, Anna strived to keep the feeling of peace and tranquility in this place.

She had been relieved that this new boat actually had a relatively quiet motor. It wasn't that she discouraged noise in general. Certainly the laughter of children's voices, people singing around a campfire, or the playful splashing sounds of kids playing in the river . . . all that was more than welcome here. But she put her foot down to the intrusion of things like blaring radios, record players, televisions, or overly loud motorboats.

Although they did have half a dozen smaller boats with outboard motors, they were mostly used for fishing and river exploration. They also had a number of canoes and rowboats. But early on she decided to discourage water skiing. Not only did that come with noise, but it was also rather dangerous since logs were known to escape from the floating barges and lurk beneath the surface of the water, catching boaters unaware.

As a result of her commitment to peace and quiet, she managed to attract the kinds of guests who were looking for a calmer sort of river experience. More and more it seemed that guests came here in search of a healing sort of retreat, an escape from the hustle and bustle of "modern civilization."

As she guided her boat downriver, Anna felt almost perfectly happy. The only shadow over her day was the realization that there was a chance, a small chance, that Lauren might not have made it to town as planned. It was entirely possible that Eunice might've thrown a wrench into the works, or Donald might've put his foot down, or Lauren might've gotten halfway to Florence and suddenly changed her mind. It wouldn't even be all that surprising. But as Anna looked out over the sparkling surface of the blue water, and as she watched a white egret soaring gracefully over the green marsh grass, she realized this disappointment wouldn't completely devastate her. At the end of the day, she had Clark and all her other loved ones to go home to. She had the inn. She had the river. She had her health and she had peace. That was far more than she'd ever dreamed of having a few years ago. Truly, she should be perfectly happy . . . and she very nearly was.

In the grocery store she picked up her order as well as a few more things. She wasn't really sure what kinds of things Sarah liked to eat, but she remembered what a fussy eater Lauren had been at four . . . of course, she had other things to fuss over now. She was just leading the box-boy outside when she saw a brassy-looking blond woman in big black sun-glasses waving vigorously at her. Wearing a tight, bright-pink top that revealed her midriff and equally tight white pants that were cut like clam diggers, she walked toward Anna in a pair of high-heeled sandals. Then Anna saw the little dark-haired girl alongside this flashy-looking woman and realized it was Lauren and Sarah.

"Hello," Anna called out. She paused to give the box-boy a tip, asking him to take the groceries on down to her boat, then hurried on over to exchange hugs with Lauren and with a somewhat reluctant Sarah.

"Maybe you don't remember me." Worried that it had been too long, Anna squatted to get down to Sarah's level, look-ing directly into her serious dark eyes. "But I'm your other grandma. The one who lives on the river."

"You live on the river?" Sarah frowned then tugged at her lower lip. "Like a duck?"

"You're right. I don't actually live on the water part of the river," Anna explained. "I live next to the river."

Sarah pressed her lips together and nodded.

Anna tussled Sarah's short-cropped hair. "Last time I saw you, you had long hair." She looked up at Lauren.

"I don't know how on earth Nanny Lou ever got a comb to go through that rat's nest," Lauren said. "I took Sarah to my beautician yesterday morning. The cut is called a pixie. Isn't it cute?"

Anna smiled at Sarah. "You look very pretty, Sarah. Do you like your new haircut?"

Sarah shook her head no.

"Don't worry, it will grow back," Anna assured her. "Now, have you ever been in a boat before, Sarah?"

"A *real* boat?"

"Yes. It's not a big boat, but it's real. And it really does live on the water. Would you like to have a boat ride?"

With wide eyes, Sarah looked unsure.

"Well, boats are really fun, and it's how we get to my house on the river. I think you're going to love it. But you'll have to wear a life jacket."

"What's a life jacket?"

"It's a vest that kids have to wear when they're in boats. In case they accidentally fall into the water. It makes them float."

"If it's a vest, why's it called a jacket?"

Anna laughed and reached for Sarah's hand. "You are a very smart little girl."

"We have some bags in the car," Lauren said as they walked through the parking lot. "I tried to pack light, but I wasn't sure how long we'd be here."

Anna looked up to see the box-boy just coming back from the dock now. She waved him over to them. "Could you give us a hand?" she asked.

"You bet, Mrs. Richards." He grinned. "By the way, I like your new boat. Bet she goes fast."

Anna laughed. "Well, I wouldn't really know about that. But she is a nice boat."

Soon they were loaded into the boat, and Anna was helping Sarah into her life "vest" and explaining what the safety rules were. Meanwhile, Lauren seated herself in the back and lit up a cigarette. Anna knew that Lauren had taken up smoking and she wasn't completely opposed to the habit, but she didn't like the way that Lauren seemed more interested in puffing on her cigarette than anything else.

"Want to help me drive?" Anna asked Sarah.

Sarah's eyes lit up. "Can I?"

"Sure." Anna led her to the front, explained how she turned the boat on and how the engine was in back, and how the controls worked. Then, once they were out in the middle of the river, she let Sarah stand on the seat and steer the boat. "We always have to keep a lookout for stray logs," she said as Sarah's little hands clutched the wheel.

"What's stray logs?" Sarah's eyes were fixed directly in front of her, as if she believed the fate of the passengers and boat were truly in her hands.

Anna explained about the logs, occasionally helping Sarah to turn to the right or the left. "Do you like driving the boat?"

Sarah nodded.

"You're doing a good job." She glanced back at Lauren. "Did you know that Sarah's the captain now?"

Lauren blew a puff of smoke, which floated over the top of her head, then made what seemed a tolerant smile as she gazed out over the water. Something about Lauren, besides her exterior, seemed altered. Anna couldn't put her finger on what it was exactly, but there was a new hardness about her daughter, as if Lauren had slipped herself into a thick protective shell. The question was why?

22

Sarah continued to warm up to Anna in the following days. Lauren, on the other hand, seemed to grow more and more chilly and detached. The outfits she wore, in Anna's opinion, made her seem that she was on some sort of manhunt. Every item of Lauren's clothing looked either too tight, too skimpy, too flashy, or all three. This, combined with her platinum blond hair, coppery tan, which must've come from hours spent lying beside Eunice's pool, and pale pink lipstick hardly gave the impression of someone who was a wife and mother. Still, it wasn't Lauren's appearance that concerned Anna most.

The most disturbing thing about Lauren was the way she interacted—or rather, didn't—with her daughter. Sarah didn't really seem to notice how her mother ignored her questions, talked over her, or even belittled her. But Anna found it hard to notice anything else.

"Do you miss your nanny?" Anna asked Sarah one morning as they went on a nature walk together.

"Uh-huh." Sarah squatted down to pick a buttercup.

"Do you miss Great-grandmother too?" Anna asked cautiously.

"Uh-huh." Sarah picked another buttercup.

To Anna's surprise, she felt relieved to hear this. It seemed a good sign that Sarah missed Eunice. "What kinds of things do you do with Great-grandmother?"

"We go to the library."

"Really?" Anna tried not to sound shocked.

"She takes me to story hour."

"Well, that's very nice of her. Do you like to read books?"

"I know my letters and numbers, but I can't read yet."

"Because you're still just four years old."

"I'm almost five."

"Yes. So do you like it when someone reads you picture books?"

"Yeah." She nodded eagerly.

"Does your mother read books to you too?"

"Mama doesn't like my books. She reads her own books."

"How about Great-grandmother, does she like to read your books?"

"Sometimes. If she's not too busy."

"How about your daddy?" Again, Anna felt cautious. Based on what Lauren had said, which wasn't much, Donald was not much of a father. Still, she was curious. Just what was Sarah's home life really like?

"Daddy likes my books . . . sometimes. If he's not busy. He likes Dr. Seuss books the best."

"That's nice. What else does your daddy like to do with you?"

"We play in the swimming pool sometimes."

"Can you swim?"

"Uh-huh." She knelt down to look at a caterpillar now.

Anna knelt, too, telling Sarah a little about the caterpillar before it crawled away. They stood, continuing to walk down the trail that ran alongside the river. "That's wonderful that you're learning to swim." Now Anna told Sarah about how her father made her prove that she could swim before she could use her canoe.

"Can I use the canoe too?"

"When you get older. I was a lot older than you before I could use it."

Sarah scowled, folding her arms across her chest exactly how Lauren used to do . . . and sometimes still did.

"Have you ever gone fishing?" Anna asked to distract her from her disappointment. When Sarah said no, but sounded interested, Anna promised to take her fishing in the afternoon. She wasn't sure if Sarah was too little to enjoy it, but she figured it would be worth the try and perhaps Clark or Marshall would want to come along with them.

<hr>

By the fourth day on the river, Lauren asked Anna if Sarah could sleep in the house instead of the cabin. "She wakes up so early," Lauren complained. "And I've been completely exhausted lately. I think all the chaos back home took a toll on me. Do you think Sarah could spend a night or two in the house with you until I catch up?"

"Sure, she can have the room next to us."

"Thanks. I worry that she might wander off while I'm still asleep and get eaten by a wolf or fall into the river." Lauren laughed like this was funny.

"Well, we don't have wolves here, but I suppose she might fall into the river." Anna frowned. "Does Sarah actually leave the cabin while you're still sleeping?"

Lauren shrugged. "Yeah."

"Oh . . ." Anna glanced over to where Sarah was swinging with a couple of older girls on the playground. She looked so happy . . . and childlike. "It sounds like Sarah misses having her nanny, Lauren. Have you noticed?"

Lauren tightened the lid back on the fingernail polish that she'd been using to paint her nails. It was the same color as her lipstick, a strange shade of whitish-pink that was, in Anna's opinion, anemic-looking. Not that Lauren had ever asked Anna for fashion advice. "Well, I don't think Sarah misses her nearly as much as I do." Lauren sighed as she reached for her sequin-covered cigarette case, then in one fluid motion, shook out a cigarette, lit it, slipped it in her mouth, and pulled in a long, slow drag with narrowed eyes. "I think I got a raw deal on that trade with Grandmother. My house gets torn to pieces and no more nanny."

Anna slowly inhaled, holding in her words, and wondering what it would feel like to take up smoking. Lauren claimed it soothed her frazzled nerves. Although what Lauren had to be frazzled over was a complete mystery to Anna. She let out the breath now, realizing that she'd much rather have fresh river air in her lungs than smelly smoke. "Sarah seems to enjoy the other children." Anna nodded toward the playground.

"Yeah." Lauren reached for her sunglasses, which were perched on top of her bleached hair. She slipped them on then looked out toward the water. "There are no kids in our neighborhood."

"Have you considered enrolling Sarah in kindergarten this fall? Some of the churches in town used to have good programs."

Lauren turned and looked at Anna. "That is a very good idea, Mom." Now she frowned. "But do you think it's terribly expensive?"

"I doubt it's too costly, but if finances are a problem, I'd be happy to help—"

"No, no . . . finances are not a problem. It's just that Donald always claims I waste too much money. All I do is buy clothes and little things." She shook her head. "If that skinflint had his way, I'd probably be forced to run around half naked."

Anna glanced at Lauren's very short shorts and the sleeveless blouse tied around her midriff to make it even skimpier. It seemed to her that Lauren was half naked right now. However, she suspected those kinds of clothes had not come cheap. Eunice had catered to Lauren's expensive taste in clothes and everything else for as long as Anna could remember.

Sarah was happy to relocate to a bedroom in the house, but it seemed that once that happened, Lauren decided to give up on any attempts of mothering whatsoever. Anna didn't mind having Sarah with her throughout the day. In fact, she loved it. The more time she spent with the little girl, the more she realized that Sarah was truly an old soul. The ways she could understand things, her grasp of language, and her ability to read people was almost uncanny. As incongruous as it seemed, Sarah sometimes reminded Anna of her grandmother. Even Hazel had mentioned that Sarah seemed to have an amazing connection to her ancestors.

"Can I wear this?" Sarah pointed to an old beaded leather cape that was framed on the wall as decoration. Her grandmother had made it long ago, back when she was just returning to the "old way" and Anna was about Sarah's age.

"Your great-great-grandmother made that, Sarah."

"Grandma Pearl?" Sarah asked.

Anna wasn't even surprised that Sarah remembered this. Already Anna had told Sarah much about Grandma Pearl, about her little cabin, the canoe, and the baskets she wove. Sarah seemed to take these stories in stride, as if it were perfectly normal to be part Siuslaw Indian, as if she'd known it all along.

"The cape is very old and it's very, very special." Anna looked more closely at the beadwork, a pattern with roses and leaves. "When you are old enough, yes, I will let you wear it."

"How old?"

Anna studied Sarah. "I think ten years old, Sarah. Can you wait that long?"

With a serious expression, Sarah nodded. "Is ten years old big enough to go out in River Dove too?"

"Yes." Anna ran her hand over Sarah's silky hair. "Ten is big enough. As long as you keep working at your swimming at your house."

Sarah promised to do that.

When Anna needed time to see to the demands of the inn, she found willing babysitters in Jill and Joanna. Both girls got along wonderfully with Sarah and never complained about having to help out. And both Clark and Marshall enjoyed the company of the little girl too. Sarah loved watching Clark "fix stuff." And she was slightly starstruck by Marshall. Truly, it seemed Sarah was in her element here. Or as Hazel liked to say, she was "happy as a clam."

Of course, while everyone else was enjoying Sarah, Anna couldn't help but wonder what Lauren was doing to occupy herself, that is besides sleeping. She usually emerged from her cabin in time for lunch. After that she'd lounge in the sun, if weather permitted, or else disappear back into her cabin. However, her absences did simplify things. And Anna hoped that perhaps this little vacation would refresh her enough to happily return to her household and parenting responsibilities. However, Anna was in no hurry to see them leave.

Just two days before Sarah's birthday, and after Anna had sent out invitations and gotten all the preparations for a big party planned, Ardelle called. "I must speak to my daughter-in-law," she said sharply. "Immediately!"

"Is something wrong?" Anna asked.

"Well, I suppose that depends on how you define *wrong*. Let me see . . . is it wrong for a wife to take her child and desert her husband?"

"Lauren hasn't deserted Donald. She simply came here for a little vacation."

"That selfish girl takes off, telling no one, leaving poor Donald in the lurch. He gets stuck with all the mess of that ridiculous remodel to deal with. How does Lauren expect that Donald can fend for himself, cook his own meals, do his own laundry, and still go to work and earn a living?"

"Isn't Mabel there to help cook and clean?"

"Eunice let Mabel go the same day that Lauren left. She said it was a waste to pay Mabel when the house was in such an upheaval."

"Oh, dear. I suppose that is hard on Donald."

"I'll say it's hard. And I've been trying to help out, but I'll tell you, Anna, I am fed up. *Fed up to here!*"

"I didn't realize—"

"No, I didn't expect you did. I know that you work hard, Anna. You always have. But that daughter of yours is the laziest thing I have ever seen. Then she up and does something like this. In the first place, there was nothing whatsoever wrong with Eunice's house. Those white kitchen appliances may have been a little out of style, but they were top of the line and worked just fine. Besides, it wasn't as if Lauren ever spent a minute of time in that kitchen to start with. And it's not likely she will now that it's nearly done—and all that avocado green—good grief, what on earth was she thinking? And I suppose she told you that they had to let the nanny go too."

"She mentioned that."

"Lauren practically ignores poor Sarah as it is. I don't know what that child will do now that she has no nanny to help pass her time."

"I suggested that Lauren put Sarah in kindergarten."

"Yes, that's probably a good idea. So, tell me, Anna, when is Lauren coming home, if I may ask?"

"I hoped they'd be around a few more days." Anna explained about the plans for the birthday party.

"Well, that's just fine and dandy. Here Eunice and I had planned a big party for Sarah too. It was to be at my house since theirs isn't quite finished yet, although it's very close. The carpet is all that's left and I heard the installation could be finished by tomorrow, a week later than we'd been promised. Even so, no one told me that Lauren and Sarah wouldn't be back in time for the birthday party. Eunice was certain they'd be back." She paused to catch her breath. "Where, may I ask, is Lauren? Is she unable to come to the phone now? Oh, let me guess, she's still sleeping."

Anna looked at the clock. It was just past ten, but Lauren probably hadn't gotten up yet. Of course, she wasn't about to admit this to Ardelle. "How about if I get her and have her call you back? She's staying in one of the cabins and it's a bit of a walk."

"Don't tell me you don't have extensions in the cabins yet?"

"I promise you that Lauren will return your call within the hour, Ardelle."

"Fine. Make sure she does!" Now the line went dead and Anna let out a sigh. She could understand Ardelle's frustration, but whatever happened to common courtesy? Perhaps it was getting less and less common.

"Is Grandma Ardelle mad at Mommy?"

Anna turned, surprised to see that Sarah was there. "I thought you were helping Jill in the garden."

"I had to use the bathroom."

"Oh . . ."

"Is Mommy in trouble?"

Anna smiled. "No, but your other grandmother would like to speak to her."

"Want me to go get her?"

Anna imagined Sarah waking up a grumpy Lauren. "No . . . I want you to go back and help Jill in the garden. Do you mind?"

"I like the garden."

"So do I. How are the cucumbers doing?" She walked Sarah to the door.

"We already picked six of them."

"Oh, good." At the foot of the stairs, Anna leaned over and kissed the top of Sarah's head. "You are truly a treasure."

Sarah giggled. "Like a pearl?" Hazel had told the pearl story by the campfire last night. Obviously, Sarah had been listening.

"Yes, like a pearl. Even better." They parted ways, and as Anna strode toward the cabins, she braced herself for the conversation she was about to have with her daughter. However, she did not brace herself for what she would see when she opened the door. Not only was the cabin thoroughly trashed, there were empty vodka bottles here and there and it reeked with the smell of stale cigarette smoke, dirty clothes, and filth.

"Lauren!" Anna shouted as she jerked the covers from the bed. "Get up!"

"Wha—what?" Lauren sat up with blurry-looking eyes. "What's going on?"

Anna pointed to the cabin. "What have you done?"

Lauren just shrugged, pulling the blankets up to cover a black lacy nightie that looked like something from a sleazy B movie.

"I do not want to get angry at you, but I'm not sure I can control myself any longer." Anna took a quick breath. "I am so ashamed of you. Ashamed to be your mother. You are like a stranger to me. I do not know why you are the way you are, Lauren, but I feel disgusted by you. Thoroughly disgusted." With one hand she picked up an empty vodka bottle, with the other she grabbed a trashy looking paperback, waving them in front of Lauren. "You are filling yourself with garbage and filth! Is it no wonder you are unable to function like a healthy human being?"

"Don't be such a prude, Mother."

"You neglect your daughter. You deserted your husband—"

"I did not desert him!"

"You didn't tell him you were going, Lauren. You left him in a huge mess. He has to do his own cooking and cleaning and—"

"*He has Mabel!*" Lauren narrowed her eyes, but the smudges of heavy makeup ringed them like an angry raccoon.

"He does not have Mabel. Eunice let her go."

"*What?*" Lauren dropped her blanket, grabbing for her cigarettes. "How dare she!"

"How dare *she*?" Anna stared at this pitiful excuse of a woman. "How dare *you*, Lauren? How dare you live like the world owes you a living? How dare you neglect and ignore your precious daughter? How dare you take advantage of my generosity? How dare you use everyone you can, whether it's me or Clark or Donald or Ardelle or even Eunice? And how dare you come to my inn and turn a perfectly lovely little cabin into a pigsty?" She tossed the book and bottle onto the bed. "I want this place cleaned up, Lauren. You put it back together just the way it was when you arrived here. And I want you to clean yourself up too. Do not come out of this cabin until you look like a decent young woman—like a wife and a mother ought to look. And then, and only then, you will use the telephone to call your mother-in-law and you will apologize to her for all your lazy selfishness!" Anna's hands were shaking as she reached for the door. "Then I will arrange for someone to take you back down the river."

Anna felt sick as she closed the door. Her knees were weak and her stomach was churning. She hated herself for losing her temper like that. But she hated Lauren even more. With clenched fists, she walked over to the edge of the river and just looked out over it, attempting to breathe deeply . . . and to calm herself.

"Is something wrong?" Clark stepped next to her, peering at her with concern.

"Oh, Clark." She turned to him with tears running down her cheeks. Then as he wrapped an arm around her, he guided her to a private place behind a tree where, like a broken dam, she let the sad, horrible story rush out of her. "The truth is, I wouldn't care nearly so much," she sobbed, "if it were only Lauren I was throwing out of here—but Sarah—Clark, what about Sarah?"

"Sarah is a resilient child. And she knows you love her, Anna. She will be all right. You have to believe that. You have to let it go."

Anna nodded, wiping her eyes on the fresh-smelling bandana handkerchief he supplied to her. Still, she knew that she would need to repair this rift between Lauren and her. She would have to apologize. And hopefully Lauren wouldn't hold a grudge for too long. She would hold a grudge, Anna had no doubts of that, but maybe in time, she would get over it.

23

May 1966

To Anna's dismay, it took Lauren nearly a year to get over it. Even then, Lauren acted differently, treating Anna with politely quiet contempt. During the past year, Anna had attempted to rebuild the bridge. She'd written many cards and letters, both to Lauren and Sarah. She had sent Christmas presents and other packages, never receiving a thank-you or any response whatsoever. Oddly enough, it was Eunice who provided an outlet for communication throughout this unsettling time. She had heard all about the angry confrontation, and in a strange way, Anna thought that Eunice appreciated how she'd raked her daughter over the coals that day.

Consequently, Anna was surprised when, out of the blue, Lauren called the last week of May. The conversation, at first, was stilted and chilly, but slowly thawed, ever so slightly. "The reason I'm calling is to make plans for Sarah's summer."

"Plans?"

"Yes. Sarah has gotten it into her head that she should go out there to see you."

"Really?" Anna felt a rush of joy.

"Yes. She keeps talking about the river and the boats."

"I'd love to have her come for a visit."

"I honestly do not know why she is so bound and determined to go out there," Lauren said flatly, "but she will not let up."

"Sarah is more than welcome here," Anna said eagerly. "She can stay as long as she likes."

"Well, I wanted to send her to summer camp, but she's begging to see you instead. And, as Donald pointed out, it would be a lot cheaper. Although I do think that, expense or not, summer camp would've been preferable."

Anna knew this was meant to be an insult, but didn't care. Lauren could poke and jab as much as she liked—as long as Sarah got to come to the river.

"Anyway, Sarah will need to come out early next week. I thought I could put her on the bus, but Donald insists she's too young."

"I agree," Anna said quickly.

"I suppose I could drive her out, but that would mean I'd have to spend a night there and I'm not sure that I'm up for that kind of abuse."

"What sort of abuse do you mean?"

"Being subjected to your harsh criticism, of course."

"I have already apologized to you for losing my temper that day, Lauren. The things I said to you were true, but I did not intend to deliver them with such hostility. I hope that someday you'll find it in your heart to forgive me."

There was a long silence now.

"So, shall we expect you on Monday then?" Anna asked.

"Tuesday is more likely."

"And you only plan to stay over one night?"

"That is unless you decide to throw me out sooner."

"Oh, Lauren." Anna sighed. "When I think of all we've been through. All I've done for you. Don't you think you could let this offense go, dear?"

Now there was another long pause.

"Well, I hope you know that you will always be welcome here," Anna said warmly. "Whether for one night or many. And I am truly looking forward to seeing Sarah again. I'm so thankful you're not opposed to her coming."

"Like I said, it was her choice. And if I wasn't going to Europe with Grandmother, I never would've agreed in the first place."

The light went on now. Lauren was in a bind. She needed someone to watch Sarah for her. No matter. Anna was happy to comply. "So Eunice is taking you on a trip with her?"

"Yes. She acts like she's doing me a great favor, but I know perfectly well that I'm only accompanying her because she's getting too old to go alone. I am her paid companion."

"I hope you'll be able to enjoy the trip . . . at least a little." Anna was glad Lauren couldn't see her skeptical expression right now.

"Yes, well, I suppose. After all, we are going to London, Paris, Rome, Athens . . . I suppose there should be some pleasures along the way."

"How long do you plan to be gone?"

"Oh, didn't I mention it?"

"No . . ."

"We won't be back until late August."

Anna was shocked. "So, will Sarah be here the whole time?"

"Is that a problem?" Lauren's tone grew sharp.

"No, of course not. I couldn't be more pleased."

"Yes, well, you've always been the domestic type, haven't you? I figured you wouldn't care."

"And Sarah doesn't mind?"

Lauren laughed, but there was a hard coldness to it. "Hardly."

"Well, I look forward to seeing both of you."

"And now I have much to do. I will see you on Tuesday."

Anna said goodbye, and although she didn't like the cool aloof sound to her daughter's voice, she did think that Lauren sounded a little bit older, a tad more mature, like perhaps she'd grown up some.

⌖

The summer of 1966 was perfectly blissful at Shining Waters Inn. Not only was Sarah perfectly delightful and no trouble at all, she was helpful and friendly to the guests as well. She seemed to innately understand that the purpose of the inn was to show hospitality and, in a youthful way, took some personal responsibility toward it. She was quick to run errands, fetch linens, take messages, deliver fresh flowers . . . whatever the task was, and completely unlike her mother, Sarah was always more than glad to make herself useful. It was as if she sensed that Shining Waters was as much hers as it was Anna's.

"Sarah seems wise beyond her years," Anna told Clark one evening after everyone had gone to bed. "I feel like she's as connected to this land and this river as I am, as much as my mother and my grandmother before me. And, you know, my people were a matriarchal society, so in all fairness, I will one day hand this property over to Sarah."

He chuckled. "Just don't go about handing it off too soon. I don't think she's quite ready for it yet."

"Speaking of being ready for something." She filled their coffee mugs. "Have you noticed anything different about your son lately?"

He gave her a quizzical look as she handed him his coffee.

"You haven't noticed him hanging around the kitchen more than usual?"

"He's always liked sneaking food." Clark opened the door for her and they went out onto the spacious second floor deck that he'd recently built for them. Attached to the house, it allowed them a spot to go out and enjoy the fresh air without having to use the stairs. This evening the river smelled ripe with new life, green and fertile and sweet. The vantage point from this deck was lovely, and watching the reflection of a sunset, the ripples of peach and rose, was like a slice of heaven. Anna sighed happily as she settled into one of the Adirondack chairs, also Clark's workmanship, and took a sip of the hot drink.

"So, what is it?" Clark sat next to her, laying a blanket over their legs to ward off the chilly air. "What's different about Marshall?"

"You honestly haven't noticed him spending a lot of time with Joanna?"

"Joanna?" He nodded slowly. "Now that you mention it. And he took her and the other kids to town for a movie tonight."

"I think he's in love."

Clark grinned. "Joanna's a very sweet girl."

"So you would approve?"

He chuckled. "Of course, why not?"

"Well, Marshall isn't finished with law school yet."

"Joanna's not finished with her college either." He frowned. "You're not suggesting they are serious enough to want to get married?"

"I don't know . . ." She grinned.

"Well, even if they are that serious, they're both adults. They can figure this out for themselves."

She nodded. "My thoughts exactly. Now if they were as immature as Lauren and Donald were when they got married . . . that would be different."

"Marshall's got a good head on his shoulders. And so does Joanna. Whatever they choose to do, they have my blessing."

"We have the perfect life, don't we?" she said happily.

"I think so. But it's not for everyone." He reached for her hand. "Take Mr. Owens in Cabin 4. He just could not believe we didn't have television out here."

"Yes, Mrs. Owens said the same to me." Anna sighed. "I asked her why she thought we needed it and she said to stay current on the latest developing news events."

"Did you tell her we take three different newspapers, as well as a couple of weekly news magazines?"

"Yes. I showed her where they were kept. But she meant the TV news. She told me they watch it every night while eating dinner."

"You're kidding. They eat dinner and watch the news?" he sounded astounded.

"That's what she said. So I asked her what kinds of things they showed on the TV news. What was so interesting that you couldn't wait until the next day to read about it in the paper, or hear it on the radio, and do you know what she told me?"

"I have no idea." He sipped his coffee.

"She said they showed scenes straight from the Vietnam War. They put real footage of real soldiers who were actually killing others or being killed, right there on the television screen for everyone to watch. Can you imagine?"

"No, I'd rather not. I've seen some horrendous photos in the newspapers and magazines. I would not like to see them on TV. And certainly not while I was eating my dinner. That's grotesque."

"She also said they showed scenes of racial rioting, where people are being shot at or hosed down—it sounds just brutal." Anna shuddered. "It's hard enough to read about those things in magazines. I don't think I'd care to see it live. And she even told me about how important the TV was when President Kennedy was shot. It seems they experienced the whole thing on TV. Everyone stayed glued to their sets. Even the funeral was televised. So was the shooting of Lee Harvey Oswald. It seems nothing is spared from the television screen."

"Good reason to continue as we are without any televisions."

She nodded. "I agree. I told Mrs. Owens that it all sounded rather stressful to me. And, do you know what, she *agreed*."

He laughed. "And yet she complains that we don't have TV here at Shining Waters?"

"Contradictory, isn't it?"

———

Anna wasn't ready to say goodbye to Sarah in August. To make matters worse, Sarah seemed even more reluctant. "Why can't I just stay here with you and Grandpa?" she asked the night before Lauren was due to come. It was past bedtime, but Anna had taken her out there for a cup of cocoa and to look at the stars.

"Because your mommy and daddy need you to be with them," Anna explained. "And your Grandma and Grandpa Thomas must be missing you, and Great-grandmother too. We have to share you with the rest of the family."

"But I want to stay here with you."

"I would love to keep you forever," Anna admitted. "But that would be selfish."

"Mommy's selfish," Sarah stated.

Anna didn't know what to say. It was true. But it was disrespectful. "When I was a child I was taught to respect grown-ups," she said gently. "Even when I didn't agree with them."

"Why?"

Anna considered this. "Maybe it was because I didn't know everything when I was a child. I'm sure I thought I did. But the older I get, the more I realize how much I don't know."

"Huh?"

Anna laughed. "I guess what I'm trying to say is that some-times people do things that are hard to understand. But if you try to be patient . . . sometimes you begin to figure out that there's a reason." Now Anna started to tell Sarah about her own mother. "I didn't understand her when I was a child. She did a lot of things I didn't like. And I know I did things she didn't like."

"Were you naughty?"

Anna nodded. "Sometimes I was."

Sarah laughed. "Did you get in trouble?"

"Sometimes. But when I got older, I felt sorry that I didn't try to understand my mother better. I realized that she had some hard things happen that I never really knew about." Anna real-ized that most of this was probably going over Sarah's head. "I know your mommy makes some mistakes. Everyone does. I think we all just need to learn how to forgive each other better."

"How do you do that?"

"Forgive?"

"Yeah."

"Well, you know how you feel when you make a mistake that hurts someone?"

"Like when I pushed Susan out of my favorite swing that time?"

"Yes." Anna nodded. "Remember how angry Susan was at you?"

"Yeah. Jill got mad at me too."

"Did you tell them you were sorry?"

"Yeah."

"Did they forgive you?"

"Susan didn't. She was too mad. She just stomped off and told her mom."

"How did that make you feel?"

"Bad."

"Did Jill forgive you?" Anna had already heard Jill's version and knew how it had gone.

"Yeah, she did."

"How did that make you feel?"

"Better."

"And it made Jill feel better, too, didn't it?"

"Yeah. She hugged me."

"So if forgiving someone makes everyone feel better, it's a good thing, isn't it?"

"Yeah. I guess so."

"So, sometimes you need to remember that with your mommy."

As Anna helped Sarah get ready for bed, she knew she needed to hear that little talk as much as Sarah did. She needed to forgive Lauren . . . again. She wanted to give Lauren a fresh slate when she arrived. But it wouldn't be easy. She was not looking forward to seeing Lauren tomorrow. She could imagine her rushing in, full of herself and her recent trip "abroad." Lauren had a knack for being a snob, and now that she'd spent a whole summer touring Europe, she would probably be looking down her nose at everyone and everything.

But the next day, and to Anna's surprise, she couldn't have been more wrong about her daughter. For starters, she seemed genuinely glad to see Sarah. She had barely stepped onto the dock when she ran directly to Sarah, swooped her up in her arms, and hugged her. Anna was so glad she could've cried.

"Welcome home," she said as Lauren walked toward her, still holding to Sarah's hand. "Did you have a good trip, in Europe, I mean?"

"It was really very nice," Lauren told her. "Educational too."

"That's wonderful." Anna opened her arms to hug Lauren. To her relief, Lauren reciprocated. "And your drive today?"

"It was fine." Lauren looked out over the river. "I forgot how pretty it is here, Mom."

"I caught a fish this morning," Sarah announced. "We're going to eat it for dinner."

Lauren laughed.

"How's Grandmother doing?" Anna asked, for lack of anything else to say. She was so shocked at this new side of Lauren. Not only was she acting more polite and grownup than ever, she was maturely dressed in a pair of neat navy pants and light blue sweater set. However, Anna noticed as she pulled out a white leather cigarette case, she was still smoking. But, to be fair, it seemed almost everyone smoked these days.

"Grandmother was happy to get home."

"We have your cabin ready," Anna told her as she glanced to where Marshall was unloading Lauren's bags. "Lauren will be in Cabin 9," she called out.

That evening, because it was Sarah's last night, they had a big bonfire with plenty of hotdogs and marshmallows on hand. Even Babette came, although her age was making it more and more difficult to travel much. But she brought a bottle of burgundy for the grownups and a crocheted hat for Sarah to take home with her. As the fire died down, the chairs drew closer and Marshall and Joanna got out their guitars and led everyone in campfire songs. Finally, after some of the guests had excused themselves and it was mostly just family and friends, Hazel told some of Grandma Pearl's stories. Anna couldn't imagine a more perfect evening . . . or a more perfect way to end the most wonderful summer.

24

As fall came, Anna realized that Babette was aging fast. Although she wouldn't admit it, she seemed to need help. Even the simplest household tasks were starting to overwhelm her. "Mrs. Thorne, she tells me I should go to a home," Babette confessed as she let Anna into her house.

"A home?" Anna asked as she went into the kitchen, looking for a place to set the heavy box of groceries she was delivering.

"For old people." Babette frowned. "Eets where her mama lives."

Anna tried not to stare at how disorderly the kitchen looked. So unlike Babette. "Where shall I put this?" Anna tried to find a spot on the messy counters.

"I know, I know . . . ees clutter, clutter, clutter." Babette threw up her hands with tears in her eyes. "What do I do?"

"Come and stay with us for a while," Anna suggested.

"Ees too much trouble." Babette pulled out a kitchen chair. "Put the box here."

"It's not trouble," Anna assured her. "We run an inn. We are accustomed to guests. Besides, you're not a guest, you're family. Just come for the winter. *Please?*"

"But I am happy here."

"I know you've been very happy here." Anna glanced around Babette's living room now. She'd never seen it in such bad shape. Unfolded laundry was piled on the couch. Books and papers and things were on the floor, possibly presenting a tripping hazard. Anna knew Babette's balance was diminishing. Besides that, her eyesight was failing. Really, living alone was becoming too much for her. "Maybe you could get someone to come and live here then. Do you know of anyone?"

Babette shook her head.

"Please, Babette," Anna begged. "You are like a mother to me, and I would love to have you stay with us—just for the winter if you like. You can have the suite downstairs. And, if you feel up to it, you can help me with the cooking sometimes. Remember when you and Hazel ran the kitchen, back when Sarah was born? The guests raved about your cuisine."

Babette smiled. "Eet was a fun time."

"Come stay with us," Anna urged. "We'll have more fun."

"I will consider it, mon chéri."

To Anna's relief, Babette decided to give it a try. By the end of the week Clark was helping her to move into the downstairs suite. The first few weeks required some adjustments, but Babette seemed to appreciate having people around. And Hazel enjoyed having an older companion. By mid-November the two women established a daily "tea time." Every afternoon at three o'clock, they would serve tea and other goodies to anyone who was interested.

Besides writing Lauren weekly letters, Anna made a special effort to call her at least every other week. She hoped to keep the relationship moving in the right direction and realized that might be upon her to do this. During December, Anna realized that she spent most of their telephone time trying to bolster Lauren's spirits. For some reason, Lauren seemed unexplainably blue. But if Anna pressed her regarding the cause of her sadness, there seemed to be no real reason. Anna attributed it to the weather, hoping that Lauren would perk up come springtime.

Winter was always their "off" season, but Anna didn't mind this dormancy. Instead, she used this time to regroup and plan for the upcoming year. She called it the dreaming season. It seemed that, more and more, the inn was acquiring a reputation as a place of healing, and recently she'd been approached by various individuals who wanted to plan group events there. While she was open to these ideas, she also felt protective of the inn and its image. She didn't want anyone coming here who would misuse the natural properties of the land and the river. Sometimes she couldn't quite explain it, not even to Clark, but she would get a feeling about someone and as a result decline their proposal for a certain event—sometimes saying "no" to tempting sums of money.

"I know he was supposed to be a famous guru," she told Clark after she hung up the phone, "but something about the way this man spoke to me . . . well, he just sounded too self-important . . . and false. Do you think I was being too judgmental? Was I wrong to turn him down?"

Clark smiled over the newspaper in his hands. "Not at all, Anna. I think you have an excellent sense about these things."

Anna spent a lot of time with Babette, learning how to prepare some of her herbal recipes and remedies, and all the numerous uses of lavender. "I will leave my plants to you, chéri," Babette told her as they were working on a batch of marjoram oil.

Anna just smiled. "I'm sure your plants would be happy to stay right where they are planted, Babette. It's such a nice sunny spot, especially nice for growing lavender."

"Eets true. The hill is perfect for my lavender. I would hate to see them moved."

Sometimes Hazel would join them during these times. Like Anna she had a strong interest in the herbs and plants and their medicinal uses. "So much gets lost when people assume you can replace everything old with something new." Hazel sighed as she carefully copied a recipe for a gout treatment. "Hopefully I'll be around long enough to publish a manual for the use of herbal medicine."

"Oui!" Babette nodded eagerly. "I would love for young people to know these secrets. Ees so much better than taking a pill."

"I wish we had something here that would help Lauren," Anna said sadly.

"What's wrong with Lauren?" Hazel asked. "She seemed better than ever when she picked up Sarah in August."

"Yes, I thought so too. But every time I talk to her, she sounds more and more downhearted. I know something is wrong with her. And yesterday she told me that she's taking some kind of medicine." Anna tried to recall the name. "I think it was called Valium. Have you heard of that?"

"Valium for Lauren?" Hazel's brow creased. "That doesn't make sense."

"I'm sure that's what she said it was," Anna said.

"Mother's little helper." Hazel set down her pen.

"What?" Anna felt confused.

"It's what some people call Valium. It's been popular for several years now. Doctors all over the country have been prescribing it like candy to frustrated housewives and mothers. It's as if they think it's a magic pill, but it's highly addictive and really, it's not for everyone."

"Do you think it will hurt Lauren?" Anna felt even more concerned now.

"I'm not sure." Hazel pursed her lips. "I suppose it's help-ful for those women who are overwrought and excited and anxious because it helps them to relax. But, as I recall, Lauren was never a particularly active person. She slept so much of the time. I honestly cannot imagine how a depressant would be of any help to her."

"You're saying that Valium is a depressant?" Anna was surprised.

"Yes."

"But Lauren already seemed depressed." Anna turned down the heat beneath the cast iron pot. "I hardly think she needs something to make her more depressed."

"Too bad we can't get Lauren to come out here for a visit," Hazel suggested, "maybe we could diagnose and treat her." She laughed. "Of course, we could get in trouble for practicing medicine without a license. But so should the doctor who's prescribing Valium for Lauren. I just can't help but think that is a big mistake."

"Should I tell her?"

"You might question her a bit . . . find out why the doctor prescribed it, how long she's been on it, how she's been spend-ing her time."

"I'm not sure Lauren will tell me all that. She's very closed up."

"I know, chéri—you should go and see Lauren," Babette said suddenly. "Eet ees not busy here. Go, chéri. See to your daughter."

"I suppose I could go visit."

"We will prepare some things for Lauren," Babette declared. "To help her be happy again. And you will take them, chéri."

"That's not a bad idea," Hazel agreed.

"I'll talk to Clark about it."

Anna's visit to see Lauren was very dismaying. Besides enjoying some time with Sarah, taking her to school and the park and the library, the rest of the four days spent there felt like a complete waste of time. Lauren refused to try any of the herbal remedies. She insisted that she needed to remain in bed until well past noon. "I just don't sleep at night," she told Anna. "The morning is my only time to get my rest." Then, Anna quickly discovered, even when Lauren got up she remained in her bathrobe, watching soap operas and chain smoking as well as sneaking drinks from a silver flask she always kept handy. Finally, about an hour before Sarah came home from school, Lauren would begin to get dressed and do her hair and makeup.

The household routine would continue with Sarah arriving home on the school bus, coming in the back door, and stopping in the avocado green kitchen, where Mabel, who'd been rehired, would have a snack set out.

"What do you do after school?" Anna asked Sarah on their first afternoon together.

Sarah thought hard as she chewed on a Fig Newton.

"Do you do things with your mommy?"

Sarah shook her head then took a swig of milk. "Mommy is getting pretty for Daddy. I'm not allowed to disturb her."

It seemed that Lauren never emerged from her boudoir until around four in the afternoon. But, to Anna's amazement, when she made her appearance, she looked like something straight out of a fashion magazine. She no longer wore the old trashy style of clothes. Apparently her trip to Europe had "refined" her sense of style and anyone who saw Lauren on the street would probably assume she was a responsible, practical, and quite attractive young housewife and mother.

Walking through her home, which now had a strange hairy-looking carpeting called "shag" as well as some modern furnishings that seemed to be more about looks than comfort, Lauren seemed to be playing queen of the house. She would spend a bit of time with Sarah, inquiring about school, and telling her to go and clean herself up before dinner. Then she'd go over some housekeeping details with Mabel. At exactly five o'clock, Lauren would make a batch of martinis at the new bar, which sat in a corner of the living room. Not long after the drinks were mixed, Eunice would come over like clockwork, and at five-thirty Donald would arrive home from work.

Anna had a hard time grasping how Sarah fit into this strange little household. Feeling sorry for her granddaughter, she did all she could to fill Sarah's time. The second evening of Anna's visit, Donald and Lauren went to the country club. The next evening they had a dinner date with friends. Lauren invited Anna to join them, but Anna politely declined. The relief on their faces was obvious.

"Lauren and Donald seem to have an active social life," Anna commented to Eunice after Sarah had gone to bed.

Eunice nodded with a hard-to-read expression.

"Sarah seems to be left by herself a lot."

Again, Eunice nodded.

"Does she ever have friends over?"

"No . . . not that I've noticed."

"What does she do?"

Eunice shrugged as she put down the coffee table book about modern art. "She comes to visit me sometimes."

"Really?"

Eunice gave Anna an aggravated look. "Although you probably won't believe it, Sarah and I get along fairly well. Perhaps not as well as she gets along with you." She rolled her eyes upward ever so slightly. "Oh, don't think I haven't heard all about her fabulous summer spent at the river, Anna. You'd think she'd been living in Disneyland the way the child prattles on."

"We enjoyed her as much as she enjoyed us." Anna frowned. "I just wish that Lauren and Donald spent more time with her."

"Oh, Anna, don't make so much of it. Sarah will be just fine. Children seem to grow up no matter the mistakes the parents make."

"Is that how you raised Adam?"

Eunice's brows arched slightly. "What are you suggesting?"

"I'm not suggesting anything, Eunice. I'm just curious. I never had a chance to learn too much about Adam's upbringing. I know his father died when he was younger. And from what I heard, it seemed you spent quite a bit of time and energy on him. Weren't you two rather close?"

Eunice seemed to soften now. "We were close. Adam was my right hand after his father passed. I depended on him for everything. He was my—my best friend." Her voice broke slightly.

Anna leaned forward. "He was a good man, Eunice. You did a good job raising him."

Eunice looked truly surprised. "You truly think so?"

Anna nodded. "Oh, he was a bit spoiled. But you expect that with an only child. I was a little spoiled too."

Eunice blinked. "*You?*"

"In some ways I was. But I was also a hard worker. And Adam was a hard worker too. But he also knew how to play. I think one of the things that drew me to him was his sense of fun and adventure. He was always so full of life and fun. That was very attractive."

"Yes," Eunice said eagerly. "He was full of life, wasn't he?"

"I sometimes wonder what it would've been like if he hadn't been hurt like that . . . in the war."

Eunice nodded sadly. "I do too. He never should've been in active service."

"Why?"

"He wasn't like that. He'd never been the sort of boy to play with guns or roughhouse like some boys. I remember how he tried to rescue a bird that flew into the picture window, putting it in a box with a tea towel, hoping that it would live . . . how he cried when it didn't." She sniffed. "He was too tender-hearted to march with a gun."

"And yet he seemed eager to go." Anna remembered her dismay when he'd been so enthusiastic to join his buddies and head off to war.

"That was his devil-may-care side . . . he loved adventures and had no idea what the war would really be like."

"He found out quickly." Anna tried not to remember the look in his blue eyes when he returned to them . . . as if the light had gone out.

Eunice was crying now, sitting by herself on the strangely-shaped sofa and wiping her eyes. Anna went over and sat next to her, wrapping an arm around the frail shoulders. "I wish we could've been friends," Anna confessed, "all those years when we were both suffering . . . I wish we'd known that we both missed him."

Eunice nodded then quietly blew her nose. "I always blamed you, Anna," she whispered. "I felt you stole him from me . . . and then he never came back."

"The war took him from both of us."

"Yes . . . I think you are right."

Now they just sat there for a long moment and then Eunice stiffened, squared her shoulders, and said it was time for bed. Anna stood, offering her a hand to help her up.

Eunice paused after she stood, looking intently at Anna. "I have found that anger and bitterness become rather cumbersome the older I get."

"It's better to just set those things aside."

"Yes . . . I suppose so."

Anna walked her through the house, going through the kitchen and to the back door. "It's dark out, Eunice, do you mind if I walk you home?"

Eunice looked surprised and then relieved. "If you'd like."

Anna smiled at her. "I would."

Neither of them spoke as they walked down the brick paved path toward Eunice's little house, but at her door, Eunice thanked Anna. "And don't worry too much about Sarah," she said in a strangely gentle voice. "I will try to see that she's not too lonely."

Anna reached over to grasp and squeeze Eunice's thin hand. "Thank you."

So, as it turned out, Anna's visit seemed to have no impact whatsoever on Lauren, but the connection she made with Eunice made it all seem worthwhile.

25

Babette died in the early spring. She passed peacefully in her sleep just as the daffodils began to bloom. Although Anna was saddened to lose her dear old friend, she knew that Babette had lived a full and satisfying life. And Anna felt very thankful to have known her. Following Babette's funeral, Anna was stunned by two things. First, she'd had no idea that Babette was ninety-four years old. Equally surprising was that Babette had left all her worldly goods to Anna.

"What will I do with her house and land and everything?" she asked Clark as they left the law office in Florence. "I already have my hands full at the inn."

He shrugged. "Hold on to it, let me make some repairs on the house . . . then why not just wait and see?"

"Yes . . . you're right. No hurry to figure it all out today. And, really, I'm honored that Babette left it to me."

Of course, it wasn't until Anna began to sort through Babette's house that she realized just how much Babette had really left to her. Anna had always known Babette was wealthy. She'd grown up hearing stories of Babette's first husband Bernard and how he found gold shortly before his demise. But Anna didn't realize how many "treasures" Babette had squirreled away in her house. Whether it was fine china, sterling silver, crystal, or fine French linens, Babette had always had the best of everything. Besides that, she had jewelry, antiques, and most amazing of all, hidden beneath her bed in an old porcelain commode, of all things, was what Clark estimated might be several thousand dollars' worth of gold coins. Anna nearly fainted.

Although Clark wisely suggested that most of the coins be locked in a safe at the inn, Anna decided that some of it would be sold and used to finish the much-needed repairs to Babette's property. Her plan was to restore the old house to its original splendor and perhaps one day use it as annex to the inn.

Summer came and, to Anna's delight, Sarah was allowed to visit again. It seemed that they picked up right where they'd left off, though Sarah was a year older. But still, she loved helping—whether in the kitchen or the garden or even in the laundry, she never complained. Anna hoped that Lauren might come out and join them for a week or two and she tried numerous times to entice her, but Lauren wouldn't hear of it.

"I have my commitments here," she told Anna.

Anna wanted to question this. She'd seen what Lauren's days consisted of, but she knew that it was pointless to pick a fight with her daughter. Instead she focused her attention on Sarah and her guests. Plus, they were now preparing for a wedding. Marshall and Joanna had gotten engaged in May and the ceremony was set for the last week of August. Sarah had been invited to be a junior bridesmaid and couldn't have been happier.

Again, it was another nearly perfect summer. Despite a long spell of cool and cloudy weather, not unusual on the Oregon coast, the rooms and cabins at the inn remained full. Then, as time for the wedding drew near, the inn began to fill up with family and friends of the wedding couple. Anna encouraged Lauren and Donald to come. She even promised them the use of Babette's lovely house, which was now fully restored, but the invitation was declined. Instead Anna invited Clark's ex-wife Rosalyn and her husband to occupy it. Perhaps that was a good thing, since Rosalyn could be somewhat demanding and Marshall seemed to appreciate having a bit of distance between them.

Dorothy and her mother baked the wedding cake, and Anna and Jill arranged the flowers, most which came from Babette's gardens. It was a simple outdoor wedding, similar to Anna and Clark's, but Marshall and Joanna both insisted it was absolutely perfect. Fortunately it didn't rain until the happy couple was well on their way to their honeymoon.

August came to an end too soon, and it was time to say goodbye to Sarah again. Instead of Lauren, Donald came to pick her up, arriving just before noon, which meant he'd been traveling since quite early in the morning. Anna encouraged him to spend the night and refresh himself. He looked tired, with dark shadows beneath his eyes, but he refused, saying he needed to be at work the next day.

Sarah blinked back tears as goodbye hugs were exchanged. Anna felt her heart was breaking. Everything in her wanted to beg Donald to just leave Sarah here, to demand that he allow his daughter a bit of happiness and a normal childhood. Instead she told Donald that Sarah was welcome to visit anytime . . . anytime at all.

"Eunice isn't well," he told her as Sarah's bags were being loaded on the boat.

Anna frowned. "Is it serious?"

"I'm not sure." He glanced at his daughter. "But I think it will cheer her up to see Sarah."

"Please give her my best," Anna told him. "And tell her I'll write."

He nodded with a slightly grim expression.

"And how is Lauren?" she asked quietly. Sarah was already in the boat now, offering to help Clark with the wheel.

"She's the same." He glanced away as if uncomfortable.

"Oh . . ." Anna didn't know what to say. "Well, if I can ever be of help, Donald. Or if Lauren ever wants to come out here to, well, to have a break . . ." Her voice trailed off as she wondered what Lauren could possibly need to take a break from. "Of course she's always welcome. You both are."

Now Sarah came back to the side of the boat, looking expectantly at Anna. "Aren't you coming into town with us, Grandma?"

"Sorry, sweetheart, I have to fix lunch and dinner. Remember Joanna and Jill aren't here to help now."

Sarah's dark eyes grew shiny with tears as she tugged on the strings of her hooded sweatshirt, but she nodded bravely.

"I love you," Anna mouthed to her as a big lump lodged in her throat.

Sarah mouthed the words back then quickly turned away, putting her hands to her face. Anna knew Sarah was crying. She called out a husky goodbye, waving and wishing there was another way to do this. Clark tossed her a sympathetic glance then steered the boat out onto the sparkling river and revved up the motor.

As she walked to the house, Anna let her tears fall freely. As a child she had hated to cry, thought it a weakness, but the older she got, the less she worried about such things. In fact, she reminded herself as she paused to look back, tears, like the river, sometimes brought healing too.

Anna couldn't have been more surprised when she received a phone call from Eunice in early November. Eunice wanted to know if the inn had room for her and Sarah to come for a visit the following weekend. "You and Sarah want to come here? To the inn?" Anna spoke loudly, wondering if this was a bad connection, or if she'd heard it wrong.

"Yes. Sarah only has three days of school next week and I thought it would be nice to take a trip out there."

"You're driving here?"

"No, no, I'm too old for that. I had hoped that Lauren would drive us, but she's not feeling up to it, so I have hired a car."

"You hired a car?"

"Do you have room or not?"

"Of course we have room," Anna assured her. "And you know you're welcome."

Eunice told her the date and time of their arrival. "And thank you for writing to me," she said finally. "I'm sorry I haven't written back yet. My hands are so shaky these days, it's difficult to write clearly anymore. But perhaps we can talk when I get there."

"Of course," Anna said eagerly. "I can't wait to see you, Eunice."

"Yes, well, thank you." Now Eunice said goodbye and Anna replaced the receiver and turned to Clark as he placed a log on the fire. "Will wonders never cease."

"That was Eunice?" His brow was creased with concern.

"Yes." Anna explained the details of the phone call.

"Very interesting."

"Remember how she and I talked openly last winter?" Anna reminded him. "Well, I get the feeling that she has something else on her mind." Anna was so excited she couldn't sit down with her book now. "The best part is that she's bringing Sarah with her, Clark. Four whole days with our granddaughter. I can hardly wait."

"I feel sorry that Mother won't be here." Clark chuckled as he turned a page. "I suspect she'd be rather amused by all this." Hazel had signed a teaching contract at a small private college in Washington. As much as they missed her, they knew how happy it made her to teach again. Sharing her wisdom with others always ignited her. Besides, they knew she would be back here in her favorite little cabin during the summers.

"Eunice has changed dramatically," Anna assured him. "In fact, I wish your mother could witness it for herself. But at least you'll be around to see how she's softened in her old age. And Donald said she's been having some health issues. Maybe she's worried . . ."

"She might want to mend her wicked ways before she runs into those pearly gates and St. Peter is pointing the opposite direction," he teased.

She shook a finger at him. "Have a heart, Clark. Poor Eunice is old and ailing."

"Sorry." He smiled sheepishly. "I'll try to be more like you, Anna. Forgive and forget, right?"

She came over to his chair, leaned down, and kissed him on his cheek, feeling the stubble scratching her chin. "Just be you. That's all I could want."

The next few days passed quickly as Anna pulled out all the stops to get the rooms in order for Eunice and Sarah. Sarah was no problem, since Anna decided to let her stay in her usual room upstairs. Anna knew how much she loved it there. However, she went to more effort for Eunice. She planned to put her in the downstairs suite that adjoined to the fireplace seating area. Really, it was their most comfortable space.

Even so, Anna thoroughly cleaned everything from top to bottom, washing the large sliding glass doors until they shone so clear that the river seemed just a breath away. And she made up the bed with a set of Babette's finest lace-trimmed sheets and down pillows, as well as a luxurious satin comforter and a French jacquard throw. She also put one of Babette's beautiful porcelain lamps on the bedside table, along with a crystal vase filled with fresh fall-colored mums. The suite wasn't exactly "lodge" style now, but she knew that Eunice wasn't overly fond of rustic décor anyway. Hopefully she would appreciate that Anna had made an effort to make her feel special and at home.

When the boat arrived, Anna was surprised at how much Eunice seemed to have aged since she'd last seen her. She seemed unsteady as Clark helped her off the boat. "Welcome," Anna said as she placed a firm hand beneath Eunice's elbow. "Watch your step."

"All right, first mate," Clark said to Sarah as she tied off the rope. "Can you help me with the bags?"

"Aye-aye, sir." Sarah made a mock salute then grinned at Anna. "Hi, Grandma!"

"Hello, darling girl." Anna blew her a kiss.

"I saw a fish jumping on the river," Sarah said with excitement.

"Wonderful!" Anna called out as she guided Eunice up the dock. "I'll just get Great-grandmother settled in her room while you help Grandpa. Okay?"

"A-okay!"

Anna slowly led Eunice, pacing her steps to match. "Did you have a good trip?"

"It was a very long drive," Eunice said.

"I'm glad the weather hasn't turned yet. We're expecting a little storm by this evening." She steadied Eunice as they stepped from the dock onto the path. "We're putting you in the downstairs suite," she explained. "Clark made a fire for you."

"That will be nice."

"I hope you can manage the stairs into the house . . . for mealtimes." Suddenly Anna felt worried. What if Eunice was too unstable to climb stairs? "Or else we can bring your meals down . . ."

"I just need to put my feet up a bit." Eunice said a bit breathlessly. "I'm worn out now, but I should be fine by dinner."

Anna got Eunice settled in her room, promising to return with a tea tray. As she hurried upstairs, she wondered if this visit was such a good idea. Although Clark had built a roof over the outdoor stairway, the weather could still sneak in on a stormy day and the thought of Eunice making her way up during a torrential rainstorm was a bit unsettling. Why hadn't she considered Eunice's age and health? Probably because Anna was so used to Hazel, who was a couple years older than Eunice, but as spry and energetic as ever. Eunice seemed to be fading fast.

To Anna's relief, by the time she returned with a tea tray complete with freshly baked pastries and fruit, Eunice looked a bit sturdier. Settled in front of the crackling fireplace, her feet were propped up on the ottoman and the jacquard throw was over her lap. All things considered, she looked at home and comfortable.

Anna arranged the tea tray on the table then sat down in the other club chair. "I'm so glad you could come, Eunice. I know we're rather rustic and this isn't exactly our best season, but I'm very pleased you and Sarah could make it."

Eunice nodded. "Speaking of Sarah, she and Clark dropped my bags off, and it sounds as if she's enticed him to take her for a quick fishing expedition before the storm comes. She is determined to catch us a fish for dinner."

"Bless her heart." Anna laughed as she poured the tea.

"This room is very nice," Eunice said. "Much more elegant than I remembered."

"Babette left me some lovely things." Anna handed her a cup. "I thought you might appreciate them."

"Thank you." Eunice took a sip. "And now I'm going to get straight to the point. I came here with a specific purpose in mind."

Anna simply nodded as she picked up her own cup of tea, leaning back in the chair, waiting for Eunice to continue.

"I realize that I owe you an apology, Anna." Eunice looked directly at her. "For years I have been very unkind to you. Before I die, and that might not be too far from now, I want to say I'm sorry."

Anna smiled sadly.

"I think back to some of the cruel things I said and did to you over the years . . . how I called you terrible names and put you down. Do you have any idea why I picked on you so much? Why I belittled you so much because . . . well . . . because of your Indian blood?"

"I'm not really sure." Anna frowned. The truth was, she'd often wondered why someone like Eunice, who could act the perfect lady at times, could be so unfeeling and coarse at other times.

"I've given it a lot of thought this past year . . . one has time to spend time thinking as one's body slows down." She sighed. "I have come to the conclusion that the reason I attacked you for your Indian heritage was because it was the only weakness I could find to attack you for."

Anna said nothing as she studied the skin over Eunice's creased brow. It was so thin that it was almost translucent.

"At least it seemed a weakness to me, Anna. Now I suspect I was wrong."

Anna smiled wistfully. "I see my Siuslaw roots as a strength. Although my own mother did not."

"Yes, and I was always threatened by your strength," Eunice confessed. "For that reason I attacked you, tried to make you seem less than you were. But I see now that it was my own weakness that made me act so ungraciously. I do hope you will forgive me."

Anna pressed her lips together. Absorbing the enormity of this confession, she took in a long, deep breath. "You are completely forgiven, Eunice."

Now there was a long silence, and Anna noticed a tear slipping down Eunice's powdery cheek. She watched as Eunice fished a wrinkled handkerchief from her sleeve and dabbed at it. "It is so easy for you to forgive." Eunice slowly shook her head. "I have never understood how that was possible . . . to forgive others when they've wounded you deeply. It is not easy for me."

"I suppose it's something I learned as a child. My grandmother was always very forgiving."

"And your own mother?"

Anna sighed. "She was not always as gracious . . . not when I was younger anyway. But as she aged, she changed."

"Yes . . . age does change us." Eunice looked out the window, toward the river. "It really is beautiful here, Anna. I can admit to that now."

"Even on a cloudy day like this, I still love it here. There's no place else I'd rather be."

Eunice took a slow sip of tea then set her cup and saucer on the side table, folding her hands in her lap. "Did Adam ever tell you about his father, Anna?"

"I don't recall him saying much. I know that Mr. Gunderson built the lumber mill and was a good provider for his family. But I never got the sense that Adam had been very close to him . . . and I know Adam was in grade school when his father died."

"Adam's father was a cruel man." Eunice pressed her lips together and shuddered. "We never spoke of him, I'm sure, because we wanted to forget. He was a harsh taskmaster, and the truth is I was not the least bit sad when he died."

"I never knew."

"No, I didn't think so."

"Did you love him when you married?" Anna was surprised she'd asked such a personal question, but there it was . . . already out there.

"*Love?*" Eunice made a sarcastic sounding laugh, almost a cackle. "No, my dear, love had nothing to do with our marriage. I wouldn't call it an arranged marriage per se . . . but it wasn't far from it. The Gundersons were a wealthy timber family while my family barely scraped by." She sighed. "It may be hard to believe, but back then all I had going for me was my appearance." She laughed again.

"I've always thought you were a very attractive woman, Eunice."

"Thank you." She made a weak smile, smoothing her hands over the throw.

"Is it your late husband . . . that you have a problem forgiving?"

Eunice nodded sadly. "You see . . . I have been taking Sarah to church. She enjoys Sunday school and I attend the services."

"That's wonderful, Eunice. I'm sure Sarah must appreciate that." Anna reached for a cookie, breaking it in two.

"She does. But I am growing increasingly worried."

"Why?" Anna leaned forward, studying Eunice's troubled expression.

"The preacher at church spoke specifically on forgiveness not long ago. He stated that, according to the Bible, we are forgiven in the same way we forgive others." She held up her hands helplessly. "And, for the life of me, I *cannot* forgive Mr. Gunderson. I do not have the slightest idea of how one does that."

"Oh . . ." Anna dabbed her mouth with a napkin.

Eunice peered intently at her. "What shall I do?"

Anna laid her napkin aside, gathering her thoughts. "This is what I believe about forgiveness, Eunice. When someone hurts us and we refuse to forgive that person . . . we might think that our resentments will punish that person, or our hostility will place that person in some sort of prison. Do you understand what I mean?"

"I think I do."

"But that kind of thinking backfires. Our refusal to forgive someone just hardens our hearts, and we are the ones who are punished. We are the ones who end up in a prison of sorts."

Eunice twisted the handkerchief in her hands. "So how do you escape this prison? How do you forgive someone when you still hate him?"

"When I need to forgive someone . . ." Anna thought specifically of the times she'd had to forgive Eunice. "First of all, I ask God to help me to do what I'm unable to do on my own. After that, I remind myself that the person who hurt me might be suffering something I don't understand. I believe that creates empathy and empathy is very empowering. Finally, I try to release my own pain."

"How do you do that?" Eunice's eyes looked hungry.

"I try to consciously let go of the anger. Sometimes I've even imagined myself bundling it together and throwing it all into the river. Then I stand there and watch it float away . . . down to the ocean, never to return."

Eunice gazed out the window with a puzzled expression. "You *throw* it into the river . . . ?"

"I'm sure that sounds overly simplistic. But I appreciate simplicity."

"Whereas I, on the other hand, have been overly complicated. At this stage of my life, it becomes painfully clear. I fear that my complications have nearly suffocated me." She sighed and leaned her head back, closing her eyes. "And now, I think I must rest."

"Yes." Anna stood, gathering the tea things. "Rest well."

Eunice didn't answer, and Anna quietly slipped out. As she returned to the house, she replayed parts of their conversation and just shook her head. Eunice was making a real effort to straighten out all the fragmented pieces of her life. As Anna stood at her kitchen sink, she prayed that forgiveness would be within Eunice's reach . . . that she would be able to let things go. Anna prayed that Eunice would find real peace and healing.

26

Anna wasn't surprised to learn that Eunice had passed on just three days after Christmas. However, she was surprised that Sarah was the one who called with this information, and even more surprised that Sarah was the one who found her great-grandmother dead on her kitchen floor.

"She was making coffee," Sarah explained sadly.

"I'm so sorry," Anna told her. "Are you all right?"

"Yeah." Sarah sniffed. "I miss her, but I knew she was ready to die."

"You *knew* this?"

"Pastor Dalton came to visit Great-grandmother before Christmas," Sarah explained. "She told him that she was going to die soon. She asked him to talk to me about it. So I wouldn't be afraid when it happened."

"Dear Eunice," Anna said gratefully. "How thoughtful of her."

"But I still got scared," Sarah confessed. "I never saw a dead person before. Not in real life anyway. I've seen it on TV. But that's different."

"Yes. But you know that dying is just a part of living, don't you?"

"I guess so."

"Everything that lives must die. It's the way we get to the next part of life."

"Pastor Dalton said that Great-grandmother is in heaven."

"I believe she is."

Sarah let out a long sigh. "I hope so. I know some people thought she was too mean to go to heaven. But you don't think that, do you?"

"Not at all, Sarah. It took your great-grandmother a long time to learn how to be kinder to people. But in the end, she did learn."

They talked awhile longer, then Anna asked about Lauren.

"Do you want to talk to Mommy?" Sarah offered. "She's right here."

Anna looked at the clock to see that it was after five o'clock, Lauren's martini hour. "Sure, Sarah, I'd like to speak to her, please."

Lauren's voice sounded tired and gruff . . . as though she wasn't eager to speak to her mother.

"I'm sorry about your grandmother, Lauren. I'm sure it must be hard on you."

"I'm sure you're very sorry." Lauren's words dripped in sarcasm.

"I am sorry," Anna protested. "I'm sure it is a great loss to you. I know you two were very close for many years."

"You're probably *glad* she's dead."

"Oh, Lauren!" Anna wondered if Sarah was listening to her mother's words.

"You never did like her, Mom. You probably wish she'd died a long time—"

"*Lauren,*" Anna said firmly. "Eunice and I got quite close recently. She came to visit me just last month and I will not listen to you going on like that. I hope that Sarah didn't hear you speaking that way."

Now there was a silence and Anna wondered if Lauren had hung up.

"I am sorry for your loss," Anna said again. "I'm sure that you'll miss her."

"Thanks for your sympathy." Now Lauren hung up.

Anna replaced the receiver and sat down at the kitchen table and cried. She wasn't crying over the end of Eunice's life. All things considered, it sounded as if Eunice had made a fairly graceful exit. No, these tears were for Lauren.

Poor, poor Lauren. What would it take to get to her? Would she follow in her grandmother's steps by waiting until she was in her final days to figure things out? Anna hoped not. She bowed her head and prayed, first for Lauren . . . and then for Sarah.

⁓⊶⊷⁓

The next few summers seemed to arrive too slowly and then, just like that, they ended too quickly. But always the highlight for Anna was getting to have Sarah spend time with them, watching her mature, depending on her more and more to help with the inn, seeing Sarah's true character, her many gifts and talents steadily emerging . . . it was purely delightful. Even as Sarah came into her preteen years in the early seventies, Anna couldn't help but be amused to see her granddaughter's fashion focus change from practical tomboy to wannabe hippie. Complete with her little tie-dyed shirts, frayed jeans, love beads, and fringed moccasins, Sarah insisted she was only exhibiting her inner self in her outward style. And, really, Anna didn't mind the changes. Not nearly as much as Sarah's parents did, particularly Donald. Sarah claimed that she often had to sneak her clothes out of the house in a paper bag just to keep her dad from seeing.

But Anna was used to seeing guests from California dressed in a similar way, and she felt that Sarah was simply going through a fashion phase. Anna even helped Sarah to construct some interesting items of clothing by transforming old pieces of lace and linens and ribbons and things into one-of-a-kind smocked tops that actually looked rather attractive, in a bohemian way. In fact, something about this manner of dress reminded Anna of how her grandmother used to create interesting garments. Of course, that also reminded Anna of how her mother would frown to see Grandma Pearl walking into the store, especially if customers were around. She'd obviously been embarrassed by her own mother's appearance. Perhaps for that reason Anna was even more determined never to treat Sarah like that. For the most part, she and Sarah were "completely simpatico," as Sarah liked to put it.

However, it was in the summer of 1975 that Anna began to grow somewhat worried for her granddaughter. Although Sarah was only fifteen, in so many ways she seemed much older. Sometimes she even seemed more mature than Lauren. Yet, being only fifteen, Sarah could also act and react like a typical adolescent. And like so many of her contemporaries, Sarah was growing increasingly impatient with her parents, teachers, and leaders in general. Anna was somewhat relieved that Sarah still seemed to respect her grandparents. However, Anna feared that wouldn't last much longer, not with Sarah questioning all forms of authority. Anna didn't voice her opinions, but she suspected there could be trouble ahead.

"Mom is just plain lazy," Sarah said one morning as she and Anna were paddling canoes on the river. Sarah had long since taken over the River Dove during the summer and was very adept at maneuvering around and was even able to catch fish from the canoe—a talent many experienced fishermen marveled over.

Anna knew better than to respond as Sarah complained about her mother. She'd already learned that to attempt to defend Lauren would only escalate the one-sided conversation into an argument. Besides, Sarah was right. Lauren was lazy.

"She never wants to do anything," Sarah continued. Now she started listing all of her mother's faults in regard to laziness in general. Finally Anna could take no more.

"I understand how you feel about your mother's lack of incentive," Anna said gently. "But I think that your mother is truly her own worst enemy in that regard."

"I've heard you say that before and it sounds like a cop out to me." Sarah's dark brows drew together. "What does it really mean?"

"It means that your mother is one of the most unhappy people I know. And I believe what others see as laziness is an inability to function. Really, Sarah, think about it. How would you feel if you lived most of your life in your bed the way that she does? Would that make you happy?"

Sarah stopped paddling, then shook her head. "Not at all. I'd hate it."

"So, while I agree with you that your mother *appears* lazy, I do feel sorry for her."

"I feel sorry for her too," Sarah said defensively. "I just do not understand her."

"Nor do I."

"She makes her own choices," Sarah continued. "I mean it's not like someone is holding a gun to her head and saying, be unhappy, stay in bed, turn yourself into a vegetable."

"That's true. But as one wise person put it—perhaps even an Indian, I'm not sure—unless you've walked a mile in someone's moccasins, you probably shouldn't judge them."

Sarah laughed. "Well, Mom would *never* wear moccasins."

Anna grinned at her. "You know what I mean. Now I'll race you back to the dock." Of course, Anna knew that Sarah would win. But at least it would put an end to this particular conversation. It wasn't that she wanted to avoid the Lauren topic altogether, it was simply that it seemed to do no good to talk about it too much. It frustrated them both.

Anna had made every attempt she could think of to help Lauren. She'd invited her for extended visits, offered to come out to Pine Ridge in the off-season to help out. She'd even offered to take Sarah on full time until Lauren got back on her feet again. But all offers were flatly turned down. "I'm perfectly fine," Lauren always told her in way that suggested Anna had stepped over a line by calling.

Anna's last call, just months ago, was because Sarah had informed her that she was seriously worried that her mom was taking too many pills. Sarah feared that Lauren's life was in danger. Naturally Anna had tried to help. But as usual, her offers were brushed off.

"I'm just fine," Lauren had said indignantly. "I went to the country club last night and I played bridge on Tuesday. Ask anyone who knows me and they will tell you that there's absolutely nothing wrong with me, *Mother.* You're the only one who seems to think there's a problem. Maybe the problem is with *you.*"

And so Anna had left it at that. Really, what choice did she have?

But to Anna, it felt as if Lauren was stuck—as if she could neither move forward or backward. Just stuck. Sarah probably thought it was even worse than that. And it seemed that no one, not even Lauren's latest psychologist, was able to help. Anna's one consolation about Lauren, at least when it came to Sarah, was that, as a result of Lauren's inabilities, Donald had seemed to step up. In many ways, he had exceeded all of Anna's expectations for him as a father. Not only that, but Ardelle had gotten more involved with Sarah after Eunice's passing. So perhaps there truly was a silver lining tucked into this perennial dark cloud named Lauren.

It wasn't until Sarah's last day at Shining Waters that she told Anna something truly unsettling. "My dad is having an affair," she stated in a matter-of-fact way. Anna concealed her reaction to this, simply nodded as she kept her eyes on the river before them and slowed the boat's engine down. They were in Clark's new fishing boat, a hefty thirty-foot cruiser that he often took out on the ocean. Heading into Florence, where Donald planned to meet them and drive Sarah back home in the same day, Anna knew they were ahead of schedule and more than halfway to town, with no need to hurry.

As the boat slowed, Anna turned to study her granddaughter's profile. Standing tall and proud, Sarah had a defiant look in her eyes. A long, dark strand of hair flew across her face, but she simply looked straight ahead with a firm jaw line. Anna considered asking if she even knew what an "affair" actually was, but then remembered that kids nowadays seemed to know a lot more about everything. Probably a result of too much television. "How do you know this?" Anna quietly asked.

"I've seen him with her."

Anna tried to hide her shock. Sarah had actually seen her father with another woman? What had she actually seen?

Sarah faced Anna now. "I haven't actually *seen* them, seen them. It's not like I caught them in bed or anything." She pushed the hair from her eyes. "But I've seen them together in Dad's car. I recognized the woman. Her name is Sharon Kross and she's a secretary at the mill. Naturally, Dad has no idea that I know about them."

"Is it possible you're wrong?" Anna asked gently. "Just because you saw them in a car together doesn't mean they are—"

"I saw them *making out* in his car, Grandma." Sarah tilted her head to one side with a sly expression. "*Kissing.*"

"Oh . . ." Anna nodded as she turned off the engine, simply letting the large craft drift downriver with current. "Then you're probably right."

"Of course I'm right." Sarah scowled. "The big question is what do I do about it?"

Steering the boat to the right side of the river, Anna bit her lip. "I honestly don't know, Sarah. What do you *want* to do about it?"

"Nothing."

Anna considered this. Really, was it a child's responsibility to do something if she thought one of her parents was having an affair? Or if the other one was using too many prescribed drugs? Where did one go to find these kinds of answers? Anna felt in over her head. She pulled the boat over to the side of the river and turned off the engine. "Sarah, I feel like I should have the answers for you. The truth is, I don't. I'm very sorry that your father is, well, possibly involved with another woman. And I'm sorry that your mother isn't doing a very good job of mothering." She let go of the wheel and put her arms around Sarah, pulling her close, hugging her tightly. "I wish I could fix everything for you. I have always wished this." She released her, pushing another strand of hair from Sarah's eyes. "But then I remember the way I was raised. And it wasn't idyllic either."

"But you grew up here, on the river." Sarah's eyes looked hungrily over the water.

Anna nodded. "Yes. But my parents had some problems too. My mother lived in fear much of the time."

"Fear of what?"

"Fear of her Indian heritage. She tried to hide it, tried to pass herself as white, even disowned her own mother more times than I care to remember. That was hard for me . . . and confusing."

Sarah smiled at her. "But you turned out okay."

Anna smiled back. "And so have you."

Sarah nodded. "And, just so you know, it's not like I'm completely devastated by what Dad's doing. I mean it seems like everyone is doing it. No big deal."

Anna wanted to challenge that, to say that it was a big deal and that no one should break a marriage vow. However, it seemed Sarah had enough to worry about.

"At least I have good friends," Sarah assured her.

"That's true," Anna agreed. One of Sarah's best friends, Kelly Rogers, had come out to stay on the river for most of July. The two teens had seemed very close. It reminded Anna of how she and Dorothy used to be as girls, and she'd been encouraged by it.

"So, really," Sarah said lightly. "I don't need parents."

"Yes, you do," Anna reminded her. "Unfortunately, you might not always be able to count on your parents . . . for everything. But you do have Clark and me, sweetheart. And you have your other grandmother too. If you ever need anything, you know you can call us. And remember you're always welcome here on the river. You're getting to an age when you might be able to make a decision like that yourself." Anna was thinking that if Lauren's marriage failed, if Donald and his new girlfriend became an issue, Sarah might need another place to live . . . it was possible that the rules would change.

"I know, Grandma." Sarah made a brave smile. "But, really, I'm okay. I'm so used to taking care of myself anyway; it's no big deal what happens with my parents. Oh, I might feel a little bummed. But as soon as school starts I'll get back to my own routines and I won't even care what Mom and Dad are up to. You know what I mean?"

Anna tried to act like she understood this as she restarted the boat's engine, but her heart longed to snatch Sarah away from her parents, to insist she stay here on the river, enroll in the high school in town, and just live a "normal" life. However, Anna knew there was probably no such thing as "normal." Not here and not in Pine Ridge. Besides that, she'd heard rumors that a lot of the local teenagers were getting involved in illegal drugs. Even if the rumors were overblown, she certainly didn't want to expose Sarah to anything like that.

To Anna's surprise, Donald was already at the docks. However, she almost didn't recognize him. Wearing a bright-colored paisley shirt and bell-bottom pants, it looked almost as if he were imitating a college kid. "Hello, Donald," she said politely, trying not to stare at the bulky gold chain around his neck. Since when had he taken to wearing jewelry?

"I got here earlier than I expected," he said as he reached for Sarah's bags. "Thought we might make it home before dark."

Anna nodded as she reluctantly handed him a duffle. "If you're sure you need to go back today."

He shrugged. "Might as well. We can still get home before dark."

"That is, unless, you want to go fishing." She was trying to think of something, anything, to entice Donald into staying another day, a way to give her an opportunity to confront him about his new girlfriend. "This is Clark's new boat and he loves taking guests out on the ocean with it. You could catch a salmon to take home with you."

He nodded as if just seeing the boat. "Nice boat. And that's a tempting offer."

"You know you're always welcome at the inn."

"I know." He sighed. "But I really need to get back." He play-fully punched Sarah in the arm as she climbed off the boat. "Hey, aren't you even going to say hello to your old man?"

"Hi, Dad," she said in a sullen tone.

He rolled his eyes upward. "Teenagers these days. Got no respect for their elders."

Anna controlled herself from reminding Donald that he hadn't exactly been a choirboy as a teen. The way he'd chased after the pretty girls had given their mothers plenty to worry about . . . those were memories she had tried to put behind her. However, it seemed that some people never outgrew their past selves.

Realizing Donald was determined to go, she exchanged final hugs with Sarah, promised to write, then told Donald to drive safely and to give Lauren her love. She watched them walking away and, with a lump growing in her throat, she slowly maneuvered the large boat away from the dock. She wasn't sure if her tears were for Lauren and a marriage that was probably doomed, perhaps from the start, or for Sarah and the challenges she faced.

But as she looked out over the blurry scene of blues and greens, like a lens out of focus, Anna suspected these tears were for herself. She was grieving. Mourning the loss of her sincere, spirited, bright-eyed, energetic girl—the child who'd believed in dreams and ideals was being replaced by a slightly jaded and somewhat cynical adolescent. And the whole thing made Anna very sad. As she guided the boat back upriver, she prayed for Sarah to remain true to herself, and then Anna prayed that she wouldn't lose her sweet Siuslaw princess forever.

27

Anna found it difficult to believe they'd been running the inn for more than fifteen years now, and harder to believe that she and Clark had been together even longer.

"Do you know that a lot of guys my age are considering retirement," Clark said as he unfolded his napkin. It was January, their off-season, as well as Clark's sixtieth birthday. Hazel had just called to wish him well, and now they were enjoying a quiet candlelit dinner for two . . . and reminiscing.

"Do you want to retire?" Anna asked.

He firmly shook his head. "Are you kidding? Retire from what? I am living the life that I love, Anna. I wouldn't change a thing."

She smiled in relief. "I don't feel old enough to retire yet. I don't even feel like I'm fifty-five," she confessed. "I remember when my mother was this age . . . and I thought she was so old."

He chuckled. "Well, you don't seem old to me, darling."

"Maybe age is simply a state of mind." She passed him the potatoes au gratin. "Take Babette. She lived like she was youthful almost her entire life. I had no idea how old she truly was until the end."

"But then there was Eunice," he pointed out. "She was younger than Mom, but she seemed to fade rather quickly."

"I think some of her lifestyle choices might've taken a toll on her health. Perhaps if she'd learned to forgive others earlier on . . ." Anna thought of Lauren now. In some ways she seemed to be following in Eunice's footsteps. But this was an evening to celebrate, not to be somber. And so she changed to Hazel. "Now your mother is an inspiration. There's someone who knows how to grow old gracefully," Anna dished out some asparagus. "It's hard to believe she's pushing eighty and still going strong."

"She is going strong, but she told me just now that this will be her last year to teach."

"Oh?"

"She said that the atmosphere on campus has changed drastically over the past several years. She says the students are apathetic and antagonistic to the point where it takes all pleasure from teaching. It's as if they just don't care."

"It seems much of the country feels the same way." She sighed. "Thanks to things like Watergate and the mess in Vietnam, Americans just seem to be fed up."

He frowned. "It's sure not like it used to be. Even during the worst of times . . . the Great Depression and the war, people maintained optimism . . . they still practiced patriotism. When I hear of kids burning flags and protesting everything and anything . . . turning on and tuning in, dropping out . . . well, it's just a shame."

Realizing the celebratory conversation was taking another dive, Anna picked up her glass of burgundy, holding it up for a toast. "Here's to you, Clark, the most wonderful man in the world and the love of my life. Happy birthday, darling!" She smiled.

His eyes glowed with warmth in the flickering candlelight. "And here's to us."

"And to growing old gracefully together." As they continued with dinner, keeping the conversation uplifting and positive, Anna told him about some new ideas she'd been considering for the inn. "I want to host some events that focus specifically on grace and mercy," she explained.

He nodded, listening.

"Ironically, Eunice is the inspiration for the idea."

"You don't say."

"I realize that many people have difficulty forgiving others, letting go of old hurts, healing from deep emotional wounds. I've had that conversation with many of our guests . . . people who have a hard time moving forward in their lives."

"You know, it almost seems that our whole country is struggling with this, Anna."

"So, in my small way, I'd like to offer a special week now and then where that is the whole focus. I would make books available, perhaps even hire an inspirational speaker and maybe some musicians."

"I like the sound of it, Anna. And I read in the paper that we have some good folk singers in town. Maybe you can hire them."

"I'll try to get the word out to our regular guests first. I thought perhaps we could send a flyer or brochure. And then I might do some advertising."

"Maybe Mom could write an article."

She nodded. "Good idea."

They came up with a few more ideas, and in the following days Anna decided on specific dates and began to implement a real plan. She had just hung up the phone after speaking to a local print shop about making flyers when it rang again. To her surprise, it was Lauren, but her voice sounded so weak and so sad, Anna knew something was seriously wrong. Her first concern was for Sarah. The last letter she'd received from her granddaughter had sounded more rebellious and angry than ever. Anna had written back, trying to share some wisdom, but she had no idea how it had been received. "Tell me what's wrong." Anna said gently.

"Everything." Lauren let out a choked sob. "My whole life is falling apart, Mom, and I am seriously considering quitting."

"Quitting what?"

"*Life.*"

"What do you—"

"I mean, I've had enough. I'm ready to call it quits, hang it up, adios amigos."

"Oh . . . Lauren." Anna tried to gather her thoughts.

"No matter what I do or how hard I try, nothing ever turns out right."

"Maybe you're not trying the right things," Anna said gently.

"What's that supposed to mean?" Lauren's voice was edged with anger now.

"Just that I worry about you, sweetheart." Anna took a deep breath. "It's just that pills and alcohol are not a substitute for happiness." There, she'd said it.

"For your information, I'm off the pills and alcohol."

Anna wondered if she'd heard her wrong. "You're no longer using prescriptions, Lauren? You've quit drinking?"

"Didn't Sarah tell you I was in a clinic during all of November and part of December?"

"She mentioned you took a vacation." Anna tried to remember exactly what Sarah had said the last time they talked. Very little of their conversation had anything to do with Sarah's parents. Anna had hoped that was a good sign.

"Yes, that's what I told Sarah, but I figured she knew the truth. Of course, she's so wrapped up in her own life, it's not as if she cares about mine."

"That's fairly typical of a teenager, don't you think?"

"Maybe . . ." Lauren let out a long sigh.

"But that's wonderful news, Lauren. If you've really gotten free of the pills and alcohol, you should be feeling pleased and proud, darling!"

"I feel like I'm a complete failure as a human being."

"Maybe you just need to adjust to—"

"Adjust to the fact that my life is completely *worthless?* Really, Mom, I don't know what the point is anymore. I have no reason to go on. Nothing, not one thing, is working for me. Nothing in my life is any better now."

"Give yourself time, Lauren."

"Time for what, Mom? More pain? After all I've done, all I get is pain and more pain. I feel like I'm beating my head against the wall. And for what?"

"Do you want me to come to Pine Ridge?" Anna offered suddenly.

"*No!*"

"But, Lauren, it sounds like you need someone to—"

"All I need is to get out of this horrible place." She started to sob now. "There's nothing here for me, Mom. *Nothing!*"

"Oh, Lauren, please, come out here. I'll do anything I can to help you, darling. It sounds like you've worked hard, you've made a good start. Let me help you now."

"I think I should come out there . . ."

Anna felt a rush of hope. "Yes," she said eagerly. "You know you're welcome here, Lauren. Please, *do come.*"

"It's weird . . ." Lauren's voice grew very quiet now. "I can't really explain it, but when I think about the river . . . it's like I can feel it calling to me. Do you think a river can do that? Actually call to someone? Or am I going crazy?"

Anna considered her words. "I do think the river attracts people to it, Lauren. I know how much I missed the Siuslaw all those years I lived in Pine Ridge."

"I never thought of it like that before . . . never really cared one way or another. But something changed when I was at the clinic. I started to hear what sounded like the river, like it was calling to me. But the shrink said it was from getting off the drugs and booze. A lot of people go crazy in those places. He said it would go away. But I still hear it sometimes. Like last night, I had this dream about the river. Then I woke up and I thought I could still hear it. I could hear the river calling to me. Do you think I can hear it, Mom?"

"I don't know." Anna felt nervous now. Maybe Lauren was experiencing some kind of delirium. Maybe she needed more professional help. Or maybe she simply needed the river. "I'm not an expert, Lauren, but I do think you should come here. I don't see what it could hurt. In fact, I'm sure it would help."

"Do you really think so?"

"Yes! Come stay with us. And if you like, we can come and get you."

"No. I can drive, Mom."

"And Sarah? I know she has school. Will she be all right without you?"

Lauren made an unhappy sounding laugh. "No worries there, Mom. Sarah is quite grown up these days. She's made it crystal clear; she has no need of a mother . . . or me."

"Yes, but—"

"Besides, she has her grandmother . . . and her father." Now Lauren started crying again.

"You're sure you're up for the drive here?" Anna asked with concern. "Remember, it's wintertime and you could have snow on the mountains and—"

"*Yes, Mother.*" Her voice grew aggravated now. "I'm not a baby. I can drive perfectly well, *thank you very much!*"

"Yes . . . I'm sure you can."

"Anyway, it'll probably take me a few days to figure everything out. I'll let you know."

"And call me if you need anything," Anna urged. "Anything at all."

It wasn't until Anna had hung up that the seriousness of the conversation fully hit her. What Lauren said about ending it all . . . was she really thinking of taking her own life? Or was she simply being melodramatic? Anna remembered back when Lauren had first found out she was pregnant, and how depressed she'd been that Donald had broken up with her. She had sometimes been overly dramatic then, even threatening to throw herself into the river a time or two. Hopefully, her talk of the river calling her had nothing to do with anything like that.

Anna went out to where Clark was working on the new boat house and told him that Lauren was coming to visit.

"That's wonderful," he said.

Anna frowned. "Yes, I'm glad she's coming." Then she explained about how Lauren had stopped using alcohol and prescribed medications, as well as what she'd said about wanting to end her life and how the river was calling. "She said she could actually hear it, Clark. Do you think that's normal?"

He shrugged. "Who knows what's normal for her? Do you think that her years of alcohol and drug abuse have given her hallucinations?"

"I have no idea. Do you think it's foolish to have her come if she's really unwell?" Anna glanced out to the river. This morning it was gray and somber, flowing fast with lots of undercurrents. Maybe a lot like Lauren.

"I don't know." He scratched his head. "But at least you won't be distracted with guests. Having her here in the off-season should make it easy for you to give Lauren all your attention."

Anna nodded. "If you don't mind, I think I'll insist she stays in the house with us. I don't like the idea of her being alone in a cabin . . . or even in the suite."

"Yes, I think that's wise."

Anna went to work getting Sarah's room ready for Lauren to occupy. Hopefully Sarah wouldn't mind and, really, there was no reason she should know. Anna also put in an order for groceries, wanting to ensure she had some of the things that Lauren used to like. However, she hadn't seen Lauren for several years. In many ways, she didn't even know her daughter. Not really.

Anna was caught completely off guard when Lauren arrived in town the very next day. Because Henry had passed away a couple of years ago, there was no boat service on the river these days, but Lauren called from the grocery store and Clark insisted on going out to fetch her.

"I've got the roof on the boat," he assured her as she handed him an umbrella for Lauren. "And there are some blankets in there if she gets cold."

"I could come," Anna offered, looking out to where the rain was blowing sideways with the gale-force winds.

"No." He firmly shook his head. "You go ahead and stay here and stay warm."

"I'll get dinner started." She kissed him. "Thank you."

"We'll be okay," he assured her. "You and I . . . we can handle this."

She just nodded. She understood the meaning of that statement. She knew he was aware of how concerned she felt for Lauren. Last night she'd had a nightmare about Lauren. Waking up, she'd felt cold and shaken and confused. Then she'd prayed. Right now, prayer seemed her only tool.

28

The first two days of Lauren's visit were cloudy and gloomy and generally uneventful. It was reminiscent of the time Lauren had spent with them at the beginning of her pregnancy. Aside from mealtimes, where she would sullenly pick at her food, Lauren stayed to her room and mostly slept. Anna decided that was probably for the best. Let her emerge on her own timing. She'd been through a lot and perhaps just needed some peace and quiet.

To Anna's relief, she saw no sign of pills or alcohol. It seemed that Lauren really had managed to get beyond her addictions. However, it was clear that something else was still wrong. Whether it was depression or just sadness, Anna couldn't be sure. On the third day the weather turned sunny and Anna enticed Lauren to sit out on the upper deck for their afternoon tea.

"Clark says we're going to have a spell of warm weather," Anna said as she tucked a lap robe over Lauren's legs. Lauren looked pale and thin, with dark shadows under her eyes. And she had aged considerably. Anna had been enticing her to take some herbal supplements, hoping to build her up physically. But it was Lauren's spirit that was most disturbing. She seemed partially dead inside. "I'm so proud of you," Anna said as she refilled her cup with chamomile tea. "So glad that you've really managed to get free of your chemical dependence. I've read up on it a bit, and it sounds like it does take time to recover completely. So I hope you'll go easy on yourself, dear. Give yourself time."

Lauren looked at her with sad blue eyes. "What if time can't help me, Mom?"

Anna made a small, forced smile. "But you wouldn't know that it couldn't help, dear, not until enough time passed."

"Donald has left me." Lauren turned to look toward the river now.

"I'm sorry."

"After all I did to get well. He—he left me, Mom." Her voice broke.

Anna didn't know what to say. She handed Lauren a handkerchief.

"I did it for him, Mom."

"Did what?"

"Went to the clinic—got clean and sober. Donald had threatened to leave me if I didn't go. So I went . . . for him."

"But didn't you do it for yourself, Lauren? It's your life. Didn't you do it for you? And what about Sarah?"

Lauren shrugged. "I did it for Donald, Mom."

"But he left anyway . . ."

"Yeah." Lauren called him a bad name.

Anna bit her lip and wished she could think of something encouraging to say.

"I asked him . . ." She paused to wipe her nose. "I asked him if he wouldn't have left me if I was still, you know, using the pills and stuff."

"What did he say?"

"That he'd decided to leave me long ago. And that he would've left me whether or not I'd gone to the clinic."

"I am sorry," Anna said again. "But I'm curious. If he left you, who is with Sarah right now?"

Lauren gave her an exasperated look. "He's still living at home, Mom. He agreed to stick around until I get back. But our marriage is over. He has emotionally left me."

Anna reached over and put her hand on Lauren's, looking deeply into her daughter's eyes. "I know it's hard, dear. But the important thing is that you've taken the steps to get healthy. Your life is on track. I know it must seem hard for you right now, but you are on a good road."

"A good road?" Lauren narrowed her eyes. "*Alone?*"

"You're not alone."

"I mean alone without Donald, Mom."

Anna wanted to question if she'd ever really had Donald in the first place.

"I'm not one of those women, Mom, the ones who are all liberated and able to be single." She shook her head. "That is not me!"

"And that's fine, Lauren. There are other men. And when you get really healthy and when you are on top of this, you will—"

"I am thirty-six years old, Mom."

Now, despite her resolve to be understanding, Anna laughed. "Thirty-six is quite young."

"Thirty-six going on seventy," Lauren said bitterly.

"I was nearly forty when I married Clark."

"You're different."

"Yes, but you are changing, Lauren. I can sense it. You are going to get stronger. You're going to embrace life and—"

"Maybe I should embrace life right now." Lauren set her teacup aside and stood so suddenly that the blanket fell to her feet. "I think I want to take a walk."

Anna blinked. "Yes, I think that's a good idea. Do you want company?"

"No." Lauren put her hand on the railing. "I need to do this on my own, Mom."

Anna just nodded. "All right."

Now Lauren went down the stairs and Anna just stood there watching her leave. "Have a good walk, dear."

Lauren didn't answer, just kept going.

Anna felt uneasy as she picked up the blanket and tea things. Perhaps it was unwise to let Lauren go off by herself. Lauren had never really been much of an outdoors enthusiast. What if she wandered too far, or got lost? Anna decided to clean up the tea dishes and set some things out for dinner and then she would go on a walk of her own. She would try to act perfectly natural, not as if she was worried about her daughter's state of mind.

After about thirty minutes, Anna wandered down for her walk. First she wandered around the grounds, and even asked Clark, who was painting exterior trim on the cabins, if he'd seen her. "No." He smiled. "But that's great she decided to get out and get some fresh air and exercise. That should help lift her spirits." He held up his paintbrush. "I'm making hay while the sun shines."

"And I won't keep you from it." Anna continued, going down the main nature trail, the one the guests usually liked most because it went along the meadow, through the woods, and finally returned along the river. Clark had built benches and stopping spots along the way. And Anna had enticed wild-flowers to grow in certain areas. All in all, it was a charming little hike and only took about an hour to complete. As Anna came to each rest stop, she hoped to discover Lauren pausing to catch her breath. But there was no sign of her.

It wasn't until Anna was on the river portion of the trail that she began to wonder about the boats. Was it possible that Lauren had taken a boat out? Lauren had never been very interested in boats before, and Anna hadn't heard any of the boats' motors starting up, but with all Lauren's talk of the river calling her, perhaps she'd taken out a rowboat.

Anna stopped by the boathouse to see that all the rowboats and canoes appeared to be in place. Then she looked over to the dock, where she kept her own canoe, the River Dove, handy for her own use. She realized it was missing!

"Clark!" she called out as she jogged over to where she'd last seen him. "Do you think Lauren took my canoe out?"

He set his brush back in his pail and frowned. "I don't know. I haven't seen—"

"My canoe is gone," she breathlessly told him. "Why would it be gone?"

His brow creased. "Do you think she—"

"I don't know." She turned, calling over her shoulder. "But I'm going to take the boat out to look."

"Maybe you should check the house first," he called back. "Make sure she's not there."

"Yes." She paused. "You're right."

"If she's not there, tell me, and I'll take a boat out too."

She was not there and within minutes, both Clark and Anna were in motorboats, Clark going east and Anna going west, promising to meet back in thirty minutes, which would be shortly before the sunset. With a pounding heart, and silently praying, Anna wove the boat back and forth along the river, scouring along the inlet and marsh areas and even calling out from time to time. But there was no sign of Lauren or the canoe. Finally Anna knew it was time to return to the inn. Perhaps

Clark had found Lauren by now. Maybe they were both sitting in front of a crackling fire, enjoying a cup of hot cocoa. But when she reached the dock, Clark's boat wasn't there. And it was getting dusky.

She ran up to the house, yelling for both Lauren and Clark, but when no one answered, she grabbed a coat and a couple of flashlights and blankets then ran back down and tossed them into the boat. She was heading upriver. Less than a mile up, she spotted Clark's boat alongside what looked like Jim Flanders's skiff. But as she got closer, she could tell from Clark's expression that something was wrong.

"Jim spotted the canoe," Clark quickly told her. "Over by his place."

"And Lauren?" Anna looked hopefully at Jim.

"The canoe was upside down," Jim explained. "I was worried you'd had problems. So I ran down there to check. But no one seemed to be with it. I looked around awhile, just to be sure something wasn't wrong, then I hauled the canoe over to my dock." He held his hands up.

Anna looked at Clark. "But what about Lauren?"

"She's not at the house?"

"I checked. She's not there." Anna felt tears coming to her eyes. "We need to keep looking!" She handed him a flashlight and blanket.

"I'll keep looking too," Jim told her.

"The canoe was at your place." She pointed upriver. "Which means it could've drifted from even higher up the river."

Clark suggested they split up and Jim said he'd get a couple more neighbors to help. No one actually said what they were looking for, but Anna could see it in their eyes. They were looking for a body.

With trembling hands, she guided the boat along the south side of the river, shining the flashlight along the edges, occasionally calling out Lauren's name. But the further she went, the more disheartened she felt. She could see other boats out now, maybe a half dozen or more, all moving slowly, shining lights through the darkening sky and river. The sounds of motors rumbling, the occasional call or whistle. The eerie image filled her with dread and she knew she was close to despair. "Lauren!" she cried out. "Where are you?"

Anna continued to search and to pray, but as minutes turned into hours, her hopes of finding her daughter alive grew dimmer and dimmer. She hated to give in to her dark doubts, but ever since this hunt had begun, Lauren's words had been haunting her. Had the river been calling to her? Had Lauren believed the river was her way out, her escape from the pain of her life? Had Lauren taken her own life?

The wind was picking up now and Anna's boat ran into a partially submerged log, nearly throwing Anna out of the boat. She looked out over the area where the other boats were slowly searching, shining their lights, and realized she couldn't ask her neighbors to risk their lives like this.

"Clark!" she yelled loudly, making her way to the center of the river. "Come here!" Before long, the other boats clustered around her. She knew that they thought she'd found something. Instead she thanked them for their help. "I can't ask you all to stay out like this," she said, choking back tears. "It's getting cold and windy and I just can't expect you to—"

"Don't you worry about us," Barry Danner called to her. "We'll keep looking until we find her." Barry was Dorothy's brother. He and his wife, Janice, had retired to the river several years ago.

"I just don't want anyone getting hurt," she said between her tears. "And I have to tell you that there's a chance that, well—" Now she broke down completely.

"Janice, you go with Anna," Barry insisted. "You get her home. This is men's work."

"Yes," Clark agreed. "Thank you."

Soon Janice climbed into Anna's boat and took over the helm. Meanwhile, Anna hunched over and let the tears just flow. Back at the inn, Janice walked Anna up the stairs and, once they were inside, Anna confided her worst fears to Janice.

Janice hugged Anna. "Dorothy has told me a bit about Lauren's struggles. But don't give up, Anna. I've been praying all evening for Lauren and I have a feeling that God isn't finished with her earthly life yet."

Anna wiped her tears and put the kettle on. "I hope you're right." She looked out the window, over the darkened river and swallowed hard. "More than anything in this world, I hope you're right."

As they had tea, Anna felt guilty for being so weak. "I should be out there looking for Lauren too," she told Janice. "Maybe I can go back out now. I can't just—"

"No," Janice insisted. "We'll wait here The men will handle it."

Anna stood and began pacing now, wringing her hands with each step.

"Do you have any guests now?" Janice asked. "I know this is the off-season."

"No. Not until the first weekend of February." Anna suspected Janice was just trying to distract her.

"But you have someone in Babette's house?"

"No." Anna shook her head, continuing to pace. "Not now."

"But I noticed the light on as we were coming to the inn."

Anna turned and stared at her. "What light?"

"In Babette's house."

Anna frowned. "What do you mean?"

"As we came downriver, on our way here, I saw the light on. In the kitchen."

"A light in the kitchen?" Anna was trying to process this. "But no one is . . ." She stopped pacing. "Do you think? I mean, is it possible? Babette's house isn't that far from where Jim Flanders found the canoe." Anna was already grabbing for her coat. "I'm going over there to check."

"I'll come too."

Soon Anna was pulling up to Babette's dock. Janice jumped out and tied it off and they both ran up the trail to the house. Halfway up, Anna stopped in her tracks, pointing to the dimly-lit front window where a white shrouded figure was moving. "What—is that?"

Janice let out a little shriek. "A ghost!"

Anna grabbed Janice's hand and together they continued up to the house where, with a trembling hand, Anna beat loudly on the door. Then to her surprise and delight, Lauren opened the door. With a white comforter wrapped around her like a cape, her face was pale and drawn. "Mom!" she cried.

Anna took Lauren in her arms. "I thought you were dead."

"I tried to call the inn," Lauren said. "No one answered."

Anna turned to Janice. "Will you go tell the men, please? To call off the search."

Janice nodded with wide eyes. "Yes. Of course. Oh, I'm so glad Lauren's okay!" She paused to hug both of them. "I'll go tell them now!"

"Do be careful," Anna called out happily, as she closed the door. Then she turned to Lauren. "What on earth happened?" She pointed to the comforter. "And why are you wearing that?"

"Because my clothes were soaking wet." Lauren led Anna into the living room where a pitiful fire was smoldering, "I don't even know why I took your canoe, Mom. I was so angry and confused. I honestly don't even remember getting into it or what I planned to do. But there I was just paddling away and I'm sure I wasn't being very careful. You know I've never been very good in a canoe." She sat down in an easy chair and sighed loudly. "I accidentally let go of the paddle and it was caught in the current and I tried to grab it, and the next thing I knew, I was in the water."

"Oh, dear." Anna went over to poke the fire to life, layering on some more dry kindling and a couple more small logs.

"And you know I've never been much of a swimmer."

Anna nodded, sitting down across from her, listening.

"The water was freezing cold, and it was moving pretty fast too." She looked at Anna with wide eyes. "I was so shocked, but I started to dog-paddle for shore and suddenly I was being pulled down. It must've been an undercurrent, sucking me down and turning me around. I fought to get back up to the surface, but the force of the water wouldn't let go. It was like I was stuck. Like a giant hand was holding me down."

"*Oh, Lauren!*"

She nodded somberly. "I really thought that was it for me. I was going to drown. I was going to die." She pulled the comforter more tightly around her chin. "But in that same moment, I realized I didn't want to die. I had thought I wanted to die before, that I had nothing to live for. But suddenly I changed my mind."

Anna studied her closely. "You really didn't want to die?"

"No." Lauren firmly shook her head. "In a split second, I realized that I really, really wanted to live. And yet there I was about to drown—for real. Isn't that ironic?"

Anna just nodded.

"So I kicked my legs and I flailed my arms, and the whole time I was praying, begging God to help me. I wanted to breathe the air again. *I wanted to live.*" She stood now. "And when I made it to the surface I was so happy. I knew I wanted to live—really live. Can you believe it?"

Anna stood up and took Lauren in her arms again. "I can believe it, Lauren. You have so much ahead of you. So much to look forward to. Of course you want to live!"

"And you know what I think?" Lauren had tears in her eyes.

"What?"

"I think the river helped save me."

Anna just nodded.

"It was the river calling to me. And it allowed me to fall into it. And then it tried to give me what I thought I wanted."

"By holding you down?"

"Yes. But then it gave me a second chance."

Anna smiled. "The river is a good one for that. Second chances."

"I honestly don't know how I made it to shore," Lauren continued. "I can't even remember exactly. All I remember is that when I climbed out I was freezing cold. It was just getting dark and I saw this house up here and I climbed up the hill and kind of just collapsed on the porch for a while. When I came too, I was shivering and shaking from the cold. So I banged on the door, but no one came. And, well, I guess I broke in."

"You *broke in*?" Anna hadn't noticed any damage.

"Actually, I found a key under the flowerpot." She made a sheepish smile.

Anna nodded, remembering where she'd hidden a key.

"Do you think I'll get in trouble?" Lauren looked around the pretty room. "It's such a pretty house. Do you know who owns it?"

Anna chuckled. "As a matter of fact . . . I do."

"Who?"

"I do."

Lauren blinked. "What?"

"I own this house. It used to belong to Babette. I'm sure I brought you here once when you were a girl. Don't you remember?"

Lauren shook her head.

Now Anna explained how Babette had left it to her and how she sometimes rented it to vacationers. "But most of the time it's just empty." She ran a finger over the dusty side table. "I suppose I should consider selling it . . . someday."

"Don't sell it," Lauren told her. "It's a wonderful house."

"No, I won't sell it. Not anytime soon. Sarah loves it too." Anna went over to the window. Looking out over the river, she saw the lights of a boat pulling into the dock. Probably Clark.

"You know, Mom, it feels like both the river and this house saved me today. Does that sound ridiculous?"

Anna turned to look at her daughter. "No, it doesn't sound ridiculous at all. I think that this river and this house, and perhaps the well wishes of Babette up there in heaven, combined with a number of people praying and searching for you down here, as well as God himself . . . were all at work to save you today." She smiled. "And I'm so thankful they did, Lauren. Infinitely thankful."

29

In the days following Lauren's near-drowning, Anna got to know her daughter in a whole new way. For the first time that Anna could remember, Lauren was being painfully honest about herself, her life, and many of the bad choices she'd made along the way. Anna had tried to conceal her shock when Lauren admitted to having had an affair ten years ago.

"So I guess it's not fair to blame Donald for everything," Lauren conceded as they folded laundry together.

"Did you know that Sarah's aware of Donald's infidelities?"

Lauren paused from folding a towel. "Well, I guess that doesn't surprise me."

"I think it was upsetting for her."

"I doubt she's too worried about it now."

"Why not?"

Lauren laughed. "Haven't you heard?"

"What?" Anna paused from ironing a pillowcase.

"Our Sarah has her first boyfriend."

"Oh . . . ?" Anna felt a small rush of worry.

"Oh, yeah. She thinks I don't know about it. But I heard her talking on the phone the night before I left. His name is Zane Emerson. And Sarah is smitten."

"Have you met him?"

"No. I think his family is new to town."

"Do you know *anything* about him? How old he is? Where he lives?"

Lauren laughed. "You sound like a mother hen."

"Well, I do feel protective of her. Sarah's been through a lot." Anna sat down the steaming iron.

"Sarah is a smart girl. She knows how to take care of herself."

Anna wasn't so sure. Even so, she knew there was no point in upsetting Lauren about this. So far, Lauren seemed to be getting calmer and steadier each day. And, really, what was so concerning about Sarah's first boyfriend? After all, she was going on sixteen and kids seemed to grow up faster these days. Still, Anna felt concerned. And she hoped that Donald was doing a better job of being a father than he'd done of being a husband.

To Anna's relief, Lauren seemed in no hurry to get home. More and more she seemed to be settling into the slow, easy pace of life on the river. And she was helping out too. Sometimes it seemed like more work to show Lauren how to perform a simple task than to just do it herself, but Anna believed it was worth the effort. As business in the inn picked up, Anna discovered that Lauren was gaining more confidence, both in her ability to manage certain housekeeping chores and in herself.

As spring vacation drew near, a time when the inn was usually fully booked, Anna asked Lauren about inviting Sarah to come out for a visit. "I thought the two of you might enjoy staying in Babette's house," Anna explained. "It would be a good chance for you to get a little better acquainted with your daughter."

Lauren's eyes lit up. "You know, that's not a bad idea."

"Do you want to call her?"

Now Lauren frowned. "It might go better if you call her, Mom. The two of you seem to have a better connection."

Anna nodded. "Sometimes it's like that between the generations. I always felt more at ease around my grandmother than my mother."

After dinner, Anna called Sarah. First she visited with her a bit, then she told her about how well Lauren was doing. Then she explained her idea about having Sarah and Lauren staying in Babette's house.

"I already have plans for spring vacation."

"Oh . . . ?"

"Yeah. A bunch of us are going to a concert."

"A concert? Wouldn't that be a one-day event?"

"Actually, it's a series of concerts. It'll be really cool. We're going to camp at this park."

"We . . . ?"

"Oh, you know, Kelly and me, and some of our other friends from school. Then there will be all these other kids there too. We'll all just hang out and listen to music and stuff."

"And your father knows about this?"

"Sure."

"I've read about some of these concert gatherings, Sarah. Often there are illegal drugs present and—"

"Oh, *Grandma!*" Sarah's voice was full of disappointment. "I thought that you, of all people, trusted me more than that."

"I do trust you, Sarah. Completely. But I worry about other kids . . . I'm not sure I trust them."

"Well, I'll be with my friends, Grandma. You can trust them. They're good kids. Like me."

"Yes . . ." Anna said slowly. "I'm sure they're good kids. And I know you're a good kid. But my concern is just that . . . you're still a kid, Sarah. And I suppose it's selfish on my part, but I just don't want you to grow up too quickly."

Sarah laughed. "Don't worry, I won't. And I'll tell you what. If it's okay for Kelly to come out there with me, we'll both come, after the event is over. Will that make you happy?"

"What makes me happiest is knowing that you are well and happy, Sarah. And, of course, I would love to see you. And you know that Kelly is welcome. Any of your friends are welcome. Well, as long as we have room."

"You are the best grandmother in the universe!"

"Well . . ."

"But I have to go."

"Oh . . ." Anna said knowingly. It was a Friday night. "Do you have a date with Zane?"

"How did you know?"

"A little bird told me."

"I can't believe Mom figured that one out." She sounded honestly surprised.

"Your mom is getting better every day, Sarah. I really think you'll barely recognize her when you get here."

"Well, I'll have to see that to believe it."

"Then you should see your mother in less than two weeks, sweetheart. And, please, do take care and *be smart!*"

As it turned out, Sarah did not see her mother, or her grandmother, in two weeks. To Anna and Lauren's disappointment, she never made it out to the river during spring break at all. And, although her apology sounded sincere, her excuse was flimsy. "Kelly is putting together a surprise birthday party for her boyfriend and I promised to help," she told Anna on the night before she was supposed to arrive.

"I will miss you," Anna told her.

"I really am sorry."

289

"I'm just glad you made it home from your concert camp out in one piece," Anna said.

"Yeah . . . it wasn't exactly like I thought it would be." Sarah's tone was hard to decipher.

"Was it a disappointment?"

"No . . . not exactly. Just different." Then she claimed she needed to go and, once again, Anna felt cut off and distant. When she explained Sarah's change of plans to Lauren, she seemed only mildly surprised.

"You know Sarah has a mind of her own, Mom. Better get used to it."

"I'm thankful she has a mind of her own. I'll just miss her."

Lauren seemed dismayed. "But now that Sarah's not coming, I suppose I won't be moving over to Babette's house tomorrow."

Anna considered this. "Well, I don't see any reason for you not to go over there, if you want. That is, if you're all right about being alone."

"Really?" Lauren brightened. "You don't mind if I go over there?"

"Why not? You've already cleaned the place up and freshened the linens and even put in some food. Why not enjoy it?"

"Thanks, Mom."

"And if you have time, maybe you can start working on the gardens." Anna had already pointed out some maintenance that the lavender and other plants needed. Of course, she'd assumed Sarah would be there to help too. But perhaps this would be a good test for Lauren. What and how much would she be able to do on her own?

"And, don't worry, I'll still come back and help you over here too," Lauren assured her as Anna and Clark helped her to load her bags into a boat that evening. "I'll make sure to be here in time to do lunches and I'll stick around until after dinner to help clean up too."

Anna hugged her. "Thank you, Lauren. You don't know how much I've appreciated your help."

Clark took Anna's hand as they watched the little boat cutting through the smooth surface of the water. It was hard to believe only six weeks had passed since that awful night when Anna had felt certain she'd lost her only daughter. How was it possible for a woman to grow up so much, in such a short amount of time?

"Do you think she can handle it okay on her own?" Clark asked as they walked back to the house.

"I think so." Anna nodded. "And even if she has difficulty getting back here to help me, I don't think I'll really mind. As long as she stays on track over there. Mostly I just want her to succeed, you know?"

He squeezed her hand. "I do."

Several teens were horsing around in the play area. They were some local kids Anna had hired to help at the inn this week. They came each morning in time to clean up after breakfast then worked all day until after dinner. So far the kids were having such a good time three of them had already signed on to return for summer. Working at Shining Waters Inn was becoming the premium summer job in the area for young people. And Anna loved having them here.

"Maybe we should offer to hire Sarah and her friends this summer," Anna said as they went inside.

"I see where you're going with this." Clark closed the door. "You think if they were all on the payroll, it would be easier to keep your granddaughter nearby."

"Is that too manipulative?" Anna sighed. "I want Sarah to visit us because she wants to . . . not because we pressure her."

Clark hugged her. "I know you're disappointed she didn't come. But I also know how much Sarah loves you, Anna. Even if she goes through a rough patch of adolescence for a while, she'll be back with you before long. Count on it."

Anna nodded. "I'm not naïve enough to believe that Sarah will escape adolescence unscathed. I just hope she fares better than her mother did." She chuckled. "In some ways it seems like Lauren has barely emerged from her adolescence . . . it's been a long time coming. Even so, I'm glad she did."

Lauren's progress seemed to be ongoing and permanent. Not only did she keep her promise to continue helping at the inn during the remainder of spring vacation, she volunteered to take on even more responsibilities as the season kicked more fully into gear. It seemed as if she couldn't learn things fast enough. And new challenges no longer intimidated her. By May, Lauren was helping with the business side of things as well as handling much of the shopping too. She continued living in Babette's house and seemed to enjoy her independence. And she even grew fond of gardening.

"I love Babette's house," she told Anna one afternoon. They were going over some bookkeeping details for the upcoming summer. "But if you need to use the house for paying guests, I'll be fine moving back here."

"I don't think that's necessary." Anna removed her reading glasses. "Why not just plan to stay put for the duration of summer?"

"I can hardly believe it, but I honestly think I could live there happily forever. Every morning I wake up and look out over the river and, whether it's sunny and sparkling or gray and gloomy, I just feel so glad to see it. Being in that house, living next to the river, caring for the flowers, I just love it, Mom."

Anna smiled. "Do you know how happy that would make Babette?"

"And you too?"

"Of course, Lauren. It makes me very, very happy."

Lauren peered curiously at her. "But you don't look very, very happy, Mom. Is something wrong?"

Anna paused to consider her next words. "The truth is, I'm starting to feel worried about Sarah."

Lauren frowned. "Why?"

"Last night I called her. We didn't talk for long . . . and I didn't want to mention it to you, but it worries me. She sounds different."

"Of course she's different, Mom. She's a *teenager*."

"It was something beyond that, Lauren. And when I asked her about coming here for summer, and if she planned to bring Kelly and her other friends, you know my idea to have them work here and earn money, well, Sarah didn't sound terribly interested."

Lauren looked concerned now. "That is different. Do you think she's actually considering not coming?"

Anna simply nodded.

"Sarah was usually counting the days until school ended by this time. She'd be all packed and ready to go two weeks before summer vacation began. And I really thought she'd be thrilled to have her friends come here with her—that was such a great plan, Mom."

"Apparently it wasn't great enough."

"I don't understand this at all. It really doesn't sound like her."

"I know . . . like I said, she seemed different. Our conversation felt uncomfortable, as if we weren't really connecting. I finally asked if anything was wrong, but she was quick to claim that everything was fine. So I asked about her dad and she acted as if nothing had changed with him either. I even asked her if she needed you to come home."

Lauren nodded. "I would go home . . . if Sarah wanted me."

"She said she doesn't need that either." Anna rocked the pen between her fingers. "But I'm not so sure."

"Should I call her?"

"I don't think it would hurt."

"When I get back home after dinner tonight, I will definitely call her. And I'll offer to go home . . . if she wants me there. And maybe even if she doesn't." Lauren ran her fingers through her shoulder-length, golden-brown hair, now tinged with gray. It was no longer that flashy platinum blond, but Anna felt it actually made Lauren seem younger and softer somehow. "Somehow I will try to find out what's going on with her."

As it turned out, Lauren had even more difficulty getting through to Sarah. Anna wasn't particularly surprised when Lauren reported on her phone call. Just disappointed.

"I don't know what to do with her," Lauren confessed as they cleaned up after breakfast the next morning. "She insisted that she didn't need me to come home. And she pointed out that if I came home, Donald would have to move out." Lauren sighed loudly. "As if I was forcing him out of his own home. Can you imagine?"

"It is awkward."

"So do I stay here? Or do I go home?"

"I honestly don't know, Lauren."

"This generation of kids is different," Lauren said. "They seem to be a lot more independent than I was."

"Independence can be good." Anna dried a platter.

"But I think it can be bad too." Lauren set a saucepan in the dish drainer. "And I'm afraid it's all my fault, Mom." She turned to Anna with tear-filled eyes. "If I'd been a better parent, if I'd tried harder . . . I know Sarah must blame me for a lot of her—"

"It does no good to throw blame around."

"Sarah said she wasn't even sure if she even wanted to come out here this summer," Lauren confessed. "I asked her if it was because of me. I told her that if my presence here was the problem, I would go home." She used a dishtowel to wipe her tears. "I don't want to go back there, Mom. But I will do it if I have to—I will do it for Sarah."

"Oh, Lauren." Anna felt her own eyes filling with tears now.

"I thought maybe I was the reason—that she didn't want me to be here while she was here. But she told me that had nothing to do with it."

"Did she tell you why she didn't want to come?" Suddenly Anna wondered if it was because of her—had she been too pushy, too intrusive? She knew teens needed their privacy. Maybe Anna had crossed over some invisible line.

"She said I wouldn't understand."

Anna just shook her head. "I guess all we can do is be patient and pray for her to come to her senses, Lauren. Maybe a few days of being stuck there in Pine Ridge will make her think twice. She's always enjoyed her time here. And with the other teen workers, she'd be sure to have fun. Plus, there's Clark's new boat and the ocean fishing expeditions. Sarah liked that so much last summer."

"I just don't know what to say, Mom." Lauren set the tea towel down. "Except that I'm sorry. I told Sarah I was sorry too. I still can't help but think it's my fault. I wish I could go back and do everything differently now. It wouldn't be easy, but I'd do it—for Sarah's sake."

"All you can do is keep moving forward, Lauren. Both for you and for Sarah. You need to keep doing your best. In time, Sarah will come around. I know she will."

"She kept making a point of telling me that she was almost sixteen and that she was going to get her driver's license," Lauren shook her head, "acting as if that meant she was all grown-up. But since when is sixteen grown-up? I just don't understand."

Anna didn't really understand either. But she knew there wasn't anything she could do about it. Just like Grandma Pearl would say . . . everyone has to paddle her own canoe. Anna just hoped that Sarah's canoe wasn't about to be swept over a waterfall.

30

A couple of weeks into June, and not long before Sarah's birthday, Donald called the inn to ask if Sarah was there. "Here?" Anna grew hopeful. "Is she coming here, Donald?"

"I don't know."

"What do you mean you don't know?"

"I mean she took off and she didn't tell me *where* she was going." He sounded irritated.

Anna sat down on her bed. "When did she leave?"

"I'm not sure."

"What do you mean you're not sure?"

"Well, she and I got into a big fight a few nights ago. The next morning I went to work, as usual, and I figured she was off with her friends, probably trying to teach me a lesson. I guess I sort of came and went . . . just like we always do. It wasn't until Mabel said something that I realized Sarah wasn't even here."

"May I ask what you fought about, Donald?"

"Does it matter?"

"It might."

"Fine. If you must know, it was over my girlfriend. She was here at the house and Sarah didn't much like it."

"Oh . . ."

"Anyway, I reminded Sarah that this was *my* house too, and that I'm the one who goes to work and pays the bills and that I can have people over here if I want to."

"I see . . ."

"Don't judge me!" he snapped. "You don't know what it's like around here. First Lauren falls apart on me. Now Sarah's acting like this. You don't know what I've been through."

"No, I don't know what you've been through, but mostly I'm concerned about Sarah, Donald. What makes you think she might've come this way?"

"Because she's not with Kelly. And that's where I figured she'd be."

"Is it possible that Kelly is simply helping to hide Sarah, to get back at you?"

"I know for a fact Sarah is not there. I just spoke to Kelly's mother. She assured me that they haven't seen Sarah for a couple of days."

"So Sarah's been missing for *how* many days?"

"Two or three."

"Well, she's certainly not here." Anna stood and stared out the window. "And we haven't heard from her."

"Well, if you do hear from her, could you please let me know?"

"Of course. But, in the meantime, what do you intend to do about this?"

"I guess I should call the police."

A chill ran through Anna. "Yes . . . you need to do that."

"Although I'm not sure there's much they can do. If she doesn't want to be found, that is."

"Why would she not want to be found?"

"Because I think she's run off with that no-good boyfriend of hers."

"Zane?"

"Yeah. I went by his place and he was gone too. No one seems to know or even care about where he's gone off to either."

"And he's been gone several days as well?"

"It sounds like it. He's older than Sarah. Just graduated and I suppose he thinks he's grown up enough to take off and take Sarah with him." Now Donald let loose with some off-color language.

"You really think he and Sarah . . ." Anna took in a deep breath.

"Yeah. But that's not even the worst of it."

"It gets worse?" She felt shaky inside.

"You bet. This Zane is a druggie."

"Oh, Donald! What makes you say that?"

"All you have to do is to look at how he dresses and his long, shaggy hair to know it's true. I'm sure that everyone in town thinks so too. Why Sarah ever took up with someone like that is way beyond me."

"Oh, dear!" Anna felt sickened.

"Well, I better call the police and tell them to start looking for her."

"Please, Donald, let us know as soon as you find out any-thing. We'll do the same." She hung up the phone and went out to the living room where Clark was just bringing in a box of groceries. Holding back her tears as she set down the box, she tried to calmly tell him about Sarah. But before she could finish, she was in his arms and sobbing.

"Is it possible she's coming here?" he asked after she'd finally managed to pour out the whole story.

"Oh, I wish she'd come here." Anna was pacing now, trying to think of a plan, wishing there was something she could do, but knowing it was out of her hands.

"I'll finish unloading the groceries," he told her. "I expect you'll need to tell Lauren."

"Yes . . . Lauren." Anna felt a heavy sadness as she went to look for Lauren. How was she going to break this to her? And especially after Lauren had been making such great progress? What if this set her back? Anna knew that Lauren blamed herself for some of Sarah's recent problems. How would she react to this?

Anna found Lauren with some of the workers. Waiting until Lauren was finished explaining the new work roster to them, Anna asked her to take a walk.

"Is something wrong?" Lauren asked as Anna led them down the trail.

Anna just nodded. "It's Sarah."

"Oh, Mom." Lauren stopped walking and grabbed Anna's arm. "Please, just tell me—tell me *now.*" Her eyes were full of fear.

Anna quickly explained about Sarah's fight with Donald and how she was now missing. "And Donald thinks she ran off with Zane." Anna took in a deep breath and waited.

"Oh, no . . ." Lauren slowly shook her head, slowly started to walk again.

"Donald is contacting the police."

"Oh, dear!"

"I don't know what else to do . . . ." Anna felt fresh tears coming. "This just breaks my heart, Lauren."

"Oh, Mom." Now Lauren put her arms around Anna, hugging her tightly. "Don't you worry about Sarah. I have a very strong feeling that she is just fine."

Anna blinked at her. "You do?"

Lauren nodded. "I absolutely do."

Anna retrieved a handkerchief from her sweater pocket and used it to wipe her tears. "What makes you so sure?" she asked quietly.

Lauren smiled. "Because Sarah is like you, Mom."

"How so?"

"She is strong and resilient. She's stubborn and independent. I realize she's not quite sixteen—and I hate that she's done this—but she is really a lot older than sixteen. In some ways, she is a lot older than I am. At least she used to be. I might be catching up with her now."

Anna patted Lauren on the back. "You most definitely are." Now she took in a deep breath. "There's something else you need to know."

"What?"

Now Anna told Lauren what Donald had said about Zane being into drugs. "It doesn't sound like Sarah to me," she confessed.

"What exactly did Donald say about Zane?" Lauren asked. "Does he know this for sure?"

Anna thought hard then explained what Donald had said about Zane's appearance.

Lauren's mouth twisted to one side. "So Donald is assuming that just because Zane looks like a hippie that he's using drugs?"

Anna considered this. "I suppose that's possible."

"That sounds like Donald. He's always jumping to conclusions about people. Did he think Sarah was using drugs too? She's been dressing like a hippie for years now. But she's never given us any reason to believe she was using drugs. Her grades have always been good." Lauren frowned. "What do you think, Mom?"

Anna shrugged. "I'm not sure. I'd like to believe that our Sarah is too smart for something like that. After all, she saw what happened to you."

"She did. And she hated it." Lauren sighed. "Sarah's always been the sensible one. Very mature for her age. I'd say that life made her that way, but the truth is, I think she was born like that. Even as a small child, she used to tell me what to do . . . like she wanted to be the parent . . . and I was the kid. She's got a good head on her shoulders."

"I've always felt Sarah was an old soul too," Anna admitted.

"I don't believe she's using drugs, Mom. I really don't."

Anna nodded. "Then I don't either. Even so, she's still missing."

"Sarah has a lot of pent-up frustration. I know it's probably my fault. Here she was with all this maturity inside of her and yet she was still just a kid. Meanwhile I was the adult and I acted like a spoiled child. You know how hard that must've been on her?"

Anna pressed her lips together and nodded. "You think that's why she left?"

"I think she decided it was time for her to call the shots."

"A lot of kids seem to be doing that these days." Anna had read articles about this very thing in *Newsweek*. She'd heard other parents' stories. The seventies just seemed to be an era when people did whatever they wanted . . . usually without even considering the consequences.

"Sarah is going to be just fine, Mom. I *know* it." Lauren made a shaky smile. "Remember what you used to tell me. Sarah has to paddle her own canoe." She shook her head. "And I'm sure she can do a better job of paddling a canoe than me. Unlike her inept mother, Sarah probably won't tip her canoe over in the middle of the river."

"You're right," Anna agreed. "Sarah is adept in a canoe."

"I'll bet that she shows up here," Lauren assured her. "Probably by the end of the week."

"I hope you're right." Anna reached for Lauren's hand and turned them to face the river. "Just the same, let's pray for her. Let's ask God to watch over her, to protect her, to guide her back home." And that was what they did, there on the banks of the Siuslaw. They prayed that Sarah Pearl would safely find her way home. "Really, that's all we can do right now," Anna admitted after they said "amen." Then, as they continued to walk, Anna was reminded of her ancestors. Certainly they'd been through some very hard times, and yet here she was—she and Lauren—descendants of a very troubled people.

"You know that your great-great-grandmother lived on the banks of the Siuslaw," Anna told Lauren as they walked through the wooded area. "Her name was Little Flower, but it was later changed to Anna."

"Like you." Lauren bent down to pick a buttercup, handing it to her mother.

"Yes." Anna smelled the tiny bloom. "Little Flower lost both her parents to smallpox when she was only three years old."

"Who took care of her?"

"Relatives."

"The smallpox epidemic was brought here by the moving man."

"That's the white man, right?"

"That's right. Little Flower's life was relatively calm for a few years, but when she was about Sarah's age, she and her people were forced off their land and sent to the reservation." Anna told about how the Siuslaw were herded like animals, forced to walk for days and days on the beach, and finally placed on the reservation up north. "The ones who survived were placed there for *reeducation*," Anna explained. "That meant they were supposed to go from being Indian to being white. The women and girls were taught to cook and sew like white women and to speak English. The men mostly died." Now she told about how her great-grandfather was shot for trying to find food. "Although many of them were starving, they were not allowed to hunt or fish or gather their native foods."

Lauren turned to Anna. "I never knew this . . . not any of it."

"Then it's time you knew." Anna continued to tell her of the hardships of their ancestors and how, finally, the few surviving Native Americans were given parcels of land. "It was a small token compared to the land they used to occupy. And it was only made available to those who knew how to file a land claim. Thankfully, my great-grandmother and her sister figured it out." Anna smiled. "We come from a long line of smart women."

Lauren chuckled. "Wish I'd known that sooner."

"My grandmother, Grandma Pearl, inherited this land from her mother. Grandma Pearl and her first husband built the first cabin, the one that Hazel stays in now."

"Yes." Lauren nodded. "Hazel has told me a little about Grandma Pearl. She sounds like she was an interesting woman."

"The River Dove was her canoe."

"Ah . . ." Lauren smiled. "I'm glad I didn't sink it for good."

"I think the River Dove is unsinkable." Now she told Lauren about how Grandma Pearl returned to the old ways, how she befriended other Siuslaw women and how they tried to relearn the way their ancestors had lived. "But it was hard. So much was lost, so many stories forgotten. But Grandma Pearl did her best to preserve it." She put a hand on Lauren's shoulder. "Do you know why I'm telling you this now?"

"I'm not sure. But I like hearing about it."

The trail was coming alongside the river now. "The Siuslaw were a matriarchal society, Lauren. That means that the inheritance is passed down through the women. And someday, Shining Waters will belong to you."

Lauren's brow creased. "I hope that's not for a long, long time, Mom. I wouldn't be ready for it now."

"It will happen at the right time, Lauren. And then, one day, you will hand it on to Sarah." They stopped walking now, turning to look at the river, which was sparkling like diamonds in the bright sunshine.

"What an amazing heritage."

Anna nodded. "It's a heritage of mercy and second chances, Lauren. From our ancestors to me, from me to you, from you to Sarah . . . for eternity." With misty eyes, Anna gazed out over the shining waters as she prayed for her granddaughter's canoe to remain sure and safe and sound . . . and to turn around toward home.

Discussion Questions

1. Teen pregnancy has never been rare, and before legalized abortion it was even more common. Yet Anna seems blindsided by Lauren's pregnancy. Do you think she should've seen this coming? Why or why not?

2. Although Anna keeps a gracious front for Lauren's sake, she expresses deep humiliation to Clark. Why do you think she feels such shame?

3. Why do you think Anna is so comforted by Babette's reaction over Lauren's pregnancy? How would you react to a friend in Anna's situation?

4. Anna seems to innately understand that Eunice is "broken." How do you think she learned this? Or is it a gift? Explain.

5. Eunice has been the difficult person in Anna's life. Describe the difficult person in your own life and how you deal with her or him.

6. Hazel always seems to bring a stabilizing force to the inn. What quality do you most admire in her character? Is there someone like that in your life? Explain.

7. Anna's new grandbaby resembles the Native American side of the family, which upsets Eunice. Do you think appearances and family resemblances play a part in your family's relationships? Explain why or why not.

8. Lauren and Donald's marriage seems doomed from the start. How would you have advised this young couple? What did you see as their biggest stumbling block?

9. Do you think Anna should've been more involved in her daughter's life? Or less? What might she have done differently?

10. Some women seem more maternal than others. Why do you think Lauren was so lacking in these skills?

11. They say it takes a village to raise a child, and it seems to take one to get Lauren on track too. What do you feel is the most important quality of community?

12. Anna and Sarah seemed to bond right from the beginning. Is there someone in your family you feel bonded to in a similar way? Describe.

13. Sarah is naturally drawn toward her Native American heritage, but Lauren has never shown any interest in it. How do you explain their differences?

14. Eunice seems to soften up with age, and her relationship with Anna improves. Why do you think that happens?

15. How did you react to Eunice's final visit at the inn, shortly before her death? Were you surprised to hear the rest of her story? Relieved?

16. It seems that Sarah changes too quickly, transitioning from the sweet granddaughter to the jaded adolescent. What do you think most contributed to this change? What, if anything, might've prevented this?

17. Lauren's 'ah-ha' moment came in the river. Have you ever experienced a moment like that? Describe it.

18. It seems things are always changing in Anna's life and yet she remains relatively serene and stable. If you asked her why that was, what do you think she would say?

Coming Soon

*The final chapter in Melody Carlson's heart-warming
The Inn at Shining Waters Series*

River's End

1

June 1978

Despite halcyon skies and only a slight sea breeze, the air felt chilly today. Or maybe it was just her. Anna pulled her cardigan more tightly around her as she looked out over the sparkling river. Perched on the hand-hewn log bench, she stared blankly toward the river and, surveying her old faithful dugout canoe, let out a weary sigh. She'd gotten up extra early this morning. Planning to paddle the Water Dove upriver, she'd wanted to soak in the sunshine, breathe the fresh summer air, clear the cobwebs from her head, and gather her strength for the day.

She'd imagined paddling hard and steady upstream, and finally, after her arms grew tired, she would turn the canoe around and allow the river's current to carry her back home—back to Clark and Lauren and the Inn at Shining Waters. But now she felt it was useless . . . futile even. She simply didn't have the strength to pull the dugout down the riverbank and into the water. Planting her elbows on her knees, she leaned forward and buried her face in her hands. A praying position, and yet she had no words. Nothing left to pray. Already she felt emotionally drained, and it was still early morning. How would she ever make it through this painful day, her beloved granddaughter's eighteenth birthday? It didn't seem possible that Sarah would've been eighteen by now.

More than two years had passed since Sarah had vanished from their lives. As far as they knew she'd run off with her boyfriend, Zane. She'd only been sixteen—just a child—and yet old for her years. Anna had tried to appear strong, hoping that eventually Sarah would return to them. In the meantime, she put her energies into working hard alongside Clark and Lauren. The three of them, connected in their silent grief, cooperated with each other as they kept the inn going and thriving, making constant improvements, increasing the business, faithfully serving the never-ending roster of eager guests.

It was for the sake of these guests, and even more so for her family, that Anna had maintained a positive outlook as she went through her daily routines. But beneath her veneer of hopeful confidence, the concerns for her granddaughter's welfare had dwelled in the shadows. How was it possible that Sarah had so completely disappeared? Without a word—not a single letter or phone call—the sixteen year old had seemingly vanished from the face of the earth. And for two years, despite her family's best efforts to locate her, Sarah still was not found. What did it mean?

Anna's unspoken fear was that Sarah had come to serious harm—that perhaps she was even dead. Otherwise, she surely would've contacted them. At least, Clark had said early on, she would've contacted Anna. Because, as he pointed out, the bond between Anna and her granddaughter had always been a strong one—symbiotic. Besides that, Anna felt it uncharacteristic for Sarah to be so selfish and inconsiderate as to cut them off completely. Even in adolescence and amidst her parents' marital troubles, Sarah had been thoughtful and mature. She wasn't the sort of person to intentionally put others through such pain and misery. As hard as it was to face it, the only logical explanation was that something had happened to the girl. Something tragic.

Still, no one ever voiced these mute terrors. Saying the words out loud would make it seem too real. And so Anna and the others had clung to the hope that Sarah was alive, that she had simply chosen to separate herself from her family, and that someday she would return. But as months passed, and as one year slipped into the next, Sarah's name was spoken much less frequently. And if her name was mentioned, there was always an uncomfortable pause that followed . . . a quiet, awkward moment that would linger before the conversation resumed itself.

But realistically—as painful as it would be—it might be easier if they were informed Sarah was actually deceased. At least they could properly grieve for her then. They could hold a memorial service to remember her and to celebrate the years of her life that had been so sweet . . . so innocent . . . so pure. Perhaps they might even build a monument of sorts—at the very least a special plaque or carved stone. They could set it right here by the river, and it would be a quiet place where they could come to think and to grieve and to remember Sarah's short but beautiful life in their midst.

Anna sat up straight now, gazing out over the river again. But in lieu of the crisp and clear diamond sparkles on the surface, she now saw a blurry watercolor image instead. It all looked murky and distorted . . . and hot tears ran freely down her cheeks. She hated to be weak like this, to give into this kind of sadness and despair. But it all seemed so senseless, so unfair that a grandmother should outlive her granddaughter. It was just wrong.

She pressed her lips together, using the palms of her hands to wipe away her tears. This would not do. She had to remain strong today—as much for Lauren's sake as for her own, because she knew Lauren would be especially mindful of her only daughter today. Eighteen years ago, Sarah had made her entrance into this world. And although Lauren hadn't really been prepared for motherhood, it had been a happy day for Anna. She had felt an immediate bond with her granddaughter.

As difficult as it would be, Anna was determined to pull this off. She intended to make this a good day. If any words were spoken of Sarah, they would be positive words, remembering all the sweetness that the girl had brought into all their lives—despite the brevity of her stay. Anna took in a slow, deep breath and stood. She would be strong and of good courage. There would be time enough for tears tomorrow.

As Anna turned toward the house, she heard the sound of a boat's motor coming up the river. Pausing to listen to the rhythm of the engine, she couldn't help remembering the old comforting sound of Henry's ancient boat. How she missed that deep chortling echoing along the hills of the river. She missed Henry too. As well as Babette . . . and so many others. Times and people had changed over the years, but the Siuslaw River remained the same, moving out to the sea, being pushed back gently with the incoming tide, always on the move.

Her people had lived alongside and loved this river for countless generations. Her grandmother's old stories made references to them. According to Hazel's research, the Siuslaw had been a matriarchal society. And Anna had known that it was the women who had handed down the traditions and what little belongings that were accumulated in a lifetime. Anna had always hoped to do the same, to leave a timeless inheritance for the generations that followed her, from Lauren, to Sarah, to Sarah's descendents. But it seemed that was not meant to be. Perhaps the heritage of the shining waters was going to end far sooner than she'd expected.

Anna was nearly at the main house when she heard the boat's engine slowing down, and when she looked over, she saw it veering toward their dock. It looked like the Greeley's Groceries boat. In an attempt to increase business, the store in town had decided to make deliveries on the river during the tourist months. Mostly, Anna supposed, because the youngest Greeley boy wanted an excuse to have a motorboat. But their groceries had been delivered yesterday, and she wasn't expecting anything else today. Cupping her hand over her eyes, she peered out to see Bobby Greeley at the helm. And sure enough, he was stopping at their dock.

"Hello, Bobby," she called out as she walked toward the dock to meet him. "What are you doing out—" She stopped herself as she stared in wonder at the waiflike dark-haired girl huddled in the back of the boat. Wrapped in an olive green woolen blanket, she looked at Anna with large, dark eyes. Sad, hollow eyes.

"*Sarah?*" Anna felt her heart give a lurch. And suddenly she was running down the dock. Blinking in disbelief, she stared at the girl. "Is that you? *Sarah?*"

The girl nodded mutely as she stood, letting the blanket fall onto the bench behind her. "Grandma," she said quietly.

"*Oh, Sarah!*" Anna grabbed the rope from Bobby and hastily tied it, then climbed into the boat and threw her arms around the trembling girl and began to sob tears of joy. "I can't believe it. I cannot believe it!" Now she held Sarah back with straightened arms, looking deeply into her eyes just to be certain she wasn't imagining this moment. "It really is you!"

They were both crying now, hugging each other tightly until finally Anna knew that she needed to get Sarah up to the house. She glanced at poor Bobby, who was watching with troubled eyes, as if he wasn't sure what to do about this awkward display of emotions.

"I'm sorry, Bobby," Anna told him. "I'm just so overwhelmed. This is my granddaughter, Sarah. I haven't seen her for years."

"That's okay, ma'am."

"Thank you for bringing her out to us," Anna quickly told him. "I, uh, I assume you'll just put the charges on our bill."

He nodded.

"Come on, Sarah." Anna helped her out of the boat. "Let's get you inside." She looked around the boat now. "Do you have any bags?"

Sarah simply shook her head. Now Anna studied her granddaughter more carefully. She looked painfully thin beneath a long, raggedy dress of faded blue calico that reached nearly to her bare ankles. She had on worn leather sandals, and her long dark hair was uncombed and dull looking. Anna put her arm around Sarah's shoulders, holding her close as they walked up the dock.

"Is my mother still here with you?" Sarah asked quietly.

"Yes. She helps with the inn."

Sarah stopped walking. "I don't want to see her."

Anna looked into Sarah's eyes now. "Your mother has changed, Sarah. A lot. She's like a different person."

Sarah's dark eyes seemed even darker. "I don't care. I don't want to see her."

Anna didn't know what to do.

Sarah looked back to where the boat was pulling away from the dock. "Maybe I should just leave and go back to—"

"No." Anna's hold on Sarah grew tighter. "You can't leave. Not until we talk." She hugged Sarah close to her again. "We have been worried sick about you, Sarah. You have family here. We love you. And even if you and your mother have your problems, you still belong here with us. Do you understand that?"

Sarah just sniffed.

Anna looked into her eyes again. "This is your home too, Sarah. This is your river. Clark and I, and Hazel, and your mother—we all love you."

Sarah still seemed unsure.

"Please, trust me, Sarah," Anna said quietly. She was desperately trying to think of a plan to ease Sarah back into their world. Her old room in the house might feel too confining, too close to the rest of them. Plus, Anna knew Lauren was already in the kitchen working on breakfast. And since the summer season had just begun, the inn was full. But then Anna remembered that Hazel's cabin, the same cabin that once belonged to Anna's grandmother, was unoccupied right now. Hazel was touring in Asia and wouldn't be home for a couple of weeks.

"I know," Anna told her. "You'll stay in 'The Oyster.' "

"Grandma Pearl's cabin?"

Anna smiled as she hooked her arm into Sarah's. "That's right. And that would make Grandma Pearl very happy!"

Some of the guests were milling around the grounds now. Some said hello and some just looked curiously at her and Sarah. She knew that Sarah looked like someone who had stepped out of a different world, almost like she'd been living in a different era, and she knew that Sarah probably had a story to tell. And Anna certainly had plenty of questions. But not right now.

"You look tired," Anna said as she opened the door and led Sarah into the sweet little cabin.

"I am." Sarah went over to the table by the window that faced the river and, running a finger over the grain of the pine, looked out with a wistful expression.

"I want you to make yourself at home," Anna told her. "If you like, I won't even tell your mother that you're here yet. You can have a shower, and I'll bring you down some breakfast and some clothes and things. You'll eat, and you'll rest, and then we'll talk." She stroked Sarah's tangled hair. "Okay?"

Sarah just looked at her. Her eyes reminded Anna of those of a frightened doe.

Anna put both her hands on Sarah's cheeks, once again peering into those troubled, dark eyes. "You are *home*, darling. This river and this inn and even this old cabin—they all belong to you just as much as they belong to me. Do you understand what I'm saying to you?"

Sarah still looked unsure, but at least she nodded.

Anna hugged her again. "You are home, Sarah. At long last, you are home." She kissed Sarah's cheek and promised to return quickly with some food. And then, feeling as if she had wings on her feet, Anna ran up to the house, wondering with each step how she would share this good news.

Want to learn more about author
Melody Carlson and check out other great fiction
from Abingdon Press?

Sign up for our fiction newsletter at
www.AbingdonPress.com
to read interviews with your favorite authors, find tips
for starting a reading group, and stay posted on what
new titles are on the horizon. It's a place to connect
with other fiction readers or post a
comment about this book.

Be sure to visit Melody online!

www.melodycarlson.com

What They're Saying About...

The Glory of Green, by Judy Christie
"Once again, Christie draws her readers into the town, the life, the humor and the drama in Green. *The Glory of Green* is a wonderful narrative of small-town America, pulling together in tragedy. A great read!"
—Ane Mulligan, editor of *Novel Journey*

Always the Baker, Never the Bride, by Sandra Bricker
"[It] had just the right touch of humor, and I loved the characters. Emma Rae is a character who will stay with me. Highly recommended!"
—Colleen Coble, author of *The Lightkeeper's Daughter* and the *Rock Harbor* series

Diagnosis Death, by Richard Mabry
"Realistic medical flavor graces a story rich with characters I loved and with enough twists and turns to keep the sleuth in me off-center. Keep 'em coming!"—**Dr. Harry Krauss, author of *Salty Like Blood* and *The Six-Liter Club***

Sweet Baklava, by Debby Mayne
"A sweet romance, a feel-good ending, and a surprise cache of yummy Greek recipes at the book's end? I'm sold!"—**Trish Perry, author of** *Unforgettable* and *Tea for Two*

The Dead Saint, by Marilyn Brown Oden
"An intriguing story of international espionage with just the right amount of inspirational seasoning."—**Fresh Fiction**

Shrouded in Silence, by Robert L. Wise
"It's a story fraught with death, danger, and deception—of never knowing whom to trust, and with a twist of an ending I didn't see coming. Great read!"—**Sharon Sala, author of *The Searcher's Trilogy: Blood Stains, Blood Ties,* and *Blood Trails.***

Delivered with Love, by Sherry Kyle
"Sherry Kyle has created an engaging story of forgiveness, sweet romance, and faith reawakened—and I looked forward to every page. A fun and charming debut!"—**Julie Carobini, author of *A Shore Thing* and *Fade to Blue.***

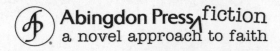

Abingdon Press fiction
a novel approach to faith

AbingdonPress.com | 800.251.3320

Abingdon Press fiction
a novel approach to faith

Plan your escape.

For more information and for more
fiction titles, please visit
AbingdonPress.com/fiction.